Oonagh

Oonagh

MARY TILBERG

Cormorant Books

Canada Council **Conseil des Arts**
for the Arts **du Canada**

The publisher gratefully acknowledges the support of the
Canada Council for the Arts and the Ontario Arts Council
for its publishing program. We acknowledge the financial support
of the Government of Canada through the Book Publishing
Industry Development Program (BPIDP) for our publishing activities.

Printed and bound in Canada

Library and Archives Canada Cataloguing in Publication

Tilberg, Mary
Oonagh / Mary Tilberg.

ISBN 978-1-897151-18-1

1. Irish — Canada — Fiction. 2. Fugitive slaves — Canada — Fiction.
3. Immigrants — Canada — Fiction. I. Title.

PS8639.I54O65 2009   C813'.6   C2007-906474-4

Editor: Marc Côté
Cover design & image: Angel Guerra/Archetype
Text design: Tannice Goddard/Soul Oasis Networking
Printer: Friesens

This book is printed on 100% post-consumer waste recycled paper.

CORMORANT BOOKS INC.
215 SPADINA AVENUE, STUDIO 230, TORONTO, ONTARIO, CANADA M5T 2C7
www.cormorantbooks.com

For Tasha

L'homme est né libre, et partout il est dans les fers.
Man was born free and everywhere he is in chains.

— JEAN-JACQUES ROUSSEAU, *DU CONTRAT SOCIAL*

One

For a long time afterward I carried him within me. I felt the contours of his smile on my face, as if he were smiling out of my own features. I lay warm beneath quilts in the little room below the roof in my sister Mairi's house. Life went on. I heard her young daughter wail and our brother Michael's children clatter in and out of the rooms below me, their voices like sparrows. I heard Mairi pacing in the next room as she spun wool; some days she worked the loom, the beater thumping like my own heart. Chauncey's heart in me. I listened and felt no guilt Mairi was doing my job. Nothing was to keep him from surfacing in my mind. I smiled to think of his laugh that could bounce around the village, echoing against the wall of forest to the west and north against the hills. I listened for the sound of his voice.

For hours I lay on my back staring as the bright day slipped around the room, as light faded into darkness. Once, the rain ceased for a while in the night. The moon rose and peered right in at me with its big face. Then it too was gone, and slowly, slowly, the birds began to twitter in the maple outside the window. Day crept in again like a thief. I turned my face away from that rogue and slept.

I kept my belly warm with both palms spread. A broody hen. No one could budge me from my nest. No one tried. It seems to me now that for much of the time it rained, sometimes a soft patter on the shingles, sometimes a thundering deluge. I thought of our brother

John, how it had rained then too, raining all over Connemara for John and young Adam Keane, hanged at the crossroads. I would fall asleep and awake in tears. "Our Johnny," I'd cry. Mairi would come and sit silently in the darkness by my side, holding my hand, her palm cool on my forehead.

"Only a few more months," I said to her once, patting my belly. In the pale light of the dawn she turned away from me. My hands were hot on my skin. Look, I wanted to tell her. My breasts have swelled. My belly is rising like new dough. I am carrying Chauncey in me. The child will have her father's dimples, the deep centre of a pansy on each cheek. But Mairi rose and went away into the day. I turned my face to the wall. I reached under the pillow for Mam's stone carving and held it in my hand until it seemed to pulse with warmth like a live thing.

Sleep closed over me like a lough. I swam in it, a fish breathing underwater. Chauncey often swam with me, his face laughing with those dimples I loved to kiss. Through the sunlit water I marvelled at his tightly curled eyelashes, at the dappled light reflecting in his black eyes. His hair sparkled. When I reached out to touch his slender ribs, to stroke the muscles of his stomach, he laughed and darted away through the water like a seal. How marvellous this ability of his. I swam like this for hours, days, until some slight noise of the world above brought me to the surface. Usually it was Daniel, Michael's boy, standing at the doorway, peering in. He was so serious, half-afraid I think now, that perhaps I had drowned in my sleep. He came to empty the chamber pot. I never left the room; I hardly left the bed. He was so sweet and uncomplaining, my brother's young son. I treasured his presence, because the moment he peeked in at the door it was as if Chauncey were sure to follow. Daniel had brought me so many messages, and each time I'd given him a hug to pass on to Chauncey. Then once again Daniel was gone, carefully clumping down the stairs with the heavy chamber pot. I drifted off.

Once I awakened to see Daniel standing by my bed, smiling shyly. With a surge of joy I asked, "A message for me?" He turned and fled.

I froze. For a suffocating instant, out of a darkness spitting snow, leering demons thrust torches at me. I shrieked and clapped my hands over my eyes. Silence. My room again, sunlight flickering in through the window. What an absurd mind to conjure such a scene. Mairi entered with Daniel close behind her. Had I shrieked aloud? I held out my hands to them both, my eyes brimming. *Look at the sunlight on the walls!* My fingers made a leaping hare on the wall. *Look, Daniel.* I laughed at their long faces and held out my arms. But Daniel hung back by the door. "He has to go home now," Mairi said. "It'll be dark soon."

Then one day, abruptly, heat suffused the room. Mairi opened the window and the scents of lilacs blew in. Lilacs! Was it spring? I looked at Mairi as she turned from the window and saw how big she was with child. I had forgotten. She sat on the bed behind me and began brushing out the wild grapevines of my hair. "Is it spring?" I asked her.

"Indeed," she sighed.

I stared at my hands, slack on my flat belly. Empty breasts. Hollow. And then I understood. I was suddenly a cave full of howling wind. No day, only darkness, only a winter wind whirling in me, a cold sea dragging me down. Mairi held me against her breast. She held my head up above the water. She breathed her own breath into my nostrils. She cursed me. She blessed me. "Damn you!" she cried. "Hold on to me."

Two

For nearly twenty years I cast about the way forward into the telling of this tale. Many hours I strained my eyes in dim candlelight, writing paragraph upon paragraph, which all too cruelly by morning proved insubstantial to the memory I carry. The writing sagged, the edifice sadly unable to bear the weight. And so the years slipped away. Lately, though, I've come to understand that what was once a personal story has in time become part of the fabric of history. I can no longer shirk my responsibility to record for future generations the truth of our experiences. My niece, Samantha Corcoran, awoke me to this necessity when she inquired after the manuscript she has seen me labour over many nights of her childhood. On the evening of the great Frederick Douglass's speech in Toronto a few months ago, Samantha asked me when I thought to publish my book. "After all," she said solemnly, "you aren't getting any younger. Who will write it if you die?"

SO I BEGIN WITH Connemara and the house where I was born the fourth of eight children. Ours was a poor district, but we managed year by year. It was my mother's deft hand at spinning and weaving that brought us through many a difficult period, and she passed on these talents and skills to my sister Mairi and me. Our father and elder brothers worked our small plot and worked for the landlord, tending his sheep and cattle. Our father had built the cottage himself when he first moved here from the Claddagh. The land was rough, good only for grazing. To enrich the potato plots we went down to the sea each year and hauled home baskets of seaweed. We had a cow once and a donkey when times were good.

ONE DAY IN THE spring of 1831, I spent the afternoon sitting in my usual spot by the shore. Below, the sea sucked and slapped into the narrow inlet where we collected seaweed. I was wrapped up in the grey shawl, my back against the massive, triangular end stone of a wall. Who'd placed such a large stone as that? How did they move it? Da, he'd only grunted when I pointed it out to him the last time we came down for seaweed.

"Before me time," he muttered. Meaning before he arrived forty years earlier. He was a silent man, hard to know what he thought about anything. Each time I visited this place I made sure to replace any smaller stones fallen from around the large one. *Spalds suit walls as well as big ones.* So the saying goes. There was true satisfaction in fitting the most suitable spald in snugly. It's the smaller stones, the spalds, tucked in to prop up and wedge the large stones, that lend the greater beauty, the patterns and colours, to the wall. Still, it was the immense solidity of the end stone that drew the eye. Perhaps Nature itself had placed it here and men in a distant age had used it to guide their building of the wall to the sea. I pressed my back against its cold smoothness and gazed at the restless water, and the island, brilliant green now in the setting sun.

A narrow spine of a stone wall climbed up from the sea and over the summit, dividing the island almost in half. One side of the island was barren, grey-green boulder-strewn, overgrazed by the landlord's cattle, while on the other side the brilliant green grass grew tall among clumps of trees, pine and hazel scrub, awaiting the livestock. No creatures at all this afternoon.

As a child I'd watched smoke rise and drift from the chimneys of eight stone houses on the island, where Da's aunt Margaret and three cousins lived. On Sundays I'd wait for them to row over for tea. There was Robby, the smallest cousin, his hair a flaming red, waving from the boat his da was rowing. Where was Robby now? He'd disappeared with his family; Da had no idea. If Robby were alive, he'd be about Liam's age.

Not a single house on the island was left whole, thatch roofs yanked off and burned. The people dispersed. Aunt Margaret died in Athenry, we'd heard that much. Then nothing more. John, seventeen, thinking he could do something to stop the constables from evicting the people. All that trouble. He, little Michael Leary, and Adam Keane arrested for their agitation. Accused of being Ribbonmen. They didn't deny it at all. The look on Da's face and Mam collapsing in the court. The Leary boy, not twelve, they'd shipped off to slave in Jamaica. But Johnny and sweet Adam Keane. No, even now I can't think of them without this rushing into my chest all the storms off the Atlantic.

The branch in the hedge lives long after the hand that planted it. So many things outlast human life. Stone walls. Gravestones. The sea, constantly washing the shore. John left no artifact that we can hold and marvel at. He left no child with his brown eyes and bright hair. On a hillside overlooking the sea, a rough gravestone marks his resting place, his name, John Corcoran, the dates, 1804–1821, chipped into the stone by Michael just before he left for Upper Canada. The rainy winds from the sea will wear them away. The words don't tell the story.

THAT TERRIBLE MORNING, MAM sent me into the hills with a basket to collect tansy. She'd intended to dye some fine wool yellow to make a baby garment. I was up in the hills overlooking the village and the sea and the island just off shore, keeping a watchful eye on the dark clouds surging over the ocean, when all at once heavy smoke billowed from the houses on the island. I stared, uncomprehending for a moment, then bolted down the rocky hills, yelling until my breath came out in sobs. By the time I'd run all the way into the village to warn of the fire, soldiers were already yanking Johnny, Adam Keane, and little Michael Leary through the crowds in the village street, ropes around their necks, young rams for the slaughter. Mam, heavily pregnant, ran alongside shrieking, trying to free John's ropes. A mounted officer struck her down.

If only I could have run faster, been closer to keep Mam from falling, to keep her from the soldier's whip. So many times since, I've imagined wrenching that whip away and slashing that bastard across his face. But it's the other, the crossroads where they hanged our John that is impossible to conjure, although I'd been there with everyone else in that cold rain.

I pictured Johnny as he rowed us in the currach across to the island on a Sunday, remembered him laughing as he chased me around the boulders above the house. The powerful strength of his shoulders as he hoisted me up for a ride down to the sea, how proud I was for the whole village to see me perched on his shoulders. I remember one afternoon when he and our oldest brother, Michael, competed cutting turf, their bared backs shining with sweat, and how finally Johnny thrust in his spade, stepped back laughing, his arms flung wide, and conceded to Michael. "I'll beat you yet!" I can see that high sunny field with its rows of drying peat blocks, people standing about, men clapping Michael on his back, our da sitting on a boulder quietly smoking his pipe, nodding as people complimented him on his sons. Yes, easy to remember these, but it's the other I resist.

We lost Johnny and Mam the year before the great hunger that came upon us in 1822. Mairi said then she was glad after all Mam didn't have to go through the famine. "God works in mysterious ways," she said. I lay close to her on the pallet in those dark hungry days and heard her say the words "mysterious ways," and a great revulsion overcame me. Just who was this God, anyway? If He could spare Mam the starvation by taking her in childbirth, and that tiny eighth baby too, if He was so powerful, why did He let us starve? Why didn't God help? Why had He let Johnny be hanged? Anger choked me as I lay beside Mairi in the dark. I hated God. I was only nine but knew to keep my fearsome thoughts to myself.

"IT'S IN GOD'S HANDS now," Mrs. Keane said. Mam was still alive. I was kneeling by the bed, and Mam opened her eyes and stared right into mine. She didn't stop staring, but the light in her eyes seemed to fade. The hair prickled on my neck. I rose without a sound and ran out and up into the hills for help. "God," I called. "It's in your hands. You see the sparrow fall. There's my Mam. Down there, in that house." I pointed, just in case He was watching.

I sat high up in the grass. The sun glittered on the sea in the distance and on the low pink clouds, casting shadows across the far bare mountains they called the Twelve Bens. Purple heather and the bright yellow of cowslips enhanced every stony cliff and outcropping. God's handiwork. He was everywhere. Surely He could hear me. What did I expect? A voice out of the wilderness to boom down: *Go home, your mam is well.* I nibbled and sucked at a stalk of grass. Wait. Patience. Who could rush God? With my chin cradled in my hands I watched the smoke from the chimney below curl in small wisps that the wind blew away in gusts. Whitecaps on the sea. Then a cry, then several voices at once. Da rushed out of the house and away down to the village. Mairi came out and looked up to me. She was shading her eyes from the bolt of sunlight that came piercing over the summit of the hills. *Oonagh*, she cried, *oh no, Oonagh.* She was twelve, four years older than I, as tall as Mam. She started for the path, but I leaped up and scrambled even higher into the boulders so that no one would find me. And no one did for the rest of the day, until Colum O'Leary jumped down upon me from behind. "You have to come home," he said. "They're waiting on you."

THE WIND PICKED UP with a nasty bite to it. I drew the grey shawl even closer. It had been Mam's and Mairi had said I could have it. It wasn't summer yet. I shivered. Da and Liam were sure to be home soon, tired after working on the roads all day, wanting their tea. Though Heaven knew, Mona at fifteen was quite capable and had likely already added potatoes to the stew.

Still I lingered, leaning against the stone. A seal popped its dark head out of the water and gazed at me before silently slipping under again. The sun lowered into the ocean, flooding the waves with its blood red light. I wouldn't fear to stay here all night until the moon rose. When we were children Colum used to tease that I was a witch or a Druid. Maybe in ancient times I would've been. *Last night you were in my dream. By the sea dancing. I saw you!* I shoved him away, pretending to be mightily offended, but thrilled. He'd been spying again. *And anyway, stupid*, I shouted as he ran away laughing. *Druids don't dance by the sea!*

But I did. It was obvious at his words that he'd seen me whirling in this spot. This sacred place. I smiled to remember his dark head peeping up over boulders or in the green grass on the hills. Ah, Colum. He was off to sea these days, travelling the world.

I felt backwards with both hands for the rough edges of the stone, closed my eyes to better absorb the rhythmic shush of water on the rocks below, wind along the grass, the rasping of a donkey grazing on the near slope. *Oh, Mam. Let me draw in the spirit of the stone at my back, let me be stern and silent, a wise woman, not to be drawn into petty squabbles. Help me.*

RATHER THAN CLIMB BACK up to the track that ran along the coast, I scrambled along the rocky beach on the jumble of round sea-smoothed boulders. Easy to get a foot caught, to step on a rock suddenly upending. Vast tables of stone closer to the sea's edge made the going easier, but too close to the water and the stone was dangerously slick. Still, by walking here I avoided being seen by the gossips in the few houses along the road. Just where the rocks gave way to a little sandy cove, I'd catch the road as it wound through the last houses of the village and back out into the hills where our house was.

As I neared the cove in the twilight, I heard voices and came upon a couple of small boys crouched among the boulders. They hadn't seen me yet and chattered on about Natty: *Did ye see how he bawled like a babby?* They snorted with laughter. What had they done? Something made them look up. They gasped, guilty-faced. I leaped down beside them as they scrambled to their feet.

"Well now, O'Rourkes. What did you do to poor Natty?" I put my hands on my hips and glared at them. Inside I was laughing.

They shrugged and looked away and giggled when they looked back at each other.

"Come now, spit it out."

The older boy, Tom, a scrawny boy of nine, lifted his head and snarled, "We don't have to tell you nothing."

"Well, I'm asking. What about Natty? It's not his fault how he is." They both shrugged.

"Your wee cousin. You should love him. Be kind to him."

"We don't have to listen to you," said Tom.

"You're not our Mam!" piped up the younger O'Rourke, a smaller replica of his scrawny brother. They scowled at me through straggly fringes of dark hair.

"Thank God I'm not!" I laughed.

"You don't believe in God. Or Mother Mary!" said Tom.

I was that shocked to hear him I put my hand to my throat.

"Where'd you hear that?"

"You love the Devil. You are the Devil!" Both boys then leaped away from me as if they expected me to attack them.

Then I got angry, if amused. "If I don't believe in God Himself, why would I believe in the Devil? You can't have one without the other!" I grinned at the sudden uncertainty in their eyes.

"You can't?" said the older.

"No, of course not."

They gaped like fish flung on the shore.

A woman's shrill voice called. The boys ducked down, their eyes pleading with me not to give them away. On tiptoe I looked over the bank up to where Mrs. O'Rourke stood at her half door. When she saw me she scowled just like her boys and crossed her arms.

"Good evening to you, Mrs. O'Rourke!" I called cheerily.

The boys were begging me not to betray their hiding place. Mrs. O'Rourke just stared grimly, then without a word she closed the door.

"Too bad for you," I muttered.

The boys giggled. "Is she gone?"

"She's a big old crab, isn't she, your mam?"

The boys giggled louder, still crouching.

I continued on my way. A moment later a pebble struck me between the shoulder blades. Then another. One hit the back of my head. If I'd turned to see, I'd have rushed back and throttled them. Instead I took a deep breath, then another, and moved on. No more stones. I stepped calmly down onto the sand of the cove.

The tide was out. Several currachs were hauled up high above the tide line, looking like beached seals. I wove around them, digging my toes into the cold sand, relishing its hard smoothness after the uncertain rocky beach.

Mr. Dickie Clooney sat on the seawall that sheltered the road from the storm waves. A gnarled old man, he often sat there in the evening, smoking his pipe. I reached the steps in the wall next to him and started up.

"Evening, Mr. Clooney."

"Aye, 'tis that," he grunted.

I swept by him up the stairs.

"They needs a good trashing, them lads," he said, pointing his pipe at the O'Rourkes, who were just visible squatting back down in the rocks.

I smiled, mindful of my words. "They're only silly boys."

"A good trashing, I say." He took another puff and I continued up the stairs. I'd gained the top stair when he said rather loudly, "I hear yis got a letter today."

My heart lurched. "A letter?"

"Colum O'Leary brought it. He's come from America again."

"Oh, thanks, Mr. Clooney!"

Colum home, and with a letter! Must be from Michael. Please God in whom I do not believe, let Colum still be there; please make him stay for supper. But as I hurried up the stony path my prayer changed. Let him come tomorrow instead. Oh please, don't let him see me all windblown and dishevelled.

The girls must have been watching from the window. While I was still at a distance, Lizzie, our youngest, came tearing down the path, followed closely by Mona.

"Let me, let me!" shrieked Lizzie, flinging back her hands to stop Mona from passing her.

Mona passed her and yelled, "A letter's come!"

Lizzie's small face crumbled in disappointment. She halted and folded her arms tightly across her chest. Her mouth was all a tremble, but I didn't indulge her in her pout.

"Is Da already home?"

"No, no!" the girls cried.

I continued up the path with a girl on either side.

"Colum O'Leary brought it!" said Mona.

"I hope you asked him to stay for tea."

"Yes, but he had to go," Mona sighed. "He's got a heavy beard now."

"Does he? Well, he's a grown man after all, Mona!"

"It's a thick packet," said Lizzie, pulling on my hand in her excitement. I smiled down at her. "From Michael," Lizzie continued. "That's what Colum said."

"You didn't open it, did you?" I asked sternly, squeezing her hand.

"We didn't touch it," said both girls at once. I knew from their faces how each had run a finger secretively over the bulky letter when the other wasn't looking.

I ducked through the doorway of the house and paused to adjust to the gloom within. The girls crowded up behind me. Faint light from the window gleamed on the oilcloth-wrapped package on the table, the fattest letter I'd ever seen, tied up securely with twine. The girls watched me. Would I open it? they wondered. I grinned at them and clapped my hands.

"Well, let's get busy. Mm, smells good, Mona. You put the potatoes in? They'll be here soon."

DA AND MY YOUNGER brother Liam had been working on the roads since February. This was the only way to qualify for financial assistance. Things had been poorly lately, with bad harvests and little employment. With the mills in Ulster taking much of the business, fewer and fewer people brought Mairi and me their flaxen or woollen yarn to weave up on the loom. Things were not the same as they'd been when Mam was alive, weaving good cloth and knitting. How could we compete with the mills? Troubles had erupted again in many places as people refused to pay the tithes to the Church of Ireland.

People who brought me their business could not afford to pay much. Mairi lived out now, in the home of the Protestant Pastor Spring, working in his kitchen. Da and Liam worked all day for a pittance. Our family was better off than many who hadn't a shelter to sleep in. So far at least, we still had the house and garden, a bin half-full of oatmeal, some potatoes. We had the bed and table Mam brought with her when she married Da, and her loom and spinning wheel.

Voices from down the path. The men were coming. Liam was still my baby brother, for all that he was fourteen, doing a man's job. He had his eye on the daughter of the shebeen owner in the village. I teased him that he thought only of the pub and not the girl, and he didn't deny it. She was a pretty enough girl, older by two years. Liam was big for his age, joining the rest of our brothers who tended to six feet, taking after Mam's side of the family who came from Ulster. He was already taller than Da, who declared that Liam wouldn't stop growing until he was taller than Michael. *Giants, all of you,* Da pretended to grumble. *Comes from all that milk he used to swill before we had to sell the cow.*

Yes, Liam enjoyed attention for his sudden gangly height. Now if only we had enough food to fill in the spaces between his ribs.

The men clumped into the house and made straight for the wash basin. Liam stood aside as Da washed up. They seemed sunken in weariness tonight, silent as stones.

"A letter's come," piped up Lizzie.

"Yeah," said Liam, flashing a bit of a grin at her. Da settled himself in his chair at the table.

Da reached across the table and lightly touched the packet. "It's a fair size, now, wouldn't you say?" He poked it as if it were a puppy about to nip.

"Colum called out about it as we passed his place," Liam's voice muffled in the towel.

"Yes, the girls said he brought it," I said.

Liam lowered the towel from his eyes and raised an eyebrow at me. "Oh? And where were you when he came?"

I stuck my tongue out so that Da could not see.

"Out walking by the sea again, I suppose?" Liam continued, grinning. He was hoping Da would chastise me for neglecting my work. I glanced at Da.

"I finished Mrs. Kelly's cloth by noon. So?" I grimaced at Liam, who grinned back, shaking his head at me.

"We'll eat first," Da growled, ignoring us.

Mona handed me the plates one by one, and I filled them from the pot on the hearth. Mona poured hot salted milk in the large bowl in the middle of the table so all could reach it, and beside it I plunked the kish with a few steaming potatoes. Da raised his eyebrows but he didn't say what I knew he was thinking, that we'd cooked too much. Then we were eating, all eyes shifting helplessly to the brown packet that sat at Da's elbow. Da nudged it with his arm.

"Michael, I'd be guessing."

"From Canada," said Lizzie, beaming. The firelight burnished her hair to a bright copper. How wonderfully strange that in one family the hair colour ranged from blackest black, like mine and Mona's, to that of Mairi's gold. In between were the copper of Lizzie and the bronze of Liam. Michael's was also copper, turned darker with age. Johnny's had been bright like Lizzie's. Mam's a soft gold tinged with red, and Da's, before it turned grey, black like mine. Half of us, including me, had Mam's dark blue eyes, and the rest took after Da, like Mairi, whose eyes were a lovely soft brown.

As if my thoughts had summoned her, Mairi burst in the door with Josie, her betrothed. He was Joseph, like Da, but everyone called him Josie. The teasing when they were first courting, *Mary and Joseph ... Just be careful about that first-born, won't you?*

"A letter's come!" Mairi called out.

"They let you go, did they?" grunted Da at her.

"They don't know I've left!" laughed Mairi. She loved to tease Da, who worried that she was too lighthearted toward her employment. "But Bertha said I might go." Her eyes were on the letter. "Will you look at that," she breathed. "How thick it is."

"It's from Michael, from Canada," said Lizzie.

"Of course it is." Mairi leaned down and planted a kiss on Lizzie's head.

Josie settled down by the fire. Mairi turned to fill him a plate and I rose, embarrassed that I hadn't offered right away. Mairi waved me away with a laugh, but I fetched him potatoes from the kish steaming on the table and gave him a cup with hot salted milk. He smiled his thanks.

"Josie hasn't eaten yet, but I have." Mairi served him the plate of stew and he laughed at all the food thrust upon him from both sides. He ate quickly. Josie looked like he never had enough to eat, and that was entirely possible, coming from a large family of boys, all short and skinny. Josie was determined to take himself and Mairi off to Canada where Michael and Josie's own two oldest brothers lived in the same village. Every time a letter arrived, Josie eyed it with great anticipation. Perhaps it carried the passage money his brothers had promised for the last five years. He and Mairi had been betrothed for two long years, waiting to marry. If they could only get to Canada. He wolfed down the food, dipping the potatoes into the milk and practically eating them whole. Pity panged in me. Mairi adored him; she hung on every word he said, even while she teased him.

"What did you eat tonight, Mairi?" asked Lizzie. This was always her question, for the Springs were known to eat quite exotic food at times, especially when they had guests come from Galway or Athlone or Dublin.

Mairi told her about the bowl of custard with cream and apricot preserves that she had served the Springs, and how Bertha had allowed her to finish the leftovers. Lizzie's eyes widened with pleasure. But before she ate the custard, Mairi assured her, she had eaten a large bowlful of lamb stew. I glanced at Da, for he hated when Mairi spoke like this. We hadn't had lamb in a long time. Mairi glanced at me and ducked her eyes away. She dug into her apron pockets and pulled out something wrapped in a white napkin.

"Well, what do I have here?" She spoke in feigned surprise.

Lizzie sat silent, her big brown eyes fixed on what Mairi was unwrapping in front of her. A number of small golden oatcakes studded with raisins. Lizzie didn't move an inch, her eyes smiling up at Mairi.

"Did they give them to you?" asked Da sternly.

"Of course. Bertha said to take some to you."

He harrumphed as if he didn't believe her story.

"Really, Da," laughed Mairi. "I made these myself."

She divided them up among us. I ate half my portion then put the rest in my pocket for later. I savoured the sweetness of the raisins stuck in my teeth long after the rest had slipped down my throat.

Da didn't hesitate to eat his share.

SOMETIMES I WONDERED IF the Springs' God wasn't the true one. He certainly seemed to provide better for them. I'd said as much to Da once and he'd clipped me hard on the head with his knuckles.

"They get our tithe money!" he'd growled.

Da growled when he spoke. He was like a gruff shaggy dog, beard tattered and strewn with grey, eyes overhung with enormous grey eyebrows that he had me snip just so they wouldn't get into his eyes.

He was a good father. He hardly ever drank. If there'd been a regular priest in the area, he'd have had us to church every day. As it was, we said the rosary before going to sleep.

Da had no idea that what I said to please him I couldn't say with belief. For a long time I thought that to believe in God was childish. Like believing in fairies. But I kept quiet, feeling alone in this. I'd just turned thirteen when I came to my conclusions. Five years had passed since Johnny had been hanged and Mam died. Michael had emigrated with Josie's brothers to Upper Canada. I lay one night on the straw bed with my sisters and Liam. He was still sharing the straw with us, before he was moved to the little loft overhead. Everyone was asleep. Across the room, in the bed, Da snored heavily.

I'd been thinking intensely on the events of that day. Father Christopher had come all the way from Loughrea and everyone had turned out for the celebration of the Mass up in the hills, in a special place sheltered from the winds within the tumbled walls of an old castle. Mostly sheep grazed there now, but when the priest came every month or so, Mass was held in those ruins.

On this day, in a strange mood, I'd felt detached from everyone, as if seeing them for the first time and from a great height. The priest's beautiful, deep voice rang against the hills and the crowd echoed in its unison. Da, kneeling beside me, bowed his grey head. Two O'Rourke boys a few feet in front kept poking each other in the ribs, barely suppressing giggles. Their mother rapped them sharply on their heads. I thought of Mam, how she'd never hit us children. How she'd died without God's help. How Michael, now in Canada, had been excommunicated from the Church because he'd spoken of rebellion just like Johnny. The words sprang into my head: *I hate You.*

Why did the Springs have all that lovely food and us hardly any? Why did the Robertson children, whose father was a sodden drunk, but Protestant, always have good clothes to wear? And a school? Liam had only a hedge school to attend whenever Master Neill came about, the good school in the village barred to him. I'd never learn to read. I couldn't accept this as Mairi had, as Joanna Leary did, or Bridie Luby, who said women didn't need reading or writing. When Bridie had said that the other day, I'd flown into such a rage Bridie'd run home after denouncing me for being a Ribbonman.

If I was a boy, I would be! I yelled at her back.

A Ribbonman, as they'd accused Johnny. His neck broken by the rope. *No. Don't think. God, please. God, who knows when even the smallest sparrow falls.*

Father Christopher said God tests our devotion like He tested Job's. What kind of Father tests His children in such horrible ways? Whatever had poor Mam or Johnny done to offend Him? Father James said Mam was such a saint God wanted her home with him. But we'd needed her ourselves.

The voices around me rose and fell in unison. My mouth clamped shut. I looked up to the hills green and scattered with boulders, the people kneeling on the grass among the ruins of the ancient castle. That castle had been here before Christ came to Ireland. The people living then had had Druid priests. They hadn't believed in Jesus. That much I knew. Maybe not even in God. *There is no God.* For a moment I couldn't breathe. *Look around. No God to hate.*

I stood up and swayed. Da looked at me through watery eyes. He dropped his head again. *Go, now,* I said to myself and walked past Mairi's inquiring eyes and up into the hills. From a boulder high above, I watched the service, Father Christopher's voice clear even from that height. Then slowly people began to leave. The service was over. I was empty as the sky. I didn't have to hate God anymore because there was no God. People lived on earth, as did the animals. They birthed babies like the animals, needed food, water, and sleep like the animals, and died too, like any other living thing on this earth. No God sent His angels to stretch invisible wings over them in protection.

All this I mulled over as I lay beside my sleeping sisters. Although I was quite frightened at what I'd conjured up — for what if I were to die that very night and God really did exist — a wild exhilaration took hold of me. Had anyone else ever dared to think such thoughts? I couldn't imagine Da saying God didn't exist. Had Johnny? Had he died with that broken neck and gone straight to God?

MAIRI WAVED HER HAND in front of me. "Oonagh, my goodness, where are you? Come back to us!"

The whole family stared at me.

"You're such a dreamer," chided Mairi.

"Aw, she's dreaming of a certain someone who's come from America," crowed Liam.

The dishes had been cleared away and Da's steaming punch placed before him. Da reached for the packet and carefully untied the knots.

Wrapped inside in an extra sheet of waxed paper was another packet sealed and tied in string. Da worked at these knots.

"Just cut it," suggested Liam.

We all sucked in breath. Money and passage tickets. Da carefully set it all aside and took up the stiff pages of the letter itself. He handed it over to Liam, the only good reader among us. Reading was hard work and the letter trembled in Liam's hand as he bent toward the firelight. He cleared his throat.

"'Dear Father and Family,'" he read hesitantly. "'I trust this letter will find you all in good health. We are not a little worried here at the report of things in Ireland. We are all keeping well. Jane sends you her love. We are expecting our third child in September, God willing.'" This revelation was greeted with wild cheers. Da puffed on his pipe, eyes glittering under bushy brows. He gestured for Liam to continue.

"'Please find enclosed the passage tickets for Mairi and Josie. The money is for the provisions they will need for the voyage. A list is enclosed. As well, I have sent Oonagh her passage. She will be good company for Mairi on the voyage as well as after. They will have no trouble obtaining work here, as maids are in constant demand by the wealthier farmers and townspeople. Truly this is a rich country if one is willing to work hard. I only wish I could send for everyone now!'"

Liam looked at Da; Da smoked with no expression. I was seized with apprehension. Emigrate with Mairi? Mairi, on the other hand, could hardly restrain her joy. She clasped her hands to her breast. I began shaking, although the room wasn't cold. To leave this place? To leave Da and my sisters and Liam?

Liam had stopped reading and was staring down at the paper in his hands. He suddenly looked up and across at me, his eyes stricken. It was as if he'd flung a spear.

"Go on then, son. Can you not see to read? Get closer to the fire. Is that all he says?" Da's voice rumbled.

"No, there's more." Liam's voice trembled. Tears started up in my eyes. Liam had expected the passage money for Mairi; we'd all been awaiting that. But *Oonagh*? I could see that question in his face.

He continued, "'In this new land a man is respected for what he can accomplish. We are all doing very well and unafraid to voice our opinions. Josie's brothers have built a gristmill in the village, near a wonderful source of water power, and are after building a sawmill this summer. They are only waiting for Josie.'"

Mairi leaped from her stool and flung her arms around Josie's neck. He flushed in the firelight. Da glanced at them from under his lowered brows.

Liam continued, "'I hope the winter was not difficult. I will send you money as I can. We are all waiting to seeing Josie and Mairi soon, God willing, and little Oonagh too.'" Liam grinned at me. "Little Oonagh!" Everyone laughed.

I shrugged. In the five years since Michael had left I'd grown a head taller than Mairi. But I hadn't Mairi's robust body. Liam liked to tell me I'd make a good broomstick.

Liam read on, "'I know they will be sorely missed at home, but you will send them knowing they have a good future here. Next year I will arrange for Liam to come.'"

His voice squeaked, "Me? No! I'll not be leaving you, Da!"

"We know why you'll be staying, and it's not your da will be keeping you home," laughed Josie.

"No, it's a lie!" said Liam.

"What's a lie? What did I say?" Josie said in mock astonishment.

"What you were going to tell," muttered Liam.

"Oh. Now. So you can read minds! That's quite a talent!"

Mona joined in the fun, "We know a girl down at Jem's that has her eye on you, Liam. Could you be sweet on her too?"

"Aw, shut up," he muttered, his head hanging low over the letter.

"Keep reading, son, till it's finished," ordered Da. He reached over and gently tapped his pipe against the hearth stone. "Is that all?" He motioned impatiently at the letter.

Liam shook his head and took up the paper again. "'Please kiss the little ones for me and may God keep you all safe until we meet again. Your loving son, Michael.'"

"So, Da!" Mairi leaped up again and danced over to Da. "A grandfather again. How do you like that?" She hugged him around the neck. He couldn't help smiling at her fervour.

"Well, it does happen."

"Are you not pleased?"

"They're so far away," he said, patting her shoulder. "As you'll be. I'll never see your children, the two of you."

"No, hush. You'll be coming along too."

But Mairi's words were hollow. The truth was Da would probably not come and most people who emigrated never returned. As a sailor Colum could return again and again. But Michael? He'd never be back. In his letter he sounded happy and settled.

Mairi suddenly said, "Oh, Da! If we'd known this was coming we could have been married at Shrove!" She wrung her hands in dismay.

"Never mind," Da muttered. "You'll be married now. Before you sail."

Josie's face went scarlet. Mairi threw her arms around Da's neck, then whirled around the room in a frenzy. Josie reached out and grabbed her as she passed. She collapsed onto the settle in a wild flurry of laughter.

I looked at Da's grey, grizzled head bowed, his gnarled hands resting on the table. He'd stared down while Mairi was dancing in her triumph. I reached out for his hand, my eyes stinging, "I'll never leave you, Da. You'll see all my children to love them."

Liam snorted. "Oh, and who will you be making them babies with? Who is there to marry? Eh? Willy Keane, poor fellow? Or maybe old Dickie Clooney? He's always looking for a wife; I hear he's sweet on ya!" Liam fell on the floor in his laughter.

Da squeezed my hand, saying, hush now, and I stopped the tears. I tried to laugh along with Liam.

He said, "Oh, I know, I know who you'd have. Colum O'Leary! I seen you two last time he was here!"

"Shut up, you!" I wanted to thrash him.

He sat up and stared at me, his mouth hanging open. Why was he being so mean? "Up in the heather. I seen you!"

I launched myself at him to make him stop. He curled into a ball while I pummelled him. I could hardly see for my anger. Then Da roared, "Stop, the pair of yis! Brawling like a pair of silly puppies. You should be ashamed of yourselves. Especially in front of Josie here!"

He stalked to the door and went out. Josie smirked as he hauled Mairi to her feet. "Come, love. Let's leave the little ones to their games."

Liam always managed to do this to me. Mairi touched me lightly on the head as she passed to the door.

"It's getting late," she whispered. "Meet me tomorrow at the stone. After midday."

The door closed and I was left alone with Liam, Mona, and Lizzie all watching me seriously. Liam dusted himself off and reached down a hand. I thrust it away.

"Aw, Oonagh. I was just fooling."

"You didn't have to mention Colum."

"Just teasing you."

His crestfallen face. This was the thing about Liam. He never meant to be mean. He just enjoyed people laughing at the things he said, and if it meant saying things about someone else, he would. He was one for remembering jokes and stories and gossip. He'd make a fine publican. Had he really seen me and Colum?

I reached out and he pulled me up. The firelight played on his face.

"Since when did you get so tall?" I reached up to touch his cheek. Relief shone in his eyes. He reached out and hugged me as if I'd said words of forgiveness.

"I'll miss you when you go," he said.

"I'll not be going!" I said against his shoulder and tried to push him away. But he held me tight and said against the top of my head, "No, you must. It's your only chance."

Lizzie flung her arms around both of us. Mona watched, serious, unsmiling.

"Come," I said, holding out an arm to her. "Let's do the Corcoran crush." Mona smiled and slightly shook her head, as if she were too old for such a habit. But Lizzie grunted with her effort to crush us. Liam groaned aloud, "Oh my good Lord, Lizzie, what a hugger you are!" He picked her up, her long legs dangling. She squealed as he swung her about, complaining that she was getting much too heavy for this. Then he plunked her down and turned to go out the door.

"Liam!"

He paused, looking at me questioningly.

"Did you really see me and Colum?"

He only grinned and smacked a kiss in the air before closing the door after himself.

Three

EARLY NEXT MORNING, AFTER Da and Liam had left, I tossed a basin of dirty water out through the doorway without looking. There was a great yell from Colum O'Leary, standing at the threshold. I was mortified as the dirty water splattered all over his feet.

"I'm so sorry." My face flamed.

"Oh, I know my feet need a wash, but girl!" He pretended to leave. I called him back but he kept walking until he reached the wall and then he perched up on it, glancing back to see if I had followed. I set down the basin and walked forward, my heart a caught sparrow. He patted the wall beside him.

"Well, I brought you all good news yesterday."

"Wonderful news!"

"You'll be leaving with Mairi."

"Did Michael tell you?"

"Oh, yes. Wanted me to make sure you came along."

"Will you be going to Canada with us as well?"

He looked surprised. "No, I've no mind to stop sailing. But if I do, I'll settle in Boston where my sister and cousins are. That's a good place."

"Boston?"

"I'd rather be in America than in the bleeding British Empire."

"But it's different in Canada, isn't it, than here? Michael makes it sound so."

"Oh, sure. You'll like it well enough."

His hand on the wall beside mine. I resisted covering it. I wanted to raise it to my lips, kiss his knuckles, lay my cheek across his palm. If he knew my thoughts! I looked up into his face, but he was staring across the valley, green and boulder-strewn below us.

"What a country," he sighed.

I thought he meant our own stretching out before us.

"It's lovely, isn't it, this morning? I doubt I'll be leaving home after all," I said.

"You must." He tapped me on the side of my head, then tugged at my braid. "Oonagh, think. What's for you here? It's all over for people like us. They'll have your Da's place pretty soon. We'll all be reduced to wandering the roads."

"What about my da, and the children?"

"They'll be joining you soon. Michael and Jane are doing very well. I went up and saw their place. A small village, but growing fast. Much livelier than ours here." He motioned with his head to the roofs we could see below.

"Colum, come for tea this evening and tell us about Michael and Jane. What's it like there? Do they have any animals? What are the babies like? What do they have to eat?"

"All right, all right!" Laughing, he raised his hand against any further questions, "I'll come some evening. Yes. Before Mairi and Josie wed. I'm staying for the wedding, then I'm off again."

"So soon?"

"The ship'll set sail, with or without me. I have to go. You'll be leaving too."

We were silent then, gazing out over the country below. He sighed as if with a great burden. I glanced at him, at the trouble wrinkled on his forehead. Was it the sunlight on the sea that creased his eyes so? He would be old too soon. He smiled sideways at me. I loved his deep brown eyes, his mouth hidden in his new beard, his heavy brows that would one day be shaggy like my da's.

"Come now, so serious! It's good I have a decent job. I love the sea. And you. You'll be fine in Canada." He reached over and chucked me under the chin.

I waved a hand at the scene below us, "What's going to happen to everything here?"

"Aw, I know. It's a heartbreak."

At that moment my heart broke. His voice full of sad certainty. We had no choice but to leave. But I wouldn't with him. He wouldn't choose me. I could hear this in what he said. Since childhood I'd assumed I'd be Colum's wife. Last autumn we'd walked in the hills together, and although no such declarations were made, I'd assumed that actions spoke louder; I'd assumed too much.

"How's your mother? I know she's always missing you."

He laughed and picked out a small clump of moss from the stones. "My mother. Well, bless her. I do what I can. If it were up to her, we'd all stay home forever. She won't think of going to America. 'Too old to change,' she says. Her heart is set on that sod next to my da."

"And your sister?"

"Nora's married, did you know? A man from Boston. They have a babby on the way, like your Jane does."

We sat in silence in the warm sun. I kept looking at his hand again, so close to mine. A sailor's hands now, heavily veined. He'd grown his thick brown beard in eight months away.

"Colum ...?"

"Hmm." Deep in his chest.

Ah, now. I realized why he didn't look at me; was he remembering that certain day up in the hills last September? Such a thing stays on one's mind even when life continues to wash over. He was remembering, certain, and wanted to talk about anything else. I couldn't speak past the pounding of my heart.

"How's your da?" he asked. "How's he taking it, you leaving too?"

I cleared my throat, hoping my voice would be natural. "We haven't talked much yet. He should send Liam instead."

"No, Oonagh, you have to go."

"If you came with me, I'd go tomorrow," I dared to say, my heart violent.

"You'll do really fine. You're a good spinner and a fine weaver."

He ignored what I'd said. A wave of embarrassment and then the thought suddenly hit me.

"Did you get married in America?"

A hoot of laughter. "Good grief, girl!"

Could I get more embarrassed?

"Lord Jesus love us. No! I like roving too much."

"But you'll be wanting a home someday."

He shrugged, grimacing. "To tell you the honest truth, I don't think I'd make anyone a good husband. I've got a roving eye, you know. The sailor's life is for me. What do they say? A girl in every port."

I'd been waiting since September to hear from him, to see him again. Those kisses and caresses, the liberty I'd allowed him that day. I'd thought us as good as betrothed.

"Ah," I said softly. "Now I see."

"Ah," he teased. "What do you see?"

"A scoundrel."

"Oh, where? Where?" He pretended to shade his eyes and look furiously around. I glanced behind me to see both my sisters peeping out of the window. Mona quickly hid, but Lizzie was having fun spying.

I jumped off the wall and headed up to my spot in the boulders above the house. I expected Colum to follow me. I willed him to follow. I could practically feel his breath on my neck. When I glanced over my shoulder he was still slouched on the wall, his long dark hair shining red lights. Mona came out of the house and slowly walked toward him. I climbed higher. She was now talking to him and they were both laughing. Maybe he preferred her. Maybe something else had happened last autumn that I hadn't seen. Maybe he was twice the scoundrel I'd realized he was. Grief was a hot ball in my throat.

LATER THAT AFTERNOON I questioned Mona, "What did he say to you?"

"Who?" she said.

"You know." I was trying to sound unaffected.

"Colum?" I could hear it in how she pronounced his name. How had I not seen it before? We were alone in the house for a few moments. I gripped her by the wrist until she winced.

"Now tell me," I said. "Tell me or I'll break it."

"Leave me be," she hissed.

"What did he say?"

She twisted away as the door opened with Liam bringing in a load of turf. He glanced at us in surprise. We must have looked a sight, a pair of cats hissing.

"What's wrong?" he asked.

Mona stepped to his side, scowling at me. "She's acting crazy."

"What's the matter, Oonagh?" Liam's voice was gentle.

"Are you home before Da, then?" I asked.

"Yes, we're done for now. Da stopped off at Jem's."

He dropped the turf by the hearth. Mona went out. I couldn't look at my brother. He might have been younger than me, but sometimes, strangely, he seemed to be the older one. He poured himself a cup of hot water from the kettle and settled down to sip at it. His eyes continued to question me.

"Don't mind Mona," he said finally. "She's upset that you're going and she must stay and carry on with all the work herself. It won't be easy, but I'll be helping her out."

"If I go."

"No ifs. You must go. You'll get you a good husband there for sure."

"Why would I want that?" I cried. "Do you think that's what I want?"

"Every woman wants that, I think," he smiled sweetly and sipped away at his hot water like an old man, his hands cupped around the mug, his eyes fixed on me.

"Well, not this one. I'll not be like Mam!"

"Mam was a saint, God rest her." He lowered the cup to stare at me in my agitation. I was pacing.

"Do you even remember her?" I retorted.

He hung his head and I wished I could recall my bitter words. Then he said, his head still low, "You're a good woman too, Oonagh. Any man would be lucky to have you." My brother's voice shook, startling me. He looked up, about to weep. The next instant I embraced him where he sat.

"I'll just miss you so much when you're gone," he sighed.

"And Mairi?"

"Of course, Mairi too. But Oonagh, you're my friend as well. It's going to be hard."

It was true, though we were four years apart. I stroked his head and he sighed, again strangely like an old man. My little brother. I could remember him at his birth, little red wrinkled baby crying hoarsely, lying in the bed next to my exhausted Mam. I tugged at his shaggy hair.

"Come on now, will you draw me some water?"

He gulped down the last of his drink then stood and stretched to the low ceiling.

"Always making me work," he grumbled, smiling. "Why should I be after missing you at all, I ask myself." He took up the bucket and went to the door. But just before he went out he said softly, "Don't set your heart on Colum. He'll only bring you grief."

I shrugged. *Tell that to Mona.*

"He's got a girl in Boston. That's what they're saying."

"Who cares," I replied and turned to busy myself at the hearth, adding fresh peat. Liam closed the door quietly behind him.

Four

BEFORE DAWN ON THE day of Mairi's wedding, I was startled awake from a bad dream, my body prickling with fear. The sensation diminished as the images faded. By the light still muted in the window, the sun was not yet above the sea's rim. Birds trilled. In the distance Mrs. Keane's youngest rooster was trying out his silly voice, breaking in the middle like a half-grown boy's. Then the granddaddy rooster's robust full crow showed him how. A crowing contest. All with their distinct voices, just like people. A slight wind rustled in the thatch. Da snored across the room.

I glanced over at my sisters asleep beside me on the straw pallet. Lizzie next to me, then Mona, with Mairi on the far side. We did this by habit, placing the younger ones between us. Until that moment I'd never much thought of how we arranged our lives in these little details. With Mairi and me leaving, who would protect these two?

Mona's mouth was open. A small line of dried spit lay in the corner of her lips. I was sorry I'd been so fierce with her those few days ago. In the time since, I'd worked hard to rid myself of my dream of Colum, making sure that every time his name came to mind I'd deny it. I'd even convinced myself Mona was fated for him, my little sister almost sixteen. But when I voiced this to her, she'd shrieked with laughter. She liked his stories of far-off places, of sailing to Asia and America, she assured me. But anything else? I'd imagined the whole thing between them. In fact, she made me promise that I would do my best to bring her and Lizzie out to Canada as soon as possible. She told me what she truly wanted was to go to school and become a teacher. That astonished me. She said she'd followed Liam a few times to the hedge school and had sat a short distance away, trying to hear everything the teacher said.

How do we live with people so closely and never really know them at all? It was as if realizing that I was soon leaving opened up her need to tell me who she was. She wanted me to know that she'd never wish to take a man from me. Her earnestness embarrassed me, fifteen-year-old Mona trying to reassure her eighteen-year-old unmarried sister. For it was true: that's what I'd been accusing her of doing.

I looked over at her again and was startled to see her watching me as well, her eyes sleepy. I raised a finger to my lips and smiled. Lizzie was slumbering deeply. Mairi slept on her side facing us, her hands in a prayerful clasp under her chin.

"Should we be getting up?" Mona whispered.

I reached out a hand and touched her on her cheek. *Sleep*, I mouthed. Mairi reached out of her sleep and tucked Mona in to her. We laughed silently, Mona and me. I was so relieved that we were friends again. Sisters, above all, should be friends. Lizzie slept on. How many years we had slept together like this, keeping each other warm when the wind skittered in under the door and across the floor right at us? Liam too, when he'd been little, had slept curled like a little pup snug against me. Liam, now long and lean and awkward in his sudden height. Next he'd be sprouting a beard, his voice deepening like Da's. When would I see him again? It was better not to dwell on that.

The straw in the loft rustled and a moment later Liam's thin legs, his long delicate feet, dangled down. He rarely used the little ladder, simply lowering himself then dropping. His pants, raggedy at the knees, were too short by several inches; he'd grown so fast in a year. He wore Johnny's best pair from the days when we were a bit better off and he'd completely worn them out. Liam was now taller than Johnny had been.

He caught my eye. I put a finger to my lips. He grimaced, then put his own to his lips in an exaggerated imitation of me. He looked over to where Da gave out a particularly loud and complicated snore. Liam grinned down at me and then stepped out the door. A flood of cool air swirled across the floor. I snuggled in a little closer to Lizzie.

Suddenly Mairi bolted right up. She stared wildly around her, then at me as I reared up on one elbow.

"Oonagh, is it day?"

I smiled at her bewilderment. She flung back the covers from us all.

"Ho, lazies! Time to get up. A wedding!"

Mona grabbed at the blanket. Lizzie sat up. Mairi tugged away the blanket and wrapped it around herself like a giant shawl.

"How d'you like my wedding dress?" she crowed.

Da grumbled awake. He swung his feet to the floor heavily. "What a pack of wild animals."

Mairi raced across to him and flung herself on the bed. "My wedding day, Da!"

"About time, too," he growled.

"Aw, Da! You want to be rid of me!" She hugged him and he patted her back.

"Go on," he said. "Don't we have a lot of work to do today?"

"Liam's already out," I volunteered. Da peered at me. Sunlight now streamed in a narrow band from the small window and slipped along the floor up to Da's bed. He rubbed his head. "I slept too long," he said. "The sun's already up."

"It's fine, Da. You never rest enough."

"Not with such a pack as I have here." He smiled.

I was already stirring up the fire. Liam entered with a freshly drawn bucket of water.

"Good boy," Mairi said. She grabbed him into her embrace and he warned her that he would spill the water if she didn't leave him be for a moment. Joy swirled and whirled around us and even sleepy Lizzie staggered around with a big grin.

Yesterday Liam and some of the neighbour boys had cleaned out the byre and spread clean straw over the mud floor. Then with Da's supervision they had built a long plank table fastened to trestle legs. We would cover it with tablecloths borrowed from several households. The head of the table would be covered with Mam's special linen cloth she'd made herself as a young bride. Mairi would be taking this linen to Canada.

Father Christopher was coming for the ceremony. The entire community for miles around was coming, for not only was it a wedding but also a send-off for three of us emigrating. Actually five, because we'd heard that the Monaghan brothers were travelling with us on the same ship. They'd been Josie's friends for years. So many young people leaving on the same day; there'd be lots of jokes and laughter and singing and dancing and drinking, and then tears would flow.

For a week we'd been gathering together the makings of a feast and various people had assured us that they would be bringing contributions. Late spring is surely not the best time of year for a wedding, with the hungry season close upon us, but still, Pastor Spring's wife had promised to bake the bride cake, and wasn't that a generous thing for a Protestant to do? They liked Mairi in that household and wished her the best. All together we'd have enough potatoes to go around, buckets of fresh milk from Mrs. Keane's two cows, and Josie's brothers had promised enough punch for several weddings. They'd also promised no drunkenness. Josie's father sometimes had trouble with drink, and this was not only the wedding of one of his sons, but a sort of wake for those of us departing our homes forever.

MRS. O'ROURKE STOOD IN her doorway, arms tightly crossed at her breast. She always glared at me when I slipped by on the road past her house, and so I usually walked along the rocky beach. But today I was in a hurry. Indeed, I shouldn't have slipped away from the preparations with the wedding in a scant couple of hours. But my stone by the sea compelled me. I imagined myself seated at that spot, gazing out to sea and the little island. I told Mairi I had to go and she said, *Go, it may be your last visit. Say a prayer for me.* Mairi always prayed when she visited the place with me.

"Where are you off to in such a hurry then, Oonagh Corcoran?"

I couldn't believe the woman actually addressed me! She had a scowl on her face but her tone seemed quite ordinary, curious.

"Nowhere, just for a walk," I lied. I had stopped on the road and was trying to smile innocently at her. She took a step toward me.

"Do you not have a wedding to prepare?"

"Everything's ready. We're waiting for the priest." I spoke casually. "Are you coming, Mrs. O'Rourke?"

"The priest, is it?"

"Of course." Suddenly laughter triggered itself in me and I had to choke it down with a cough.

"Which priest, then?"

"Father Christopher."

"Hmmph," she said and continued to stare at me.

"Well, I'll be off then," I smiled sweetly.

"I hear you're going to America with your sister."

"Upper Canada."

"Wait here," she said abruptly, and turned back into the house.

I waited, mystified. What did this hateful woman want? She had spread all sorts of rumours about me, having caught me standing at my stone and singing to the sea with my arms outstretched.

"Come here," Mrs. O'Rourke said from her doorway. I walked closer, nervous by the intensity in her face. When I was near enough she thrust a small cloth-wrapped item into my hands.

"Your Mam and I," her voice was hoarse, "we were young girls together. That place you always go to, we used to meet there, the two of us. Did you know that?"

"No." Cold prickles went up my arms and legs.

"We did. We were best friends. She gave me that." She gestured to the small wrapped thing in my hands. "She found it close by the stone and gave it to me as a token."

I felt faint and floating. Another moment and I'd sink in this sudden sea.

"No," she said sharply. "Don't look at it now. You're going there. Keep it. Look at it there. Take it when you go to America as a piece of this place, as a token of your Mam who loved you and who loved God best."

Tears streamed down her face as she spoke. I moved toward her but she put up a hand.

"Thank you," I whispered. But she had already slipped into the cottage and shut the door.

MANY STRANGE THINGS HAPPEN in one's life, but this was the strangest that had occurred to me. I obeyed her wish and did not unwrap the item until I was sitting by the sea, my back firmly braced by the stone. Even then courage failed me for some time. I could feel the thing was hard. I wished I could have asked her how old my Mam was when she'd found this thing. I tried to imagine my poor mother as a girl with Mrs. O'Rourke, sitting here, the two of them. What did they talk about? What confidences had they exchanged? It was impossible. I couldn't evoke them at all. And then I just couldn't unwrap the thing. The cloth covering it was a small scrap of linen with a thin blue ribbon tied around it. Had my mother made that cloth? Or was it a piece of Mrs. O'Rourke's? The ribbon itself a small treasure. I had to share this with Mairi.

I looked around then with new eyes. This had been my mother's special place too. Had I been told this? I couldn't remember that we'd spoken of it. It was only the end stone of a wall. It was my imagination that had made it special. And now I had found out that others had deemed it a special place as well. Who else down the ages? My mother's mother, of whom I had one memory, stretched out on the table in the cottage at her wake? I was barely three. I remembered the tiny figure, features shrunken. Not human, unrecognizable, though people told me she was my granny. Many years later I told Mam I could remember Granny's funeral and she didn't believe me. Well, could my little granny have found this boulder too, when she was a young girl? Amazing to imagine. A chain of young girls, unknown to each other, found this place by the sea, linked through time by the pull of this very stone. I leaned my head back and wept. For my Mam. For Johnny. For my Da who would never see his grandchildren in Canada. For Liam who would stay and carry on and marry the publican's daughter. I wept for my little sisters. How would they manage? How could I leave knowing return was impossi-ble? Sure, it would be wonderful to see Michael and Jane again. But what would become of me in that unknown place? I wept for myself. When I calmed down, I realized that I had to open up the little bundle.

For what reason had she given this thing to me? Ever since she'd caught me here, she'd barely been able to look at me. On that day, towering clouds had skimmed swiftly just above the sea's horizon; the sun shot brilliant shafts on the waves thundering in, tossing rainbows up over the sea. A shower sprinkled my face, then warm sunlight. Raising my arms high I had sung aloud for all the chaotic beauty that was before me, that I was part of, my hair like long grass whipping in the salty wind. Someone snorted behind me, and there she stood, Mrs. O'Rourke, watching me sing with my arms raised, as if it were I invoking the wind, the waves on the sea, the sun.

"What are you playing at, Oonagh Corcoran?" She never simply called me Oonagh.

"Oh!" I laughed and I twirled about in front of her. "Look how the sun shines for me!" And at that moment the sun did indeed shaft out from behind a bank of clouds and hit us with its warmth.

To my surprise Mrs. O'Rourke swiftly crossed herself, then glared at me with a malevolence I couldn't understand.

"You should be ashamed of yourself, girl, and coming from a decent God-fearing family. Your Mam was a saint, God rest her."

"God! Why should we fear God? Tell me that one, please." Why did such a tongue overtake me that day? And with Mrs. O'Rourke, who would be sure to spread it around that Oonagh Corcoran fancied herself a Druid.

Again the woman crossed herself. She whispered, "Do you not fear God?"

"God?" I burst out laughing. Suddenly I wanted to see her cringe, see her drop to her knees in fear. Her attitude ignited a rage in me.

"God!" I yelled, and raised my arms skyward. "If you are there reach down and strike me dead where I stand. Wicked, wicked God for taking our sweet loving Johnny and our own saintly Mam!"

And that poor woman did indeed sink to her knees in horror, muttering and crossing herself repeatedly. *Hail Mary* ...

"Ah," I shouted. "The wrong god, then. I should be hailing Mother Mary to strike me down!"

Mrs. O'Rourke stood up and ran away without a backward glance. I felt instant remorse for scaring her, superstitious woman, and for exposing my own lack of belief to such a one as her, something I'd not done with my dearest ones. For the last two years she'd refused to give me the time of day and had spread it around that I was an unbeliever, a pagan, even a Druid. I didn't know of any Druids, but it had been whispered around that such people existed in secret.

THE PRIEST HAD SURELY arrived, and Mairi would be cross with me if I were late. But I took my time. I untied the ribbon and unwrapped the cloth. I felt Mam, smiling, leaning over my shoulder, her warm breath on my cheek. And there it was, a small, flat piece of Connemara marble, perfectly oval, the size to fit neatly in my palm, a grey stone streaked with darker tones. When I turned it over, my heart froze, for a design had been carved into the stone, chains linked around the edge and a small cross in the centre. I examined it more closely. The links were actually two snakes intertwined, deeply cut into the stone, their tails and their heads forming the four points of the cross. My mother had found this here, at the stone. Perhaps there had been other such holy relics to be found — for this is what I felt I held in my hand — and I had overlooked them all these years. I scanned the ground at my feet. No. Surely not. This was meant for me from Mam, and Mrs. O'Rourke had known that.

She'd had to give it to me. Maybe that's why she'd been so hateful, knowing she had to give up this relic. Seeing me sing by the sea; maybe my mother had sung here too. I held the stone to my lips.

FATHER CHRISTOPHER SAT AT the head of the table, and on his right Mairi and Josie, both smiling so much they could barely eat. Da sat on the left and kept nodding his head at the shouted congratulations and jokes. *Hurry up, hurry up. Eat, eat!* I'm sure Mairi was thinking. I kept catching her glance, her face flushed as if she'd been out in the sun and wind all day. She wore Mam's special linen dress and lace shawl. Several old women commented on how much she looked like Mam with her golden hair, and how sad that Mam wasn't here to see her first daughter married.

Colum sat near the door at the other end of the table. For this I was grateful because it meant that I wouldn't have to see him as I gazed on the bridal couple. The table stretched the length of the byre. Lanterns hung from the rafters and large candles glittered from one end of the table to the other. Even though the uncertain afternoon sun still shone, evening would soon be upon us. The barn itself had only two tiny windows close under the eaves and the door for light. The boys had done a fine job of cleaning it out and the place smelled of new hay. Liam had cut grass and heather in the meadow several days ago just for this purpose.

I turned to see Colum. He was having a fine time, downing the punch as if it were water, chatting with the boys, flirting with old Mrs. Keane as if she weren't old enough to be his grandmother. She beamed with his attention. He caught me shaking my head at him and shook his head back at me, sticking his tongue out; I felt scalded, the same feeling as last fall when I lay with him in the hills. I fought the tears that sprang to my eyes. I pretended to pay attention to the ladies around me who asked about Michael and Jane and our going to Canada.

We cleared away the dishes. Finally Father Christopher rose, as did the bride and groom. The ceremony was over in minutes. I hardly heard the words for the tumult in my head. I felt Colum's eyes right between my shoulder blades. It could've been us up there. Longing and loneliness and disgust: could I think only of my own sorrow on this, Mairi's wedding? I was about to faint. They embraced; everyone cheered and clapped and whistled. Then fluttery Mrs. Spring was bringing in the bride cake, gleaming in white icing, the loveliest concoction I'd ever seen. She carefully set it before Father Christopher. Mairi's eyes shone bright in the candlelight, her lips smiling. Josie leaned over and wiped a tear from her cheek. Amazing. Never thought he had it in him. There was much I didn't know. I confess: envy gnawed deep in my belly.

Father Christopher blessed the cake. He had eyebrows like our Da, and they contracted and expanded with each solemn word. He was indeed blessing the cake — a large one — for the money he would soon be jingling in his pockets, snorted the cynic in me. As if he'd heard my silent scorn, he raised his head and looked straight at me. I was mortified. His black eyes pierced right into my godless soul. Then he smiled and everyone, including me, took in a deep collective breath. Someone handed him a large knife and he set to cutting the cake into little slices so that all would be fed. One by one people came up and took a slice and left their contribution for Father Christopher. He bobbed his head and cut the cake, glancing over the room to see if anyone needed a slice. Josie's brothers were busy serving the punch. Mrs. O'Rourke sidled in through the doorway, accompanied by her five children who stared at the remnants of the cake. Father Christopher motioned for them to come forward. Mrs. O'Rourke shrank back, smiling. Of course. She had no donation. The crowd became noisier and noisier. I slipped up to Father Christopher and whispered that I would take a plateful to the O'Rourkes if he didn't mind. He simply said, "Bless you, child," and shovelled six small slices onto a dish. She saw me coming and seemed to cringe, trying to diminish herself.

"O'Rourkes!" I called out merrily. "Will you not share in our happiness?" and plunked the plate down on the table next to where they were standing. ·

Many of the people there knew how Mrs. O'Rourke had spoken badly of me in the past. They poked each other and whispered behind their hands. So what, I thought: *There you go, Mrs. O'Rourke, all is forgiven.* The children crowded up to the plate and carefully the oldest daughter parcelled out the small slices. Mrs. O'Rourke tried to smile at me. On impulse I threw my arms around her and felt her jerk wildly like a small frightened animal.

"Thank you for my Mam," I said into her ear, getting a whiff of her smoky hair, and then let her go. She stumbled a little backwards. I looked up in triumph to see Colum staring at me as if I'd gone mad. Well, maybe I had. I pursed a kiss to him, feeling suddenly daring, caring for nothing. And then people were lifting the table to the wall. Someone started up a fiddle.

AFTER JOSIE SWUNG MAIRI out in the first dance it wasn't long before the floor was crowded. One of the first people up dancing was Colum. Everyone clapped, whistling for his fine dance. One after another the boys stepped up to show off their dancing abilities. My hands reddened with the clapping. Mrs. Keane was up and dancing, her feet kicking out, and for such a round woman she was like a little thistledown. By now everyone was dancing, single or not. Three fiddles played. A roar of approval greeted old Mr. Malley with his pipe, from down near Galway. His son Jeremy grinned beside him. The girls exchanged smiles and their mothers whispered behind their hands, for Jeremy was a fine-looking, dark-haired boy, close to six feet and hefty, all of seventeen, a talented player himself. So many of our young men had left for America or Canada, or had been transported in the recent tithe and land agitations; it was heart-wrenching how eagerly the girls and their mothers gauged each new boy. Would there be no life for them without a husband? Unthinkable. But there weren't enough decent men to go around now. As for me, I'd always had my heart set on Colum and hadn't even thought to look at anyone else. Such misplaced loyalty. I looked now to see him whirling Ida Dooley in a reel.

Ida Dooley was a nice woman, never married, about twice Colum's age. Her head was thrown back and she was laughing so hard I was sure she must be peeing herself. Every woman Colum paid attention to glowed with joy. Ida, bless her, had had precious little happiness. She took care of her old parents in a rude hut close to the shore, scrabbling out a scant living washing clothes for people. Her hair was already streaked with grey and her thin cheeks permanently seamed with care. But here she giggled like a young girl. My heart constricted. I knew what she'd feel like later on tonight when she lay down to sleep, going over and over in her mind each kind, careless comment Colum or anyone else had made, chewing over these lovely moments like a sheep her cud, until suddenly the moments were swallowed, gone, and she was curled up alone on her pallet.

From behind, someone encircled my waist with hard fingers and lifted me off my feet. I shrieked.

"At your sister's wedding and you with a long face!" Andrew Monaghan, it was.

"Put me down, you big monster!" I yelped, full of sudden laughter.

"Not till you dance with me."

Andrew was one of the Monaghan brothers who would be going to Canada with us. He was Josie's friend from boyhood, a stocky youth with powerful shoulders and arms. We were the same height and could look straight into each other's eyes. I didn't know Andrew well.

"I'll dance with you!" I said and he released me. He was strong, with snapping brown eyes and a fine gold beard. His hair on top was already thinning. The fiddlers were beginning another reel. He held out his hands. I took them and away we went. I looked over my shoulder for Colum; he was dancing with Betty Reilly, Ida Dooley's cousin from near Spiddal.

"Are you excited about going?" Andrew leaned toward me with the question, whiskey strong on his breath. Usually the smell repelled me, but not tonight. I leaned closer and shouted above the noise and music, "I can hardly wait to go." I smiled into his eyes like a wanton, all the time hoping that Colum should witness. Andrew had no idea of my game, of course. Man that he was, he came even closer and told me he was planning on settling in the same area where Josie was going. We would be seeing each other there, he promised. Would that please me? I almost didn't hear his question, my mind on Colum. His whiskey breath swept over me again and I realized he was practically standing on my feet, his face in mine. I jerked back and his hands caught me. He grinned at my flush. He thought he'd overcome me with his attention. I forced myself to grin back at him then ducked my head down to escape his eyes. Andrew may have been a nice man, but altogether too proud of himself, a pride I feared. And the drinking. I'd heard stories about how the Monaghan men beat their women. As the father, so the son. Mairi and I had long ago decided against any of that family.

I caught Colum's gaze, only a few dancers away, and held it, willing that he see my careless joy, dancing with Andrew Monaghan. I stuck my tongue out at him and grinned and then quickly turned my head away for the rush of tears to my eyes.

"Excuse me," I muttered to Andrew and pushed aside his hands. "I feel sick."

Outside in the dark I didn't make it to the far wall in time before vomit surged into my mouth. The lovely supper spewed into the grass.

"Oonagh Corcoran, for shame. You haven't been drinking, have you?" Father Christopher was sitting in the dark on the wall.

"No," I muttered. "I ate too much. I'm not used to it."

"Aye," he sighed. "No one is. Weddings, wakes. That's when we get to eat like that. Nowadays," again he sighed heavily, "it's mostly the wakes."

"I'm sorry, Father." I turned to flee.

"Stay, child. Tell me, are you happy to be emigrating?"

"I'll be very glad to see Michael again." *Whom you tossed from the church!*

"Oh, yes. He's doing very well, so I hear."

"Very well." *No thanks to your church, Father!*

"Will you be coming to confession tomorrow?"

"No. I've nothing to confess." And then, "More's the pity."

To my surprise the priest laughed out loud.

"Indeed, Oonagh. Let's hope your fortunes change in Canada!"

"Oh, they will, Father!" I was lightened by his laughter. He wasn't such a grim man, not with those eyebrows that even here in the dark had a way of glowing like snowy bushes.

"Oonagh!" called Andrew from the barn door. "Are you all right?"

"She's just fine," called Father Christopher. He whispered, "Is that your young man?"

"I have no young man, nor do I wish one," I said rather haughtily.

"That will change." His soft voice was reflective. He slipped down from the wall. "Come, let's go inside to celebrate your lovely sister Mairi and her fine young man."

"I'm feeling ill, Father," I said.

He reached out a hand and gripped me tightly by the shoulder. "You're all right now. Just needed a bit of air. Take a good breath." He turned me back to the byre. "You see your sister there, wondering where you are?"

Mairi was peering out the door. I rushed forward and she threw her arms around me tightly. Thank you, thank you, thank you, she said. She didn't say what for, but steered me inside.

THE EVENING WAS ENDING. Father Christopher had long gone and now the older people were saying their goodbyes. I had danced with everyone who asked — even old Dickie Clooney, who stank like the inside of a whiskey jar — everyone, except for Colum, who remained at the corner of my eyes all night. He never came close. I'd swallowed glass after glass of water, feeling hot and sweaty as if I'd been raking hay in the sun, and the sickness I'd felt earlier was gone for now. But I felt weary. With Father Christopher gone and some of the grannies, too, we were getting ready for the last. Mrs. Reilly shooed her two youngest girls out of the door. Some folks didn't like this last dance, thought it too forward. I'd always thought it the greatest fun, but tonight, with Colum pretending I didn't exist, this dance would be misery itself. I was torn between staying and leaving.

The pipes started up, slow and mournful at first, then picking up speed, gay and saucy as the fiddles joined in. Everyone milled about expectantly. Who'd be the man to start the dance? A cry went up as suddenly whirling about in the centre with the large white handkerchief was our own Liam. We all started hooting and clapping. He twirled about the crowd, waving the kerchief, stomping to the music, then, no surprise, he stopped in front of Libby Harrington, the publican's daughter. He threw the cloth around her neck, fell on his knees, and gently drew her down. She was a wee thing, only up to his shoulder. So it was wonderful to see her kneel too in front of him and see him reach forward and give her a swift little kiss on the cheek. Then just as swiftly he was back on his feet, his face burning red, and beginning his trot around the barn. Libby rose, slightly bewildered. Who would she choose? Her eyes followed Liam, as if she wished she could go up and choose him. But that's not the way of the dance. People started to urge her to choose someone soon so we could all have our turns. She finally ran up to her own brother Niall and threw the hankie around his neck. Everyone laughed. Niall dropped to his knees obligingly and received his sister's little peck, which then released her to run after Liam and follow him, hanging on to his shirttails. The great fun of the dance was in guessing who would choose whom. If there was someone you fancied greatly, either you wished desperately that he would fling the kerchief around your neck or that he would remain free long enough so that you could do the same to him. It was always fun to be surprised, when someone picked another no one had guessed. Like when Niall came bounding over the floor and swept the kerchief around Lizzie's neck. Our little Lizzie! She dropped to her knees as if he'd used a scythe on her and everyone roared. But when he went to drop a kiss on the top of her head like some big brother, our Lizzie surprised him, for she raised her lips to him instead. Once again we laughed and some whistled. Niall had thought he was hiding his affection for Lizzie in a huge joke. After all, she was only twelve, and he a big bruiser of a fellow at fifteen. He'd thought to make us laugh and we did laugh. But more at him, for in spite of himself his face glowed red. Lizzie grinned triumphantly at us. Now whom would she choose?

On the dance went, the music varying from slow to fast, the chain of dancers growing. I wanted to leave. I was afraid Andrew would choose me and then I would have to choose, and there was only one I wanted and he was still unselected, waiting by the door. But suppose someone chose him, then whom would he choose? I began to feel sick again. I couldn't very well leave with Colum himself standing so close to the door. Why hadn't I left earlier as had some of the other unmarried girls? This dance could be fun but it could also be painful. Suppose you remained unselected to the end? The music played faster and faster and people were hooting and yelling and laughing. Then Betty Reilly pulled Andrew down with her and planted a big kiss right on his mouth and he kissed her fiercely back until the crowd started shouting "Enough!" I sank down behind Mairi's skirts so that he couldn't see me, but I needn't have worried, for Andrew Monaghan was drunk enough that he grabbed out for the nearest woman, and she happened to be Ida Dooley. I laughed aloud for I knew now how this would end. Sure enough, Ida made straight for Colum and wrapped the kerchief securely around his neck and practically tumbled him over to the floor. Everyone could hardly stand for laughing. After a sloppy attempt at a kiss, she released him and she joined the long procession that was winding around the barn now. The chosen ones. Colum cast his eyes about and came straight to me. He draped the cloth about my neck and drew me to him. The room hushed and the walls fell away. He pulled me into the centre and fell on his knees, and there on his knees his head was at my breast and all I wanted was to wrap him close. But he drew down steadily on the kerchief around my neck and I dropped to my knees, a good little prayerful maid. He took my face between his big rough hands, the scoundrel, and before all that company, gave me a kiss to last. "Enough, enough!" they were shouting. As for myself, I couldn't breathe. He was smothering me. I thrust him away and my hand lashed out to slap him for such a kiss as that in public, but he gripped my hand and laughed.

"Go choose a lover," he whispered, and away he went to join the tail end of the line, leaving me shaking. I wanted to run after him but that wasn't the game. My legs trembled as I walked up to Dickie Clooney, who was leaning against the wall smoking his pipe. I pulled that old man into the ring, him protesting and laughing, but pleased, you could see. We fell to our knees and I kissed his whiskery old cheek.

"Will you marry me?" that old man shouted as we stood up.

"I cannot," I replied and gave him another little peck on the other cheek.

"Ah, it's a shame," he laughed and everyone with him.

I hurried to join the line, digging my nails into Colum's waist through the heavy shirt he wore. I breathed in the sweet sweat smell of him and that brought back the hills of last September. It was all I could do to restrain myself from pressing closer to him, from hugging him full around the waist. Each movement of his body ahead of me shuddered through my hands and up my arms into my body.

Then I realized that Dickie Clooney was standing in the middle, the last person with the hankie. We moved in a circle about him. He would be the start of the unravelling. He circled with us until he suddenly darted forward and picked Ida and drew her into the circle. Once again the same process of falling to the knees, the kiss and then she led him to a seat. She could return to the circle and pick a partner herself. Sometimes people picked the same partners and sometimes not. Ida took Colum again and again we all laughed as she dropped him to his knees. He was soon up and I held my breath, waiting for him to come to me but he chose someone else entirely. I watched as he drew her down. He kissed her hard as he had me, to everyone's hoots of laughter, then leaped up, whirling around and slapping his heels in a crazy jig, the crowd clapping and yelling in appreciation for his antics.

The ecstasy of my being collapsed. It had been just a game, a silly dance to finish up the wedding festivity, an amusement for him. The music still played fast as people danced. A wave of tiredness swept up my limbs. Dawn with its cool air had arrived in the windows. I left the dance before anyone else could choose me or I him. It's not good luck to do that, to break the chain prematurely. But I didn't care. I felt as heavy as that stone by the sea, and as cold. Colum followed me outside. He said in a low voice, "Don't leave so early." I shook my head at him, smiled wearily, and saw how apologetic his eyes looked. How long I had known him. All our lives. At that I felt much better, a strange sort of peace stealing into me. The stars were fading in the sky above us and the sea was lit up with the dawn. I put up a hand to his soft brown beard, shaking my head. I found my voice.

"Goodbye, Colum. Take care of yourself."

"And you. Be careful of those Canadian men." His voice was joking but tender. He gave me a quick hard hug and turned to go back indoors. "Sleep well now." Those were his last words to me.

Five

THE SOUND A GROWN man makes in his anguish can terrify the hearts of his children. Early on the day of our departure, when I'm sure he thought we were all asleep, across the darkness I heard Da, a man bereft. I could not go to him for he'd spurn anyone's attempt to staunch his grief. He'd wept so last when Johnny was hanged. Mam's soft voice had shushed him as he tried to muffle his sobs. But when Mam herself slipped away on us, we never heard him cry.

Mona stirred beside me and then lay so still I was sure she too was listening. I held my breath. She sighed deeply and her breathing relaxed into sleep again.

At the sound of Mona's sigh, Da was silent. A few moments later he rose and quietly left the house. I waited, thinking he'd relieve himself and return. When he didn't, I rose and peered through the window to see if I could see him. It was still dark, the brilliant stars hanging low, but a faint thread of light lit the horizon on the sea. Mrs. Keane's roosters were beginning to crow. As I peered through the window I suddenly realized Da was sitting on the wall in front of the house, facing the sea, the bulk of him darker than the sky.

I quietly took the blanket off Da's bed to wrap around us both and crept out. The door hinges creaked and I paused on the threshold, but no one else awoke. The cold dew soaked my feet. A slight wind off the hills carried the scents of the freshly tilled soil in the garden. Da turned his head slightly as I approached but said nothing.

I settled next to him and placed the blanket around us both. He didn't refuse it. We sat on the cold stone watching the sky lighten in the east.

"A fine day for travelling," he said.

"Da. You must see what you can get for the loom."

"No," he said. "We've managed to keep it all these years. Mona may use it."

"It could bring the price of a passage ticket. They're less costly now than when Michael and Jane left. You could sell everything and with what we'll be earning in Canada you could all come by autumn."

"So many ships now, everyone leaving. These companies all want the business. That's why the price has gone down."

"What's left for any of us here?"

Da turned and looked me full in the face. The light of the dawn lit up the crags and creases of his face. He smiled, his face creasing even more in the delightful way that gladdened my heart. He turned, indicating by his head that I should turn too, to look behind us. The hills were bathed in the sunlight now pouring over the islands in the bay, blazing a path on the water. The white walls of the house shone as if newly whitewashed and the oat thatch glittered like gold. The spring grass shimmered in the wind between the chaos of the boulders strewn across the slopes and in the fields enclosed with stone walls. I knew every boulder and path through the boggy places, hummock to grassy knoll, up, up to the summit where the small lake glittered like a jewel, where turning in a circle one could see north to the bare heads of the mountains and south and west and east, the sea, the inlets, small islands and coastline itself jutting out like fingers grasping at the Atlantic. Out of sight but within our vision always, that graveyard overlooking the sea where the long green grass swept like a mantle of grace over new graves and old, where Da intended himself to lie. He knew I could see all this even as we remained in silence. He put his arms around my shoulder and comforted me as he hadn't done since I was very small.

We sat on the wall and watched the sun born again out of the sea, launching itself into the blue sky scudded and streaked with feathery pink clouds. Behind us in the house, Liam and the girls stirred awake. We watched in silence as below Mrs. Keane walked to the byre with a pail to milk her cows. Mrs. Keane and her milk cows who had saved us a few times with her generosity. In turn we'd scythed and raked and stacked her hay. I knew she'd keep her eye on Da and Liam and the girls. She was a good and loving woman who'd lost her own husband at sea almost twenty years ago. She lost her boy Adam when we lost our John.

"She's a good woman," I murmured. Da squeezed my shoulder.

"You've a walk ahead of you. You must get ready now." But he held me tightly even as he said this and so we lingered a while longer. Behind us the door burst open and our Lizzie came dashing out.

MAIRI AND JOSIE HAD come from the McGanns' house two miles west of the village and were waiting in the village by the time we walked down, all of us together, picking up Mrs. Keane as we went. The Monaghans had brought a handcart to carry our bundles and bags of provisions. We had only to walk as far as Cloch na Rón, where it was arranged that one of Da's Claddagh nephews was waiting to transport us in his boat to the port at Galway from where our ship, named *Elizabeth*, would be sailing. We loaded up the cart and several people in the crowd now gathering to see us off added small sacks of potatoes for the sea voyage. We were grateful for this generosity so early in the year. When we reached Galway, we would buy yet more provisions such as Michael had listed in his letter. Da was sad that Father Christopher had not managed to come to see us off. "Oh, he should be here. You could use his blessing," he kept repeating. I tried to comfort Da by telling him that the new priest was in Cloch na Rón and was going to bless us there. I knew Da was afraid for us in our long journey over the dark sea. I was afraid myself. I wanted to stay now. But as a leaf is caught up in a brown spring flood, so were we swept along through the village, the press of the friends and neighbours allowing us no retreat. They followed us through the village and up the winding track to the post road. People shouted advice and prayers for our safety and good fortune. I felt each stone in the path, each rut, thinking, *this is the last time I walk this.* I had to hold on to the side of the cart at times, my vision blurry.

"So, taking your wheel, are you?" Mrs. O'Neil from the village touched the spinning wheel where I'd placed it carefully in the cart. "I hear you have to take great care in those ships not to have such a thing broken. You might be better to leave it for your sisters." She was well-meaning. I smiled and she smiled back and patted my shoulder. "You'll put it to good use, I know, Oonagh. Like your mother, God rest her."

We reached the summit, with the post road in sight, and stopped to catch our breaths and to look back down the tumble of hills to the sea. From here you couldn't see the village at all, or our own house hidden in the fold of the hills. It was here we would be left to go on our way. Until that moment I had managed to keep my grief hidden, even with Lizzie hanging on to my dress. Mairi had walked the entire way holding on to Mona and Da. Liam had helped to pull the cart.

Liam stood beside me now, his face red with exertion. "I could go all the way with you, help with the cart," he suggested.

"You could come with us all the way to Canada. We'll stow you aboard like a sack of potatoes!" laughed Josie.

"You'll be coming back down now with us," Da said, clamping one hand on Liam's shoulder. "We've work to do."

And then the whole mad bunch of us were weeping, Lizzie wailing to break my heart. I don't think she had quite realized until that moment, when Da turned away to walk back down the road, that we were leaving without her and what that meant. We watched as Da walked away, not once looking back at us; I knew why he couldn't. I admonished Liam and Mona to take good care of Lizzie and of each other until we could meet again. Mrs. Keane gathered heartbroken Lizzie into her arms and slowly returned down the hill. Liam wouldn't let go, drawing Mairi and me into a Corcoran crush. I managed to reach deep into myself and come up with a smiling face and a cheerful voice.

"I'm sure Libby Harrington is waiting to comfort you," I whispered into his ear. His arms tightened around me and Mairi, and suddenly he raced away from us, disappearing too soon around a bend. I sank to the ground, weeping until Mairi pleaded for me to stop. Father Bob Shea was waiting at the quay to bless our departure. Would I be the one to delay our journey into evening? As we walked on, the cart creaking in the ruts, I kept looking back in vain for a last glimpse of Liam.

WE WERE MORE FORTUNATE than some in that we had Da's relations living in the Claddagh and we could stay with them until the ship was ready to sail. On the departure date it was still not outfitted and we heard stories afterward from some fellow passengers of the hardships this made for them. It was especially difficult for the children travelling alone, such as the three O'Neil boys, all under age fourteen, going to meet their father already in Canada, and for little Winny Deland, thirteen, with a noticeable belly, who had spent the extra three nights huddled on the wharf behind some crates.

She called herself a widow, though I saw brows raised and smirks hardly hidden when she declared herself so at the gangplank. Winny was a beautiful little brown-haired thing, but her voice raised with no temerity when asked to declare herself at the roll call. She had no family with her. Her own landlord had paid for her passage, but once in Canada she would have to fend for herself. My heart went out instantly to her as I watched her climb the ramp, holding her bundles under one arm, her other supporting a belly that predicted the birth of an infant at sea. Her landlord had taken care of her provisions. Later, when we became friends, she told me who had fathered her infant. Her landlord's son had taken care of that.

We were about one hundred passengers, all quartered in the hold on bunks. Forty-one of us were women. There were twenty-seven children fourteen and under and three infants; of these, seven were orphans, including a small girl of four under the charge of her eighteen-year-old male cousin. Thirty-seven men I counted, with no more than nine over the age of forty. Most of the men were no older than twenty-five; like Josie, they were eager to start a new life. The Walsh family, eight children and father and mother, were the largest family. All these facts about my fellow passengers I gleaned over the hours we spent together.

For the first two days we were in sight of our homeland. On the morning of the third, I walked on deck early to catch some fresh air and saw we were alone on the sea. Fear gripped me momentarily. Long swells lifted the ship and dropped it; my stomach heaved. I stood at the railing looking back to the east where the sun was struggling through the mist, where I imagined Ireland. Others gathered around me, all gazing backwards. Then James Flanerty, who was one of those young boys travelling alone, pulled out a pipe and played a melancholy air. He was a talented player and had all who listened near tears. The captain addressed us. He spoke kindly, advising us to look only forward now, that we were sure to have good lives in Upper Canada, that from now on young Flanerty should play only joyous music to make us dance. His words changed the mood and we went off to prepare our various breakfasts at the fires provided for us on deck.

The first days in what became a lengthy voyage were splendid. The wind carried us swiftly over the water. We walked on deck and breathed the fresh air. In the evenings the Flanerty boy and another young musician, Michael Quinn, played and people danced.

Then came days when the weather kept us below and the sailors yelled at anyone who dared to come above deck for want of a little air or to use a latrine. The ship tossed like a scrap of bark. The smell of seasickness served to increase our misery. I comforted Winny, who cried helplessly in my arms; she was close to her time and full of fear, longing for her own mother. Mairi was ill from the first day at sea; she was already carrying new life. In the first two weeks I myself retched often with the motion of the ship and the rank smell of the bilge water below.

Our vessel was too small for the lot of us crowded into the hold. Josie said that on its voyages from Canada it hauled lumber and was hastily outfitted to carry humans on the return. Conditions were less than proper. The slop buckets spilt as the ship pitched in the swells. When the seas were rough, most of us used these buckets rather than risk climbing on deck to the latrines in the bow. After a particularly heavy swell, one of those latrines swept overboard with a great wash of a wave. Suppose someone had been in it? To be swept overboard as one was relieving one's self, trousers down around the ankles, or skirts hitched up. I tried to make Mairi laugh at the thought of it. But she was appalled at my joke. I hushed her for she began coughing in her agitation. I looked around for Josie. He was in a far corner with the Monaghan brothers, with whom he bunked and spent most of his time.

We almost became used to the foul odours below, as one becomes used to the stink of a pigsty. We shared a berth, Mairi and me, with little Winny and two other single women, one of them, Brigid, with an infant. There was an attempt to accommodate the need for female privacy; we hung a blanket to hide ourselves when we dressed. But there was little privacy. Many times a female voice loudly cursed a man for peeking. There was no water for washing, except what the sailors hauled aboard from the sea. Drinking water was rationed in the last weeks. The voyage took two weeks longer than we'd been prepared for and most of us ran out of provisions. The captain fed us small rations from the ship's stores, a bit of salt pork and mostly a type of hard biscuit we could soak in water to soften. Hunger was not something foreign to us, at least those of us from Connacht. But some townspeople from Galway, not fine enough for a cabin but finer than we, complained bitterly. Maybe they'd never had to go without, never had to see their children's flesh melt away. This was nothing new to us. We simply lay together silently that last hungry week before we reached Quebec. Mairi held my hand constantly. *Sorry, forgive me*, she kept murmuring. I tried to reassure her but finally her plaintive, guilty voice grated on my nerves. *Shut up*, I told her.

The ship pitched and tossed constantly, sliding up mountains of sea and dropping steeply into watery valleys. Josie warned me to stay below. *Tend to Mairi and pray for God's sake*. Every freckle on his thin face stood out like a mole, his skin was so blanched. He was sick more often than Mairi. I wanted to be up on deck, storm or not, to breathe the fresh salt air. Watching those nimble sailors scrambling aloft in the rigging, I envied them the freedom of their sex. As a man, I would have been one of them, with rough hands hauling the taut ropes, shouting against the wind. All seasickness I had when confined in the hold dissipated on deck. Below, terror often rose in my belly with the loud creaking and groaning of the timbers as the ship navigated the huge swells, the unexplained bangs and clapping sounds, like so many whips cracked. With the hatches secured against the weather, the hold was dark and fetid; often no lamps were lit for fear of fire and we crouched together in our berth, clasping each other's hands against our fears.

On the fourth week at sea a storm blew up, lasting nearly a week. We went without cooking, eating only the hard biscuit issued us, and raw potatoes. Most of us were quite ill by then, with the damp from the sea water trickling through the hatches, with the foul air we had to breathe. It was in this terrible week that Winny gave birth.

A braver young woman I had not seen before. One of the other women clasped a candle to light our work. Although tears welled in her eyes, Winny never uttered a single cry in her pain. Mairi and the women of our berth had crowded in with others to make room for Winny. Fortunately at Winny's first labour pain, Sally Hill appeared, smiling and calm. She'd told us all her story of coming over to Galway from England with a man who later abandoned her. She managed by herself, being skilled in midwifery, and had birthed hundreds of babies over the following years. She took over the situation and I was grateful for her bold cheerfulness in this nightmarish place. The faint candlelight threw terrible shadows as the ship lurched up and down.

All around us people shrieked with fear at the chaotic movement of the vessel. Winny's eyes were large and black in that dim light. She pushed mightily with all the force that was in her. Brigid, a widow of eighteen with a small child at her breast, sat on the bunk, Winny's head and back propped against her as she wiped her face. I guarded the berth against curious eyes, shooing away children who were not already held fast in their family's berth.

Then came a moment when the ship rose steeply, up and up. We held our breaths, clutching at whatever would secure us. I squeezed shut my eyes for it felt as if we were rising straight up into the heavens. Everyone in the hold fell silent. The ship climbed to the summit of this tremendous swell, hovered, moments draining away, then with a terrific groaning of timbers the ship slapped down into the trough of that wave. The dark hold erupted into howling and wailing. I'd bitten down on my lip, tasting blood. Something hurtled along the floor past my feet, rolling over and over. Then Sally Hill was exclaiming, "A bonny lass, look!" as she drew out from Winny the tiniest infant I'd ever seen born. And there, in the midst of this hellish place, a tiny piece of perfection drew her first breath. Would that it could have been a breath of fresh air in a place of peace and quiet. Winny held out her arms, laughing and crying as Sally wiped the new infant with a cloth and wrapped her in a small blanket we'd readied for her. It was impossible for anyone to go on deck to get warm water from the galley for washing this new infant or for cleaning Winny, who had torn with the birth and was bleeding. Sally Hill had sent me around earlier to retrieve a bit of clean water into a basin from anyone in the hold who would contribute and that was how we were able to wash the infant's face and head clean of the birthing.

Two days later, when the weather calmed, the captain himself sent down a boiled egg for Winny with the message that each day remaining at sea she would have an egg as long as the hens laid. Furthermore, when the weather improved to allow us back on deck, we would have a christening, himself officiating. It was obvious to everyone that the child should be named Elizabeth after the ship. Because of the storm, almost two weeks remained of increasing hardship. We feared for Winny and her infant as well as others who remained ill and scarcely moved from their berths.

FROM THE BEGINNING I'D had conflict with my brother-in-law, who insisted I stay below with the women. He was now the authority in our little family. I had little choice but to obey him. People were talking about me walking among the sailors, he said. It was unseemly. Mairi agreed with him. I'd told Mairi about the sailors' lewd comments, and how I'd laughed at their suggestions and invitations, telling them I'd sooner roast in hell. Mairi was horrified. "Oonagh, they'll think you're flirting with them if you laugh like that!" She was right. Woe to any of us women who wandered alone on deck after dusk. Brigid told me how she'd gone to one of the latrines after dark and how one of the scoundrels had grabbed her breast, attempted to kiss her face, thrusting himself lewdly against her, refusing to let her go until she screamed suddenly, frightening him. Indeed, many of the women had their own such stories. I didn't tell anyone, not even Mairi, that I'd had to fight off Andrew Monaghan's attentions several times in the dark hold, when he'd corner me in an embrace, holding me tight, rubbing himself against me. His breath always stank of whisky and I wondered at his endless supply. Each time I struggled away and the last time I had kneed him hard as he tried to lift my skirt, his hands rough on my skin. He fell back, cursing me. After that incident he left me alone.

More and more I was confined below. I missed the taste of salt spray on my lips, my time of dreaming alone. On deck I could dream of Colum, for being at sea made me feel close to him. If I'd been born male, I'd surely have been a sailor. I would have sailed with Colum, inseparable companions to the end of our days. Instead, here I lay confined in the dark hold, able only to imagine sleeping on deck, the magnificent sky, the stars and moon wheeling above.

ONE MORNING WE AWOKE to the relative silence of a becalmed ship. I scrambled up on deck, ignoring the threat of gossip, ignoring Josie's black scowl. I climbed into a fog such as we had at home, when the mountains would disappear in a grey wall. If I didn't know better, didn't hear the shouts of the sailors, the creaking of the rigging, I could've imagined myself at home waiting for the fog to lift so that I might see once again the mountains behind us or the island in the channel. But here we were, far out at sea, the middle of nowhere at all, in a dense fog. A sailor standing at the rail muttered that we were not far off the Grand Banks. At any moment we could fracture upon a reef. I strained to hear the crash of breakers on rocks but was thankful to hear only the wind in the rigging as it slowly picked up. When the fog lifted, the sailor shouted, "Land!" I could not see what he was pointing out. "Perhaps," he said, "your eyesight is poor. Sure and there's land on the horizon." I had to take him on faith alone.

After the fifth week many of us had begun to sicken with the foul drinking water and the lack of nourishment, reduced as we were to rationed food. Several people were lost to illness, ship's fever, and how we ourselves didn't succumb I don't know. Mairi said God was protecting us. I didn't argue with her, but why did He protect us and not the widow Mahoney who was going to join her sons in Montreal? Why did He not rest his protecting hand on the little Jameson lad, no more than three years, who the men had to let go to the sea? Why did He dry up little Winny's milk so that her infant had no sustenance? Winny tried and tried in vain to feed the infant. She soaked a cloth in that foul liquid we had for water and coaxed the infant to suck on that but to no avail. Winny's mistake was her pride, for at first she refused Brigid's offer to nurse the child herself. When Brigid finally took the infant to her own breast, it was too late. My sister whispered it was God's mercy on Winny, and now she could truly begin an unencumbered life in the new land. She said this as we gathered at the railing to watch that small bundle, only lately christened Mary Elizabeth, barely a week old, our piece of perfection born in a storm, drop into the sea with scarcely a splash. Winny herself, feverish, lay uncomprehending in the dark hold.

Mairi said that we cannot question God's wisdom. I questioned His very existence. With no surgeon on board this little ship, we had no name to give to the illnesses that now began to take people away. Rash fever, bowel complaint, typhus? This was the year just before cholera devastated so many thousands. I've often wondered since if it wasn't the cholera already that visited us on that terrible voyage. Mairi wasted away with fever and inability to keep any food, including broth, in her belly. Three days after the sea burial of Winny's baby, Mairi lost the new life she'd started. I'd awakened to hear her groaning with pain. In the dark I felt the wetness of blood seeping from under her clothes. I tried to staunch the blood she shed and grew more terrified as her blood soaked the cloths I pressed to her. I yelled for Sally Hill. Josie came running too. He thought he was losing Mairi. Sally told him to go back to sleep for there was nothing he could do now. Sally Hill, that thin Englishwoman whose speech I could hardly understand, was altogether a marvellous healer. Together we stopped Mairi's bleeding, though we could not ease her pain. Sally Hill showed me the tiny bit of new flesh Mairi had expelled. *About four months*, she muttered. I turned away for fear of vomiting. Josie was beside himself with fear and self-loathing and regret that we hadn't remained in Connemara. I cared for Mairi best I could, keeping to myself this bitter question: *Is this God's wisdom and mercy, Mairi, to take away your early baby or is it His retribution for your sin?*

WHY WAS I SPARED? I worried about Mairi. She'd been seasick, sick from pregnancy, with not enough to eat, and now she'd lost so much blood. Her spirits were low. Little Winny, lying in the berth next to Mairi, refused to rouse herself, refused anything but a bit of broth. Except for her eyes, which seemed larger and larger with each passing day, Winny diminished right before us. Another week and she might have followed her infant into the deep. Mairi kept muttering and fingering her beads. Why didn't God strike me down, me, the pagan unbeliever? I lay at the end of the berth, curled at Mairi's feet, past hunger, sinking in and out of blessed sleep. If only I could sleep forever. When I was awake I cursed my overactive angry mind; I cursed the thoughts that roiled there, that I could share with no one. Then one day I heard the call on deck — *land* — and joined the rest of the healthy ones rushing for the ladder up. I was on deck as we rode at anchor off Quebec.

BECAUSE WE HAD SOME sickness aboard and had had several deaths, we could not disembark at Quebec. But arrangements had been made for us to go ashore on a small island down the river. Food and water would be provided, we were told. No one was to be allowed into Quebec. We were all going on to Upper Canada and the authorities wanted to ensure that we would not be spreading pestilence. They were afraid of typhus and smallpox. We were to take all our clothing, whatever we had, to wash. While we were on land, the ship's crew would clean the ship thoroughly, ridding it of rats and other vermin, as well as cleaning out the steerage where we had lived like dirty pigs for so long.

Mairi wanted desperately to accompany us, but in her weakened state we feared she might fall into the sea at the transfer from ship to small boat. She and Winny were allowed to remain on board, seated on deck. Mairi breathed in great gulps of good, clean, pine-scented air. She laughed and laughed and then began to weep. No one could comfort her. Winny beside her was in a sullen stupor. Sally Hill touched Mairi's heaving shoulders, then said, *It's in God's hands now.* The most hopeless words, if you could have heard her sigh. The sun shining on Mairi revealed how dirty she was after all these weeks. I was no better. None of us were. We stank worse than a filthy barn as we emerged from the hold, the lot of us, eyes tearing in the sudden light. The day was warm and overcast but we couldn't help gasping at the country before us. I felt apprehension at the sight of the mountains along the north shore of the river, high as those at home but densely covered in dark forest. The south shore looked well-settled with houses and barns and fields stretching far back from the river. Josie gripped my shoulder. I'd never seen him so happy, not even on his wedding day. We scrambled over the side, into the boat with our bundles of clothing and blankets. There was fresh water on the island. The ship would be provisioned by a steamer coming from Quebec.

People fell down upon the broad rocks of the shore and wept. Josie spun into dance, leaping and slapping his shins in a jig. Everywhere around us people milled about, talking excitedly, comparing voyages. Several other ships lay at anchor and had disgorged their human cargoes. The accents flowed around me. County Mayo. Donegal. Antrim. Sligo. Belfast. My ears pricked for the language of Galway and I swivelled my head to see the speakers of certain accents and voices. People's faces leaped into my vision with the terrific force of recognition only to recede as I realized they were strangers. So many of us! How many distant relatives we had! I glimpsed my father's face in the few grizzled old men who wandered lost among all the young people so glad to be in this new land. In a few years Ireland would be empty of people, the young gone, the old dying of broken hearts and loneliness. Wouldn't the fine lords be pleased then? All that lovely grassy land for their beef cows and fancy horses.

Most of the children were employed in stamping on the clothing in tubs of water. Some people were in the river itself, swishing their clothes. My eyes were caught by those little children who sat silent, intently watching the proceedings, so frail they hadn't the strength to help. Instead, their mams set them to guard the family linen drying on the bushes or flat boulders. Josie and I had no tub in which to wash, so I fastened my skirts high up on my thighs and entered the river. The water was clear and cold. Josie didn't bother to roll his pant legs up because he said they needed a good scrubbing. I feared he would ruin them but it wasn't my place to say a word. We both got to work scrubbing, especially the cloths we'd used for poor Mairi. Although I'd rinsed them with the seawater a sailor had drawn for me, they were badly stained. I didn't know if they'd be salvageable, they needed to be boiled, but at least they would be clean and we could use them for something. I plunged arms into that cold river water, again and again raising the heavy soaked cloth, my skin rapidly reddening with cold. A woman sitting on the bank near me told me I'd do better to get a stick and "beat hell out them rags." We had no soap, but a pounding would do. She was right. I got Josie to find me a good stout stick. The woman said her name was Margaret, from Ballina in County Mayo. She wanted to know every blessed thing about me and Josie, for she assumed that we were wed. I put her straight about that. She was the very curious, talkative type who can't help referring anything said to some experience of her own. I heard all about her brothers who had decided on New South Wales, where she would have liked to go except that her husband preferred taking his chances in Canada. Four years since she'd seen him but he'd be waiting for her on the docks in Port Hope.

"Now isn't that just a fine name for a town?" she said.

I hauled our linen sheet out of the water and the woman leaped up to help me wring it. I looked around for Josie to rescue me — I was weary of her talk — but he was away in the distance in a knot of men. *Well, isn't that just like him*, I thought with irritation, *deserting just when the work gets hard.*

Margaret chattered on and on. *Port Hope.* I prayed she wasn't settling anywhere near where we were going. We wrung the sheet vigorously, shouting at the little children who came running out of nowhere to bat at the huge bubble formed in the centre as we wrung it. They stood giggling in the shower of water that dripped like rain from the sheet. These children were wild beasts, running about, fighting, screaming. Where were their parents? Then a gang of terribly untidy ones, their hair tangled, unwashed, snot dripping from their noses, raced up to Margaret, screeching for her attention, each complaining about the other. I'd hardly thought Margaret old enough to have so many children, especially as the youngest, carried on a young girl's hip, was not more than two. Surely Margaret's husband had not fathered this last one! She pushed them away. *Go find yer mam; don't bother me now.* They gave her strange looks and glumly turned away. The girl with the baby looked back once with reproach.

"Whose are they?" I blurted out.

"Oh," she laughed. "Mine and me sister's. I've no patience for wee ones so I call her mother to all five. She looks after them while I look after the farm work and such. Well, I did, with our husbands gone. I don't know what we needs them men for anyway, except to plant us a little seed now and then!" She guffawed so loudly I couldn't help laughing too. She thrust out her arm and ordered me to feel the muscles.

"That's me doing all the work of a man and a woman besides."

I declined to touch her fleshy freckled arm but murmured some appropriate word of appreciation. Around us people shouted and laughed. Raunchy jokes. Somewhere a fiddle started up.

"Uh oh," she laughed. "There's the music and there's me feet." She did a little jig right there on the boulders while I tried to lay out the sheet to dry. She was in my way. Deliberately, I suddenly saw, her eyes dancing.

"What a long-faced puss you are," she said. "A bit of dancing should cheer you up. There's dancing after the sun goes down. Here, let me help you lay this over the bushes. It'll dry better than on the rocks, less chance of people tramping on it. Such fine linen! People don't care, you know. They'll tramp on anything. You have to watch so's no one takes it."

We laid out the rest of the clothes over bushes and the tall sweeps of grass skirting the bouldered shore. I didn't promise her I'd come that evening for the dancing. I planned to be back on deck to watch the sun sink into the river upstream. As if she'd read my thoughts, she said, "Did your captain tell yis that you'd all be sleeping on shore tonight? Oh yes, but no one sleeps while the fiddle plays!"

My heart was sorely dismayed for Mairi's sake. Perhaps I could wrangle my way back somehow. But when I inquired of the sailors down by the wharf, they said it was orders. All to sleep ashore and we'd reload next morning early after the provision ship had come. Ah, he didn't want a fight on his hands that old captain. With us ashore, there'd be no one clamouring for the food he couldn't provide. It would be a hungry night for us. I looked out to where our ship bobbed at anchor. It was far out enough that I couldn't distinguish people on board, but the tiny figure at the rail must have been Mairi. I'm sure she couldn't tell me from anyone else on that crowded shore.

By the time I caught up with Josie, he'd already sampled a fair supply of the local drink. How had it appeared? He smelt like raw whisky. He and his friends the Monaghans and some others I didn't know. I hadn't known Josie to drink much, but Andrew and Kiernan both drank regularly and often to excess. Andrew's eyes were bloodshot. I began to back away from the way he leered at me. But it was Josie himself who proved the pest.

"Isn't this a grand land, Oonagh, darlin'!" he said, and tried to throw his arms around me. The others with him laughed as I pushed him away.

"Get away," I growled at him. This was the Josie I didn't care a whit for. I'd seen him like this only a few times and each time he made a perfect fool of himself. "Find yourselves a rock and crawl under it," I heard myself. The next instant he backhanded me. And laughed, looking at his friends, all as drunk as he. Tears sprang to my eyes with the shock and the pain of it. I tasted blood; my lip began to swell.

"This piece of baggage is me sister-in-law, as you well know by now, Andrew." His arm was now tightly around my neck as if he were about to pummel me with the other. "Most of the time she's a good girl, but she does have a nasty bite to her. Any takers?"

Andrew laughed loudly and said, "What will you pay me?"

I swore at Josie and managed to wrest myself away. "With your poor wife sick on board ship! Shame on you, Joseph McGann." He grinned foolishly, swaying; tomorrow he'd have a splitting head and would remember none of this.

Andrew Monaghan threw his arm across Josie's shoulders.

"Don't you go abusing this fine boy," he growled. "If you were my woman, I'd teach you manners."

"Thank God for small mercies!" I almost spat the words at him. That I'd once thought him the slightest bit agreeable! At my words he raised a fist in my direction, then thought the better of it. He said, as if a big joke, "Well, we all knows what Oonagh Corcoran needs, a good deep plowing of the garden."

"It'll take more than the likes of you," I retorted, my face burning. I should have kept quiet and walked away. Why give his words any weight at all? A man like that thrives on embarrassing women. He loves to see the flush on the face and the tears of shame.

"Be polite, you!" Josie slurred in my direction. I would never again look on that man, my dear sister's husband, without remembering how he encouraged such vile talk.

THAT WE HAVE TO rely on such beings! Even our Da had at times gone on week-long drunks, drowning his sorrows, and we were supposed to just forgive the men this. At that moment, looking at Josie and the other sorry lot with him, all supposedly fine men, I resolved never to take a husband but to work hard for myself alone.

However, the future is never predictable and such resolve can melt like snow in a warm spring sun. Everything changed when I met Chauncey. He was the exception, for I never once saw him drink. He was not a saintly person, but he never drank, he told me, because it was impossible to be vigilant if one was drunk.

Chauncey. The very name makes me think of dancing, or the way a deer has of sailing through the air over a fence. I hear his voice in my ear, that low chuckle that was meant for me alone. If I'd never met Chauncey, I might've become a very sour and lonely old woman, dry and brittle as a withered cornstalk. Instead there are not enough hours in the day or night for my work, and love for people and gratitude for life itself pervades every inch of my being.

Six

"OONAGH." THE TEASING SWOON in his voice as he said my name. "Oonagh. I've never heard of such a name before. OOO now!" he said. "Ooo ooo now! You from across the water too? Same as this little squirt?" He pulled at Daniel's long hair. His pronunciation was like butter sliding off a hot oatcake. "What kinda name is that, anyhow?" His brows raised like dark half moons.

"My own," I retorted. "My very own, if you don't mind. Now, Chauncey" — here I went sarcastic, I couldn't help myself — "Chauncey? Where'd you get such a fancy name yourself?"

I meant to imply *a fugitive slave like you with a fancy name like that!*

He just threw back his head and roared laughter. He bent over and slapped both his thighs. I watched him open-mouthed, I must admit, with confusion. Beside us, Daniel, my nine-year-old nephew, was in perfect imitation, slapping his own bony little thighs. Hahaha! Was it that funny then, what I'd said?

The man wiped his eyes on his white barber's smock, so white against his dark face. He was the first black man I'd ever seen. Close up. Mairi had pointed out some men working on the docks in Montreal and I'd tried not to stare too much, lest they might consider me rude. We were coming down the gangplank of the *Elizabeth*, getting ready to transfer to the boat that would take us all the way up the St. Lawrence to Upper Canada and Mairi exclaimed, "Oh, Oonagh, look over there!" I'd looked. They took no notice of us with our bundles. They were too busy unloading and loading. I whispered, asking if they were slaves, and Josie overheard me and scorned me, *didn't I know only in the States were there slaves still, and shame on them for it.*

"Well, you got me there, Miss Oonagh, you surely did," the barber chuckled. He rubbed Daniel on the top of his head and Daniel grabbed his arm and made as if to swing off it. "But for your information, may I say that Chauncey is a fine old name signifying good luck — *bonne chance* — as they say down in New Orleans. And that's me, a lucky man. I chose my own name. Chauncey, for the reason I just said, and Taylor ... after a great man I once met. Has a nice ring to it, don't you think? Chauncey Taylor, at your service." He swept low in a bow and then burst out laughing again. This time I had to laugh with him, for I knew he wasn't laughing at me but just laughing for the sheer relief of it. "My friends call me C.T., however. People just love to shorten things up!"

"What did your mother call you?" I asked, cutting off his laughter.

"Ah," he said. "Now, now that is something else." Suddenly he reached out and grabbed Daniel up in his arms and swung him around, the boy giggling. "I bet I know what your mother calls you: little squirt. Danny boy, huh? And Daniel Corcoran when she's mad at you."

"No, she calls me Daniel," Daniel shouted.

"Is she never mad at you?"

"We have to go now," I said quickly. I was ashamed of myself, of my impertinent tongue. Speaking like that to a stranger I'd just met! We took our leave and walked away toward the mill where Daniel's father, my brother Michael, was waiting with the wagon. Halfway down the street we could hear Chauncey laughing again and I turned to see. He was talking with old Mr. Jesper. Daniel grinned up at me. I rested a hand on his shoulder.

"See? I told you. Isn't he nice?" Daniel would have spent all his time with Chauncey if he could.

"Oh," I replied. "That man's got a powerful laugh."

Daniel laughed delightedly and skipped a step. "Auntie Oonagh, you should hear his stories. You should! You'd hardly believe the half of them!"

"He's a liar, is he?" I squeezed his shoulder teasingly. Daniel wrenched away from me, his eyes flashing.

"No! It's all true."

"Aw, you'd believe anything he says, wouldn't you?"

Now he was peeved. We walked a few moments in silence. He angled a sly look at me. "I think he likes you."

"Indeed not. We just met, silly." I felt a foolish warmth in my cheeks.

Daniel continued, "I knew you would like him. I told him you would."

"Daniel Corcoran!"

"It's true. You do, you do!" He laughed and spun out of reach. The truth was Daniel's tales about Chauncey had quite prepared me to like him long before I met him. I was curious about my nephew's hero.

CHAUNCEY HAD ARRIVED IN Cobourg in the fall of 1830. It was several months before he established his barbering business. By some good fortune, my brother Michael had driven in by sleigh from the farm with his family on the very day at the end of January that Chauncey opened up shop.

Daniel left his parents and sister Meg inside the store opposite Buck's Hotel and took a stroll down the street. He was so excited to be in town instead of alone on the small bush farm. People everywhere. He walked toward a newly painted red-striped barber's pole that a man was hammering into place beside the doorway of a small shop. The pole had drawn his attention first. A small knot of people had gathered, curious, joking with the man who was hammering the pole in place, a tall skinny fellow, taller and skinnier than Daniel's da, and a few years younger. As he hammered he spoke loudly to the people gathered.

"Chauncey Taylor's my name, barbering's my game. The first five people to sit in my chair and trust my razor will have themselves a free shave and a haircut!"

The crowd laughed and grew larger by the minute.

"Hey, nigger! How do we know you ain't gonna cut our throats?" someone shouted.

"How do you know? How do you know?" The barber only laughed. Daniel craned his neck to see who had flung the insult, but there were now too many people taller than he.

"Yeah!" Another voice shouted. "You niggers killing white folks down there in North Carolina, so we hear."

"Is that so? Is that a fact? I heard it was the opposite! Well, this ain't North Carolina, is it? Praise God!" He waved his hand about and then swept low in a bow. "Chauncey Taylor, folks, at your service, lately come all the way from New Orleans, Louisiana, to this blessed land of snow and cold. No mosquitoes here!"

"Not yet," Daniel called out. The crowd laughed. "Wait until summer and you'll see mosquitoes," he added, encouraged by the laughter.

"Is that a fact? Well, young man, how'd you like to be my first free customer? A haircut — no shave!"

Again the crowd laughed and Chauncey Taylor leaned down toward him. "How about it?"

Daniel didn't know what to say. Chauncey's large eyes were sparkling. Someone shoved Daniel in the back and he lost his balance, slipping on the icy walk in front of Chauncey. He would have fallen if Chauncey hadn't reached out and caught him.

"Whoa there," he said softly and released Daniel, who backed away, eyes filling with tears of embarrassment. People were laughing, with someone, perhaps the one who'd pushed my nephew, laughing the loudest. Michael arrived just in time to witness this. He pushed through the crowd and laid a hand on Daniel's shoulder. He smiled down at his son. Michael spoke to Chauncey. "I hear you're one of the best. Saw your advertisement in the paper."

"Ah, yes, sir. Indeed. This fine boy yours?"

"My first-born." Michael's hand tightened on Daniel's shoulder, gripping hard through the heavy cloth of Daniel's coat as voices taunted in the background.

"I've invited him to be the first to have a haircut, free. First five people will get a free haircut and shave."

"'Cuts like a good-natured joke,' your blade," smiled Michael, quoting from Chauncey's ad.

The barber let out a deep laugh. "Did you like that little verse?"

"Did you make it up yourself?" asked a woman.

During Michael's words with Chauncey, several of the crowd had begun to drift away. Some of the hostile people continued to watch. Which of them had pushed Daniel?

"Well, Madam, a good poet friend of mine composed that verse. He has often himself fallen asleep while I've shaved his face or cut his hair. He is certainly confident of my abilities."

"Yeah, name him!"

The speaker was an American layabout who drank too much at Buck's Hotel, causing trouble and gambling. Daniel hated the taunting tone in his voice, his sneer, and the way he kept grinning around at his friends for support. A coward.

"Josiah Hill is the poet. You may have heard of him. He lives in York."

"A bloody nigger like you?"

Michael spoke directly to Chauncey.

"I'd appreciate a haircut for my boy here and maybe one for me, and me beard trimmed."

Chauncey motioned for them to enter his small shop. Michael had taken Daniel's hand as if he were a small child and they moved forward, the crowd following. The man Michael had thwarted yelled some obscenity but my brother kept on moving and shoved Daniel ahead of him through the low doorway into the shop. It smelled pleasingly of hair ointment and scented soap. Chauncey ushered Daniel into a large chair, but first he placed a smoothed block of wood to make the seat higher. He explained that he was a tall man and he preferred not having to bend his back all day. Michael placed himself at the door and admitted only those who said they wanted to try the barber's services.

"Do you pull teeth too?" asked one man, leaning around my brother's shoulder.

By now Daniel was seated with a clean-smelling cloth tied around his neck. He'd only ever had his mam cut his hair, so he was a bit leery of this stranger snapping the air with his scissors.

"No, I'm one barber doesn't pull teeth," laughed Chauncey, his own teeth flashing white. "What I can do," Chauncey continued as he began snipping at Daniel's hair, "besides barbering is clean clothes, any kind of cloth or silk. You spill some grease on your Sunday best, bring it to me. I have a formula for taking grease and dirt out of practically anything."

"How do you do that?"

"Ah," he said. "Now that is my secret formula. I don't tell a soul so I can't tell you. What's your name, boy?"

"Daniel."

"Well, Daniel, you just tell your mother next time she's got a troublesome stain on her silk ball gown to bring it to me for cleaning —"

"Ball gown?" Daniel hooted.

"Anything needs a good cleaning. Maybe your own wedding suit."

"Wedding suit?" Daniel hooted even louder. Michael laughed.

"I want to thank you," Chauncey said softly.

"Just you do a good job on me beard," Michael said. "It's as good as an advertisement."

"Oh. It'll be perfect."

When he finished cutting Daniel's hair, Chauncey used a large, soft-bristle brush to sweep the itchy hairs from the boy's neck.

"Close your eyes," he ordered, then swept the brush all over Daniel's face. The clipped hairs tickled and Daniel sneezed to everyone's amusement. Carefully Chauncey untied the cloth from around Daniel's neck so that the hair wouldn't get on his clothes.

"Down you go," he said. "Next?"

Michael stepped up and Daniel assumed his place at the door, smiling as people reached in to admire his new haircut with a rub of their hands on the back of his neck. He stared in some concern when Chauncey flourished his gleaming razor above his da's face, recalling what had been shouted in the street. Cut throats? Chauncey began the scrape, scrape of his blade against Michael's cheekbone all lathered in white.

"Careful with me beard, now," Michael warned, then he winked at Daniel in the small mirror in front of him.

"Always, always, sir," said Chauncey as he went to work.

BY ALL ACCOUNTS CHAUNCEY Taylor gained business in a short time. He was quick and accurate with his scissors, kept his razor sharp, and was much appreciated by the men of Cobourg and the surrounding district. Men from as far away north as the little village where we were to settle near Michael's farm came regularly to see Chauncey when they came to Cobourg for supplies or for their mail. The next Daniel saw Chauncey was in late spring. He'd accompanied his father into town for seed and other goods the family needed. This was only a few weeks before Mairi and I landed on the dock at Cobourg. Daniel went off to explore the town, hardly paying heed to Michael's instructions not to be gone too long. To his disappointment he found Chauncey's barbershop closed. He peered in through the small window but could see nothing. Then he heard someone whistling, better than a bird's song, intricate and rambling. The whistling was suddenly replaced by a fine baritone voice singing out, the words not in English. Daniel crept down the alleyway between the barbershop and the next building. There, behind the shop, dressed in a pair of overalls with his sleeves rolled up, was Chauncey, scrubbing away on a washboard stuck in a large tub. A mound of clothes waited in a basket.

So many sheets and shirts. In another basin was a small pile of wrung clothes. Beside him hung a copper kettle suspended from a tripod over a blazing fire.

When Daniel said "Hello," Chauncey dropped the cloth he was scrubbing and whipped around, his dripping fists raised in the air.

Daniel scrambled backwards.

"Boy, don't you know better than to sneak up on a body?"

"I'm sorry." Daniel flushed.

"No, no!" Chauncey laughed. "You startled me. Daniel, is it?"

Daniel was pleased he'd remembered his name. Chauncey turned back to the washtub and began scrubbing vigorously again. Daniel leaned over to see his work. Daniel had only ever seen women doing the washing, though the men could be counted upon to haul up some water and firewood now and then.

"Don't you have a wife?" he asked after a prudent time had elapsed.

"A wife?" Chauncey's eyebrows rose sharply. "'A wife,' the boy says. What makes you think I don't have a wife?"

Daniel watched Chauncey's hands plunging down into the steaming water.

"Isn't that water too hot?"

"It has to be hot to get these linens really clean."

Daniel leaned even closer to sniff the nasty smell, harsh to the nostrils. "Is that your special formula?"

"My special formula?" Chauncey looked at Daniel quizzically for a moment, then burst out laughing.

Daniel laughed too. "You have a lot of clothes!"

"Oh yes, indeed."

"So are you using your secret formula?" Daniel persisted, sniffing and wrinkling up his nose in disgust.

"Boy, you are a curious cat, aren't you?"

"Why do you need so many clothes?"

Chauncey hooted. "Do you think these clothes are all mine?"
More clothes bubbled in the large kettle over the fire; others were

soaking in a barrel off to the left. "Lord love us, child! Why would I want to own all these?" And here Chauncey grabbed a stout stick and began twisting it around in the kettle until he had a large steaming wad of a sheet wrangled onto the end.

"Out of the way!" he yelled and Daniel jumped back as Chauncey swung his heavy burden out of the kettle and into the barrel of fresh cold water. Then he pounded his stick into the barrel as if he were churning butter. Finally he wrung the cloth as best he could and dumped it into the tub with the washboard.

"There!" He wiped sweat away from his forehead with one arm. "None of these clothes is mine, boy. That's just my business. I don't mind doing the washing for folks, long as I get paid. My mama taught me to do it when I used to help her. All them heavy soaked linens and quilts. She always got me to stamp on the clothes in the rinsing tub. I brought her water too." His voice trailed off.

"Does your mam live here too?" Daniel looked around at the door, half-expecting Chauncey's mother to come out.

"No, she lives in Virginia."

"Do you have brothers and sisters?"

"Boy, anyone ever tell you what happened to the curious cat?"

"No."

"No?" Chauncey huffed.

"What happened?"

He paused in his work to stare at Daniel. "Boy, how old are you?"

"Almost ten."

"Is that a fact?"

Chauncey continued with his work while Daniel gawked on. "Daniel," Chauncey said suddenly. "Would you put another stick or two on that fire?"

"Oh, sure!" Daniel leaped to the task, very pleased to be asked to do something. Two fellows came into the yard, seeking their clothes. Chauncey went indoors to retrieve their bundles and one of them told Daniel to scram, they'd heard his father was looking for him.

IN AUGUST DANIEL ARRIVED at the barbershop when there were no customers.

"Ah, just the man I wanted to see," declared Chauncey and he rose up from his chair. He shooed Daniel outside and closed up shop, hanging a small carved wooden fish up on the door.

"Folks'll know I've gone fishing! So they won't wait around." He explained to Daniel's glee. "Let's go see if your pa will let you go fishing."

All that sultry afternoon, in the shade of overhanging willows, they sat by Cobourg Creek near where it emptied into Lake Ontario. They dangled lines into the clear gently flowing water, hoping for a nibble. Daniel pestered Chauncey with questions. Chauncey had revealed his scars accidentally. His back looked like a plowed field, all dark ridges. It had been a hot day and perhaps without thinking he removed his shirt. Daniel gaped. He put a hand out and gingerly touched Chauncey's back. Chauncey jerked away.

"What's wrong with your skin?" Daniel whispered.

"Ain't nothing wrong, boy. Forget it."

"But it's all rough. Is it sore?"

Chauncey shook his line and stared at the water dancing in the sunlight.

Daniel persisted, "Were you born like that? What made them?"

"Whoa, Buck." He tugged hard at Daniel's hair. "Boy? You could use a haircut. Come back to my shop next time you folks come to town. I'll cut it for nothing." His voice was low and casual.

"My aunts have come from Ireland."

"Oh, yeah? Well, bring them for a haircut too."

Chauncey looked serious so Daniel said, "Women don't get haircuts."

"They don't?" Chauncey's eyebrows raised high. "Not ever?"

"Nope," Daniel said emphatically. "They're not supposed to."

"Well, I'll be! Why ever not?"

"They're women!" Daniel laughed. "They're supposed to have long hair."

"Is that a fact? Hmmm ..." He leaned one elbow on his thigh and affected to think very deeply. "What about men and boys like you? Why do they cut their hair, I wonder?"

Daniel had never thought about that. "Do you cut your own hair?" he asked. He reached up and touched the springy black cap of Chauncey's hair.

"I don't need to. My hair stopped growing when I was about your age."

"It stopped growing?" Daniel was amazed. Then he laughed at Chauncey's wink.

Chauncey jerked on the line.

"A fish!" Daniel leaned over to see.

"Well, I'll be hornswoggled! It just got away."

"Aw, Chauncey! How big was it, do you think?"

"As long as your arm."

"No!" Daniel stared into the water. Then he looked up at Chauncey and caught a huge wink. "You're fooling again."

They sat for several silent minutes, then a fish struck Daniel's line. They landed a small bass.

"Your ma will be pleased," Chauncey said. He swiftly killed the fish, tied it to a string, and submerged it. He leaned over to push the catch into deeper water. Daniel saw his scarred back again. His shoulders.

"So what happened to your back?"

He shrugged, the welts like ripples. "I got whupped a few times," he muttered.

"Whupped?"

"Yep."

"Why?" At that point Daniel wasn't quite sure what *whupped* meant. He had a sickening feeling in the pit of his belly. *Whipped.*

"Well, it's like this. The first time, I was a bit younger than you are and I ran away into the woods because I didn't feel like working in the fields that day. My ma had said she'd like a fish for our supper. I wanted to go fishing, just like we're doing today."

"And your da whupped you?"

"My da?" He burst out laughing that chest-deep laugh of his. "Naw. I never had a da. Not like you do."

"Everyone has a da."

"Nope. Not this boy." He thumped himself on the chest. "I was hatched."

"What?" Daniel turned to see if he was joking again.

"Yep, hatched. Under a cabbage leaf, so my ma tells me. She brought me home wrapped up in a handkerchief."

"No! Tell the truth!"

"What? You think I'm lying?"

"You're a human being, not a bird."

He looked at Daniel then down at his arm. "Is that what I am? Well, I'll be!"

"Humans don't get hatched!"

"Oh, indeed?" He grinned slyly, the dimples hollowed in his cheeks. "So how do humans get on this earth, then?"

"Chauncey!" Daniel punched him lightly on the arm. "You know."

"No, no. You tell me. You seem to know a lot for being just a little shaver."

"I don't know nothing," Daniel muttered, feeling rebuked. They sat on the shore in silence. No more fish tugged at their lines. Then Chauncey gave out a huge sigh and began speaking.

"I stayed out in the woods for two days until they caught me. Brought me back to the farm, tied me over a sawhorse, and whupped me." He stood up suddenly, and looking around cautiously, he loosened the rope around his waist and dropped his trousers. Daniel was startled at this. Chauncey's thighs and buttocks were furrowed just like his back, criss-crossed on his thighs and a few such stripes across his shins. He quickly pulled up his trousers and tied the rope firmly, almost angrily.

"Yep. Now some a those I got when I was just your age. When I run out to the woods. Couldn't stand up for a few days. So much blood. You scared of blood, boy?"

"No."

"You ever seen someone whupped?"

Daniel shook his head.

Chauncey jumped up and demonstrated, standing spread-eagled, hunched over an imaginary sawhorse. He leaped back and pretended to be the one with the whip. He slashed through the air.

"'Take that, you worthless piece of dog shit! And that! And that!'"

"Did you cry?" Daniel asked.

Chauncey flung himself back down on the grassy bank.

"Would you cry?" he asked, picking up the pole again and swishing the line through the water.

"I'd kill them!" Daniel declared.

"Ah," he said.

"I would. I wouldn't let them whup me!" Daniel declared.

"Uh huh."

"They wouldn't catch me. I'd run far away."

"Good for you," Chauncey said.

"DO YOU CUT WOMEN'S hair too?" I asked Chauncey.

He laughed. At me, it seemed. I didn't know why. This was our second meeting. It had been my idea that Daniel have a real haircut in town today and I offered to take him while Michael conducted his business. I was eager for a trip to Cobourg and secretly curious about the barber. My brother had agreed. Daniel was looking pretty shaggy.

"I do, and I shaves them too if they need," he said, reaching for his razor from the bench and flourishing it in the air like a little sword. I stepped back. Daniel swivelled his head. I was appalled at the quick vision I had of a cut throat. I stepped back once more, involuntarily. Behind me the old cronies on the bench waiting their turn laughed at me too.

"I only asked," I said.

"Was it for yerself then?" He imitated my accent perfectly, snapping his scissors in the air above Daniel's head.

Another step back and I'd be sitting in someone's lap in that tiny barbershop.

"Goodness!" I touched my braid over one shoulder. "No, not for me, thanks."

"Well, you do have fine black hair, Miss Oonagh," said Chauncey. "I dress ladies' hair very fine. If they've a ball to go to, I can make them look like queens. 'Chauncey,' they used to say to me in Louisiana, 'Chauncey, whatever would we do without you; you're so clever.' They used to tell me that." He suspended his slender hand over Daniel's head for a long moment, his whole being gone silent. Then he shook his head slightly, as if to clear his vision. "Yes sir, ladies and gents, that's what they used to say."

He snipped at Daniel's shaggy blond hair and it fell away in clumps to the plank floor, leaving his neck vulnerable and precious, like sheep when freshly shorn. How much smaller and skinnier they look. I had a sudden thought and laughed. Daniel turned his head to me. I said to the barber, "Have you ever shorn sheep?" The thought of Chauncey working on a smelly old sheep seemed ridiculous; he was so refined in his ways, his hands slender and fine. I couldn't help giggling at the thought. One of the elderly men behind me cackled, "Sheep?"

Chauncey didn't laugh. He bent in closer to Daniel's head as he snipped.

"Indeed, you're right, Miss Oonagh. I started this illustrious career shearing sheep. That's what. I wasn't much bigger than this young fellow here, catching the creatures in the pen. Now that's a job and a half when you're a little shaver. I've done more than my share and then some. It's back-breaking work. But I guess I did a mighty fine job of it all the same. Never a snip of skin or blood drawn. That's me: magic fingers."

He turned his head and looked full at me. Grinned with those dimples. I looked away in some confusion. The word beautiful swam into my mind and a slow heat rose into my face.

He continued, "That's what gave folks the notion I could do people's hair too. Actually, on my time off, that's what I began to do to earn a little cash money for the future. I knew for a long time I was coming up to this blessed land of freedom. So on my own time I cut people's hair. Then the master, he figured I was good enough to be in business for him and there you go: *la chance!*"

As he spoke I couldn't take my eyes from his face, from the expressions that changed swiftly with each thought, like a meadow shadowed in passing clouds. He spoke to Daniel's head, but his words were somehow meant especially for me.

"You escaped, right, C.T.?" Daniel spoke to the barber's reflection in the mirror suspended above the bench.

Chauncey snipped his scissors loudly near Daniel's ear and yelped, "Oops, got a piece of yer ear, I'm afraid!"

Daniel jerked and yelled, "No!" and clapped his hand over his ear. "Ya never!"

Chauncey roared his boisterous laugh. It came from somewhere deep in his chest, the booming laugh of a much larger man. I looked to the men waiting for their shaves and haircuts. I doubt another woman had entered the shop. Smiling, I looked back at the barber, his deft fingers, an artist with the scissors. Then I realized he was looking at me in the mirror. Staring, holding my gaze. I held his a moment longer than I should have. Just like that. I couldn't breathe. He winked and chuckled softly, snipping noises at Daniel's ear until the boy cried out, "You won't do it!" and giggled. Now Chauncey took a soft brush and carefully brushed away the loose hairs on Daniel's neck.

"There you go, little lamb," he said tenderly. Daniel slid from the high chair with its extra block of wood. I handed over the coin. At first the barber wouldn't take it; said he did Daniel's hair free because he was a good friend. I insisted the boy's father would have it no other way, he must take payment. Then Chauncey bowed low over my outstretched palm and I felt his hot breath. I think he meant me to feel it. I was afraid he was going to kiss my hand. Instead he straightened and picked up the coin from my hand with cool dry fingers. I was in ruins.

"So, you'll be after having a man's haircut from now on, Daniel Corcoran. When will you have your first shave?" teased old Mr. Jesper.

Daniel shrugged. The others guffawed as we left the little barbershop. Daniel grinned at me as we closed the door.

Seven

MAIRI WHEEDLED, "OONAGH, DEAR. It's only until they've built our house and then you can live with us again, I promise you. We'll build it large enough you'll have your own room. This is a good chance for you." Her eyes pleaded with me for understanding.

"I didn't think I took up so much room; I thought I was a help."

"Oh, you are, you are," said Josie. "But it can't be comfortable for you in that corner, so far from the fire. Paddy and Lorna are quite eager that you should come to them. They have a room upstairs that you will have all to yourself. Board and half shilling a month. They've assured me you'll be granted time to spin and use Lorna's loom for your own use as well."

"Oh now, that's generous." My sarcastic tone! I bit my lip as Josie pushed noisily away from the table where we were gathered. He stomped around the room for a good long moment, his face red as he fought for control over his temper.

Finally he burst out, "Jaysus, girl! I don't know what you want! Half a dozen good men been willing to marry you right off. Good men with good farms. Denis, even. Now there's a brawny man with a roaring business. It's not every day you'll have a blacksmith of his worth come asking for your hand."

"Oh, this is what it's about, is it?" I glared at my sister and my brother-in-law.

Josie threw up his hands. "There's no fireside like your own fireside," he muttered.

I shot back with another saying, "If you want to be criticized, marry!"

Josie motioned violently to Mairi, as if to tell her to make her sister see sense. He slammed out of the house.

We sat in silence. The melting April snow dripped off the roof. The fire crackled in the hearth. Mairi leaned back and rested her hands on her swollen belly. Her hands moved, tracking the movement of the baby within. I swallowed, my chest full of pain.

"I only want to stay here with you and help when the babby comes," I whispered. "He's not much help to you, is he?"

"Oh, I'm sure he'll be." Mairi smiled weakly.

"Will he get you the water? Chop kindling enough?" I couldn't keep the tremble out of my voice.

Mairi waved a hand. "Of course, you silly. It's just that you've been here spoiling us rotten. He'll do what needs to be done, never fear."

"Why does he keep wanting to marry me off? Denis the blacksmith! God help me!" I caught Mairi's eye. We burst out laughing.

"Can you see me with that big brute, now? He'd crush me!" I could hardly speak for laughing.

"Or that skinny runt who asked you before Christmas. Oh, Lord, you'd a crushed him!"

"Or Finn! Finn! Can you imagine me with Finn McCurdy? That dirty turd with not one sound tooth in his head and his eyes bloodshot from the drink? And your Josie fixing to marry me off to that one! Good gracious, why?"

"Well," said Mairi, sobering. "It's a true thing what he said: There's no fireside like your own fireside. It's not a bad idea to settle yourself down. Not with Finn, surely. But marriage, Oonagh, your own home, your own little ones. What about Andrew Monaghan?" The last she said hesitatingly, wincing in anticipation of my response.

"Do you love Josie?" I demanded.

"Of course I do!" Mairi replied quickly, her eyes widening at such a question.

"Are you happy with him?"

Mairi paused to consider her reply. "Of course we're happy. Why wouldn't we be happy? A babby on the way and in the summer the men will be helping us build a new house." She smiled a little uncertainly at me.

What more could you want to be happy? I stared at my sister, then suddenly reached across the narrow plank table and took up both of Mairi's hands. I leaned forward and pressed my lips to them.

"I love you dearly," I said. "I'm glad you're happy. If he ever makes you sad, I'll come beat him up for you."

Mairi laughed and pulled her hands out of my grasp. "You're such a funny one, you are. But then you've always been a funny girl." She gazed at me tenderly. "Andrew has asked you, hasn't he?"

"Mairi! A Monaghan! You know what that family is like. He's the very last man I'd ever want." I shook my head. "Maybe I should say Finn is the very last. But Andrew Monaghan is pretty far down that list! No, he hasn't asked me. Mairi, Mairi ... I want to choose the man I marry. Or I'll never marry at all."

"You can't go on dreaming of things that are past."

"I'm not! How could you say that?" I jumped up and paced around the room, straightening a sampler on the wall, stirring the fire, adjusting the pot above it.

Mairi's eyes followed me as one follows the flight of a butterfly in a meadow, a slight smile on her lips. "The only cure for love is marriage, so they say."

"Hah! You just said you love Josie! I caught you." I swept in close to her and planted a kiss on the top of her head. Mairi reached up and caught up my hand.

"Oh, Oonagh, I wish some wonderful man would come along soon for you."

I drew away, my arms folded tightly across my chest. "Look, I don't mind going to work for Lorna McGann. God knows she needs help with all those children. Paddy is never there to help her."

"He's much too busy with the mill!" said Mairi.

"You don't have to defend him. I know he's your brother-in-law. Of course you'll defend him. I'm not criticizing him at all. I'm telling you I'll go and work for them —"

"Oh, Oonagh, love, thank you so much!" Mairi rose and rushed to hug me. I held out a hand to stop her.

"Wait! I'm not finished. I said I'll work there for a short while. As soon as I'm able, I intend to get my own land and my own cottage."

"Your own land?" Mairi stared at me, her mouth open in disbelief. I grinned at her astonishment.

"Whatever for?" said Mairi.

"I want my very own place, me own fireside," I declared, thumping myself on the chest. Then I dashed forward and grabbed Mairi around her thickened waist. "Can't you understand that? My own land, my own fields, my own woods, my own hens, my own sheep, my own loom —"

Mairi interrupted the list-making. "But that's why you should get married! You'd have all that!"

"No!" I shook my head vigorously. "Why can't I get it for myself? Without a man?"

"Josie is right. You're daft!"

"All right! I'm daft!" I laughed and hugged her gently. "My, what a big babby you'll have!"

"Don't go changing the subject!"

"A monstrous babby. Much bigger than his daddy ever thought of being."

"Josie's big enough!" laughed Mairi.

"Oh, I dare say!"

We hadn't laughed so much and for so long in ages. I complained that my stomach ached from laughing too much and Mairi said, holding herself in the appropriate place, that she was surely going to pee herself if she laughed more. Which set us off again. Mairi stood helplessly hanging onto the table, trying to keep her legs crossed, holding herself while I ran for the chamber pot stored under the bedstead. Giggling all the while, Mairi squatted on the pot, holding my hand for steadiness. Josie chose that moment to enter the house with his brother Paddy. Both men yelped at the sight and quickly retreated, which set us into howls of laughter.

When we'd quieted, we heard the voices of the men outside muttering.

"So what will you say?" Mairi whispered.

"Looks like Paddy has come for me already. You were so sure I'd agree."

Mairi's eyes filled with tears. "It'll help poor Lorna and you too."

"Aye, I suppose. But I won't go for long. Let me come back when the babby comes."

"I'll be all right."

"No, tell me I can come back then."

Mairi turned away.

It's Josie that wants me gone. I touched my sister on the shoulder. When Mairi looked back, I whispered fiercely, "I'll go. But stop them trying to marry me off. I won't have it!"

AND SO IT WAS that I became part of Paddy McGann's household in the village. It was still a small village that straddled the banks of a swiftly flowing little river. At the north end of the settlement rose a small stone gristmill; across the river a sawmill cast the scent of freshly cut pine. The river had been dammed here to provide power for the millwheels, filling the air with the rush of water as it poured over the wheels. For such a small village there was a goodly number of people about, wagons and oxen, folks come to the gristmill. Among the log buildings straggled along the west bank of the river were a dry goods store with its large painted sign, GRILLS EMPORIUM AND INN, a tinsmith, ALLEN BROTHERS, and Murphy's smithy, which needed no sign. A log bridge spanned the river where the waters narrowed just below the gristmill, and two frame houses, Gerald McGann's and Paddy's where I now lived, stood out on the opposite shore. Anyone could see how well the mill owners had done for themselves, with good glass in the windows and solid verandas in front with chairs to sit and rock in the evenings. Though most summer evenings the insects drove us in early.

ONE DAY IN JUNE I was delighted to see my nephew Daniel come to fetch me. He'd been sent to buy supplies by his parents and wanted me to help him. Kind as Lorna and Paddy had been in helping me to settle in with my new work, at the sight of Daniel's face beaming at me, my loneliness for real family erupted in me and it was all I could do not to pounce and hug him to death. We ran down the hill to the store, my own feet flying like a little girl let out to play.

Mrs. Grills bundled up the various dry goods Jane wanted and I was taking a moment to chat with her when we heard a horse outside. Daniel left the bundle on the counter and went out.

"That boy," I told her. "He just has to hear the clink of a horseshoe and he's gone in a flash."

"Well," she smiled slyly, her brown button eyes gleaming. "If he had a blacksmith the likes of Denis Murphy in the family, he could be apprenticed to him, now, couldn't he?"

"He could be apprenticed to him anyway," I retorted.

I moved to the door. I had no wish to continue a conversation about my unwedded state.

To my great surprise Chauncey Taylor stood beside Daniel, both stroking a tall bay gelding tied up at the rail. They didn't see me and I held back in the shadows, clutching Daniel's bundle.

"It's been a while, hasn't it? I'd say you've grown a fair bit." Chauncey ruffled Daniel's longish blond hair. "Is this your village?"

Daniel nodded. "The mills belong to the McGanns. My uncles. My Aunt Mairi is married to Josie McGann. So their babbies are my cousins, right?" Daniel ran out of breath.

Chauncey took a deep breath along with the boy and huffed it out loudly, teasing Daniel. "Now I thought you lived on a farm."

"Oh, we do, we do." Daniel gestured north. "Out that way. But Oonagh lives here now with the McGanns. Paddy and Lorna McGann, over there. See that big house with the veranda?" He gestured across the river.

"It's a big house all right."

"They got a kitchen with a stove. And a heat stove. Two stoves!" Daniel held up two fingers.

"I guess Miss Oonagh would like that."

"And a brick bake oven!"

"Well I'll be." Chauncey removed his hat and scratched at the back of his head. He looked suitably impressed; Daniel's face glowed with pride. "A lot of houses in town don't even have that much!"

"I know," crowed Daniel. "Oonagh makes the best bread in that oven. Never burns."

I bit my lip hard to keep from laughing. They still hadn't seen me but I caught a quizzical glance from the old man sitting on the porch a few feet away. I shook my head, smiling, a finger to my lips. The old man didn't crack a smile.

"Boy, where's your father?" Chauncey asked.

"Oh, he's home. He sent me to pick up some nails from Denis Murphy, and Mam wanted me to get a packet of needles and some buttons and a whole bunch of stuff. I'm going to go eat at the McGanns. Why don't you come too? Oonagh will be glad to see you."

"Will she now?" Chauncey smiled.

"Oh yes. She said you have a powerful laugh. That means she likes you."

"Hush, boy. I've brung my own lunch." He patted the bag slung over the saddle.

Now I wished I'd revealed myself earlier. Instead my feet were increasingly rooted to the boards of the porch. The old man stared straight ahead, listening, his pipe unsmoked in his hand. If only I could edge back into the store and come out noisily, banging the door.

"Is this your horse? What's his name?" Daniel stroked the horse's neck and nose. Most settlers used oxen if they had any beasts at all. Cheaper. Slower maybe, but less troublesome. The last thing you'd want is a team of runaway horses dragging you through a field full of jagged tree stumps.

Chauncey said, "I've hired that horse from Wellington's Livery in town. Buck — I think that's his name."

"Buck? That's for an ox! What kind of silly name is that to give a horse?" the boy hooted derisively.

"Oh? What would you call this good-for-nothing bag a bones, huh?"

"He's not a bag a bones! He's beautiful. I'd call him ..." Daniel peered closely at the horse's large brown eye staring back at him. "North Wind would be a good name."

"North Wind? Why?"

"I'd want him to go like the wind. And a north wind can be something fierce. So ...?" The boy spread his hands to rest his case.

"I see your reasoning now." Chauncey nodded seriously. "You want to give the horse a name it can live up to."

The boy grinned, nodding.

"That's a good thing to do."

"Daniel Corcoran, where are you?" I said loudly, walking forward and down the steps.

"Oonagh!" Daniel yelled. The horse stepped back delicately from the ruckus. "Oonagh, look who's here!"

Chauncey waved a hand and called out, "Hello!"

"Oh! Hello!" I hoped I sounded surprised enough.

"Come on, Chauncey! Come eat with us," Daniel grabbed Chauncey's hand and was trying to drag him forward. Chauncey held back, clearly reluctant.

"Have you come to give us all a shave and a haircut?" The old man finally recognized the stranger and clumped down the wooden steps toward Chauncey, his face creased in a smile.

Chauncey smiled in return and looked surprised when the old man extended his hand. They shook hands. Chauncey waved a hand around at the village. "Nice little place here."

"Huh," the old man snorted. "Not so little anymore. Compared to last year. We got the dry goods store in only last fall. And they're after building another sawmill just up the river a piece. By Jaysus, after the McGanns built that gristmill everything else sprung up here like mushrooms after a rain."

"Chauncey! Aren't you coming? Oonagh, he can come eat too, can't he?" Daniel yanked on Chauncey's hand.

"Now boy, I told you already, I brought my lunch." Chauncey grinned sheepishly at me and the old man. "Boy wants me to go eat with him."

"Your pa Michael Corcoran?" asked the old man.

Daniel inclined his head and scuffed the dust.

"You're more than welcome, Mr. Taylor," I said, but Chauncey glanced at the old man and shook his head. "Thank you, ma'am, I brung my lunch," he murmured. He gave Daniel a little shove in my direction. He whispered loudly, "You'd better go, young man. I wouldn't want Miss Oonagh mad at me for all the world."

As we walked away, Daniel rather crestfallen, I heard the old man say in the loud voice of those hard of hearing, "Aw, that girl. She's a hard one."

"Is that a fact?" Chauncey said, louder than necessary. I turned to see him leaning against the horse, stroking its fine ears, his eyes on us.

"Oh my, yes, that woman. She thinks she's too good for folks around here. Don't know where she gets that notion. She's no prize I don't reckon."

I stopped and bent down, pretending I'd stepped on something sharp. Daniel had run on ahead.

"Made a fool of Denis Murphy, so she did." The old man had his back to me, otherwise I'm sure he wouldn't have continued so loudly as if it were Chauncey and not himself who was hard of hearing. I scratched at my foot, hiding my laughter.

"Oh yes, Murphy walked around here proud as a cock, sure she'd accept him. A fine man with a roaring business. But she refused him."

"She did. Well I'll be. Why?" Chauncey practically shouted.

"Huh! Everyone knows why. She's too good for him! And for any other man hereabouts!"

"Aw, she's a bit choosy, that's all."

"Choosy! She'll be left high and dry if you ask me, and none too good for her, I say. Mind you, she's always been decent and polite to me, you know."

"To me too," said Chauncey. He looked right at me with a big grin, and now with my face flaming I picked up my skirts and ran down to the bridge.

"LOOK," I TOLD DANIEL a little later when he complained that I hadn't made Chauncey welcome enough. "Do you see the man down there by the mill pond? Did it ever occur to you that he might be wanting a little peace and quiet all alone?"

"No, he doesn't," retorted Daniel.

That evening Paddy told us that the black barber from Cobourg had asked about acquiring land in the village on which to build a shop and a cabin. Gerald McGann had agreed to sell him two small lots. "Good for business having a barber settle here," Paddy said.

Eight

FROM THE LITTLE WINDOW in my attic room, I could watch the raising of the new log buildings across the river. There was a guilty pleasure in sneaking upstairs and taking a few moments to watch the men swinging their broadaxes in the hot sun. I kept looking for Chauncey himself, but he must have been at the Front on this day. He still had business there. People meeting at the store enjoyed discussing this newest village member: *Was he not extravagant, building a separate cabin for himself when he could have a lean-to in the back of the barbershop. Did he think he was better than them? Look at Denis, satisfied with a little addition on the back of the smithy. The barber had no wife or family, after all.* So the comments went, sometimes caustic as lye. Chauncey had not yet moved up from the Front and already people were taking sides in regards to his presence among us. I kept quiet, but I was secretly proud. The barbershop sprang up right next to Grills. Farther down the river Gerald McGann had sold him a plot on the bank for the small cabin. Soon Chauncey would be right across the river, wielding his scissors and razor. What could possibly have drawn him to our little village? True, for such a small place it was the centre of a growing area, and in the last few weeks, what with the cholera scare, new people were moving in, fleeing from the towns. Maybe he'd have all the business he needed, but nothing like in Cobourg with boats arriving full of men needing grooming. As for his clothes-cleaning business, there were lots of men around here without wives to do for them, but in Cobourg it'd been the boarding houses and the richer people who had hired him to do washing. Who in this little village could afford to hire him to wash their clothes? Maybe Martha. The Grills at the inn. Most people up here would be lucky enough to have more than one set of clothes.

In the months that I'd been at the McGann's, I'd worked hard spinning and weaving, blankets mostly, but also linsey-woolsey and good woollen cloth. Once people found out my skills with wool and flax, they were more than happy to hire my services. Lorna McGann let me have the candles in the evenings when I spun yarn until my eyes burned in the dim flickering light. Often the entire household fell asleep to the sound of my wheel. The children in the next room assured me the noise of the wheel was faint.

Lorna told me that Paddy grumbled more than once, *Does she never rest?* She replied, *As long as the children can sleep with the spinning, let the girl work. It's her own time.* For that I was grateful.

Only sometimes did I stop to think that at this pace it would take a very long time to save enough to buy my own little farm. Land prices were going up. Mairi was right, no doubt. I should look for a decent husband. It'd be much simpler. But when I thought of marrying someone like Denis Murphy or Andrew Monaghan, my flesh crawled. Better to become a nun. Even if I didn't believe in all that holy nonsense. Still, sometimes I wondered if I wasn't completely daft. Where did these foolish dreams come from? Several young women who'd been on the ship with me and Mairi had since married and had infants in arms or on the way. Even that Brigid, the so-called widow with her baby. A man on a big farm just outside Cobourg spoke up for her right away. She said later that he told her he chose her because it was clear that she was capable of breeding children. As if she were a cow. But Brigid had laughed as she told me this. She was big-bellied again and full of stories about her man and the rich farm they worked together. She was most incredulous at her good fortune compared with the wretchedness she'd left behind in Galway.

Many other men from around here too had met the boat at Cobourg with an entirely speculative look on their faces. But not all of us women were willing to accept a man right away. I was glad to see Winny hired on at one of the boarding houses in town. *Let her grow a bit older* ... The scrutiny of those men watching as we clambered ashore with our bundles. But no Michael to greet us. Someone told us that Michael and Paddy McGann would be along the next morning with a wagon. *In the meantime, he said, make yourselves comfortable right here along the shore. There's no rooms at the inn.*

It was at our disembarkation where Denis Murphy himself had first seen me, so I'd been told. He was much admired in the area. Not every little village just starting up could boast of a smithy with such a skilled blacksmith as Murphy. People coming to grind their grain at the mill were doubly glad to have nails or a tool made up at the smithy.

I didn't dislike the man particularly. His skills and accomplishments were beyond doubt. I just couldn't visualize having his babies or sleeping in the same bed with a man whose odour repelled me something fierce the first time I met him. The ill breath of his mouth, a mixture of tobacco, whisky, and rotten teeth. And when was the last time he'd cleaned himself properly? No excuse for that. Da, coming in after a hard day's work on the roads or digging peat, what did he do first but strip off his shirt and thoroughly wash his face and neck and all under his arms? Mam poured a little hot water in the basin to warm up the chill spring water. *Ah, darling. That's good, that's better*, he'd mutter to Mam's sudden brilliant smile.

The news from home was grim, hunger and sickness. Arrivals spoke of continuing troubles: tithes and taxes, crop failures, no work to be had. People were organizing again, protesting to the authorities, marching in the streets, even rioting. Hard to hear of such news without worrying about Da and Lizzie, Mona and Liam. In the year since we'd arrived, Liam had sent one letter with a neighbour who'd emigrated. The landlord was now offering paid passage for anyone willing to give up his leasehold. *Da won't hear of it. He would sooner starve, he says.*

"Of course they should take it!" Michael had raged. "Why is Da being so pigheaded? Free passage? Great suffering Jesus! At least let Liam and the girls come."

Mairi had urged Michael to write with such advice. There'd been no reply yet. *But*, I'd argued silently, *listen to what some of the people are saying about the ships coming across now.* True, people were getting free passage, being shipped off like sacks of grain or culled cattle in dirty holds of ships so crowded, whole families sharing a bunk, taking shifts to sleep, the air bad, not enough food. A family we heard of had lost every single member but one little girl. Conditions were far worse than when Mairi and I had come, and that had been bad enough. At least landlords ensured cattle reached their destination alive. Michael told us that plague from Asia, cholera, was killing large numbers of people in Ireland and it had reached Lower Canada. People had died of the disease in York as well. In Cobourg people crowded the church to pray. Try as I might I could make no sense of religion. Why would I want to worship a god who needed such prayers for deliverance?

The authorities had set up a quarantine station on an island in the St. Lawrence downriver from Quebec. Maybe the very one where we'd washed our clothes. Even so, Quebec and Montreal had been badly hit and the fear was that the plague would reach into every community with more pestilent ships arriving all the time.

Da was no fool. He'd probably heard these horror tales. That's why he'd said no. I wished everyone was here, together, safe. Sometimes I couldn't sleep, worrying about Lizzie especially. Did she have enough to eat? Were they keeping healthy? It was terrible to be so far away. On such nights of worry I drew out from under the pillow my mam's small carved stone Mrs. O'Rourke had given me. I held it in my hand until it felt warm. I closed my eyes. To whom could I pray? I didn't know. All I could do was utter my prayer for my family into the darkness of the night and hold that sacred stone tightly in my hand, as if by holding this smooth stone of the old country I was able to touch my family there. But too often terrible thoughts kept me awake and I'd weep silently under the blanket. Surely Liam and the girls would come, but we'd never see Da again.

I compared our homeland, its barren hills scattered with tons of stones, to those of the neat farms down on the Front at Lake Ontario with their fruit orchards and grain fields. Even here in the bush people were making great inroads into the huge silent forests. Grain waved lushly green among the fire-blackened jagged stumps of the giant trees. There were plenty of great pink and grey boulders the men struggled to move into walls and piles. But crops grew well in this soil newly opened to the sun. Potatoes! Last fall Michael had taken surplus potatoes all the way to Cobourg. No one who was willing to work hard would go hungry in this country. If only I could reach out across the sea and pluck my sisters and Liam out of the misery that was our homeland. Michael read us the terrible symptoms of cholera as described in the newspaper until Jane cried out for him to stop. Everyone kept checking their children and each other. But how doubly bad in the old country where hunger was a constant. All manner of illness to attack those already weak from hunger. I well remembered the 1822 famine, the year after Mam died, how we finally all lay together to keep warm, to keep from needing food. That painful gnaw in the gut, the dizziness, the feverish feeling. Retching up nothing but sharp bile. Watching those you love grow gaunt. Strange that one says "grows" gaunt when nothing is growing but is in fact disappearing, the flesh from your face first, your stomach and thighs, your arms. We'd almost lost Lizzie but for the bit of milk Mrs. Keane kept supplying. She saved a number of children that way, bless her.

Blessed Mrs. Keane. Was she still alive? And my family? My thoughts touched upon the unthinkable and I'd envision the old house, door closed, as I approached. No smoke at the chimney. No laughing faces at the window. I'd creak open the door and look in and see only huddled forms on the bed. No bed, for Da would have sold that to buy food. Straw heaped in the corner. Would they still have straw? And there was little Lizzie — I had to summon up faith the family was fine and would be coming soon.

Only a year since we'd left and Ireland seemed remote. The rock where I used to sit and contemplate the sea: here I had no such place and no time. One certainty about Canada, we had to work something fierce. Through the bitterly cold winter just past, Mairi's fireplace roared with extravagant heaps of logs, yet ice formed in the corners of the room. I never felt warm except in bed under the blankets, where I'd curl up, and sometimes even then I'd be too cold to fall asleep easily. I missed snuggling up to my sisters. I'd catch myself wishing that Josie would go away so I could crawl in with Mairi to get warm. This coming winter would be much better for me at the McGanns, where I intended to stay after all, where grates in the floors let warm air into the upstairs rooms. The children warned me that it still got very cold, but no ice on the walls. The house Josie was building would have two rooms downstairs and a room above for the loom. Mairi had assured me that they'd build a little room next to it for me, but Josie had grumbled that a bed could be set up just as well in a corner of the loom room. I'd understood he really didn't want me back living with them. Perhaps he disliked me as much as I'd come to dislike him.

He'd promised Mairi a built-in brick bake oven right next to the hearth and a real cooking stove from Three Rivers, Lower Canada, better than the stove Lorna McGann had. Not only would it cook food without the extra flavouring of ashes but it would heat water and help heat the house. I secretly furnished my own dream cabin with such a stove. The only drawback was cooking in the heat of summer. Lorna's kitchen was suffocating on bake days in the height of July, even with the door and windows open. Open windows meant the house was never free of flies and mosquitoes.

We survived the winter, anticipating spring and summer, only to be besieged by hordes of blood-sucking insects. Once I'd come in from hoeing the garden and Lorna had shrieked at the sight of me. *What have you done to your face?* Sticky blood wet my right temple all down my cheek. Black flies, much smaller than a housefly but with a deadly bite, had taken out pieces of my flesh. Worse than the clouds of midges back home.

All day as I worked on one task after another, my mind ran with plans or with thoughts of my little sisters, my fingers working automatically, washing up children, cooking, scrubbing clothes, gardening, spinning yarn, or carding up the new fleeces people had brought me in the spring. Several people had complimented me on my weaving. But no one knew where my thoughts really were; people would have been surprised to know how I daydreamed of my own place. I'd plant a specific garden just for dye plants so I wouldn't have to wander all over the woods searching them out. Not that I minded wandering in the forest and meadows or along the riverbank. I was learning, both from what people told me and from my own experimentation, what tree barks and plants, roots and flowers in this new land could provide dyes. Sumac for maroons and browns, butternut husks for yellow. Oak and elder and birches and maples. All had bark one could use to varying degrees. I could use the berries that sweetened the air of the forests and meadows. But I longed for a garden full of marigolds and camomile, meadowsweet for black and tansy for yellow. Lavender and roses. For fresh beautiful flowers and dried petals tied up into linen sachets. Back in the old country Mairi had once brought such a thing home from Pastor Spring's house. A lovely smelling sachet that Mairi said was to put among your clothes in your clothes trunk. How we'd laughed at that. Then wicked Mairi had compounded the hilarity by slipping the sachet down into her bosom. *There, that's me clothes trunk!*

Next door, Martha McGann — married to the other McGann brother, Gerald, who owned the mills with Paddy — knew much about plants and dyes. She'd come from England and married Gerald in Cobourg. She had brought from her mother's garden in Sussex a variety of flower seeds and cuttings and grew a small garden in front of the house. She'd had the men fence it off from the cattle, deer, and other creatures. Every time I had a chance to walk past that garden

I did, peering in longingly at the blooms. They reminded me of Mrs. Keane's garden and the Protestant minister's wife's garden. Why hadn't our mam grown flowers? But then I remembered Mam's weary smile and the stony ground around our house. Heartsease, heather, violets, and cowslips grew in abundance in the hills above our parents' home, with lovely grass thick among the boulders, and down along the road hedges of fuchsia and honeysuckle. Fuchsia wouldn't grow here with the harsh winters. Martha had tried and lost the only plants she'd brought. She hadn't known how cold and long the winters were here. Even in the house the temperatures dipped so low plants froze. Martha had promised me cuttings for my first garden when I got married.

I did enjoy hunting the woods for new dye plants. But sometimes, too far out of earshot of the village, the forest closed in darkly. Soon every crackle of underbrush was that of a bear or wolf. I'd heard stories of bears tearing their way into people's cabins, solid doors being ripped off their leather hinges as the bear sought food, even a story of a bear swimming out to someone's canoe and tipping it for the fish in it. People warned me not to go too far alone, but to take a companion and both sing and clap stones together to make a racket so as to frighten bears away. And wolves. Yes, having my own dye plants growing at the doorstep would be beneficial.

In my imagination I was often busy planting gardens or building lovely stone walls that climbed gentle slopes, good pasture close to home, keeping my beautiful sheep safe from predators. I would have sheep one day. As I plunged my arms into hot soapy water, washing baby nappies, I envisioned placing one large stone upon another, fitting them together to build up a wall. My own farm would have such lovely stone walls like those I remembered from home. The men often complained of the multitude of stones surfacing in the soil of this new country as they turned it over for crops. Well, if one wanted to plow up the earth every year, stones were indeed a problem. But my place would have a rich stone-free bottomland along a small waterway or lake suitable for gardens and crops of wheat, rye, corn, and potatoes. I would leave the slopes above in woods and pasture. I had it all worked out. But these dreams I shared only with Daniel, who got an earful. His enthusiasm bolstered me but I felt a little foolish to be confiding in such a young child.

ONE MORNING DANIEL CAME running to fetch me. Michael and he had come to town for the opening of Chauncey's new barbershop. Lorna rolled her eyes at me when I asked leave to go, but told me to get back in time to make the noon meal.

Chauncey had set up his brightly painted barber's pole in front of his new shop. Quite a few fellows had gathered, as did a couple of curious women besides myself. We peered into his glass window that gave such good light into the room. The men cracked jokes and swapped stories. Chauncey was lathering up Bert Kenyon's face for a long-overdue shave.

"Now don't you be in no hurry," admonished Bert, eyeing the gleaming blue steel of the razor that Chauncey stropped dramatically to everyone's enjoyment.

"Me in a hurry? Don't you fear. Just relax, lean back, and let yourself drift away on a dream." Chauncey winked.

"No nicks, no cuts."

"No nicks, no cuts."

Chauncey set to work carefully scraping away the rough beard in swaths. We watched each stroke. Bert squeezed shut his eyes.

"Hey, Bert! You after courting some woman, are you?" a joker yelled from outside.

"Can't a man have a shave in peace?" Bert sat up suddenly, yelling back, his abrupt motion startling Chauncey in mid-air. Good thing the razor hadn't been on the man's skin.

"Mr. Bert, sir, you can't move around like that with no warning. I might nick you next time."

"No nicks I said!" Bert glared around the room before settling his head back against the chair. "Damn it all, I was almost asleep."

"Don't move then, please sir."

"Don't 'sir' me! I'm a red-blooded democratic Yankee. I ain't no 'sir,' no sir!" Bert closed his eyes amid the guffaws of his friends.

"Now that's a true enough fact, Mr. Taylor. This man is a damn Yankee and no *sir*, no sir!" said Denis Murphy in the doorway. I knew that booming voice without seeing its owner, his particularly pungent odour recognizable.

One of the women, Emily Cotterage, whom I knew slightly, whispered, "Now there's the one for you," and poked me teasingly in the ribs. I ignored her.

Denis Murphy bellowed, "This Yankee owes me a pinch of money and no doubt he'll be owing you too."

"Now we've discussed all that, Denis Murphy! You know I'm good for the money once the crop comes in. You'll be getting your money." Once again Bert had sat up straight in the chair and Chauncey was standing back, his razor poised. Bert continued, "Now just let this fine barber carry on with his job."

Chauncey gave us all a slow grin over Bert's head. "Well, Mr. Bert Kenyon, can you pay me the price today for this work I'm doing? I've already trimmed your hair. A good price for a haircut and shave. One shilling, sir."

"One shilling! Holy Mary, do you come from the same place in Ireland as that Murphy?" Bert stared at Chauncey, then grinned. He dug into his pants pocket and deposited a few coins into Chauncey's palm. "There. That's half right now. I'll pay you the rest tomorrow. One shilling ..." Muttering at this outrageous price, he settled himself back into the chair.

Chauncey calmly began wiping the rest of the lather off Bert's face. Only half was shaven clean.

"Hey!" Bert suddenly realized what was happening as he heard his friends snickering more and more loudly. "You ain't finished!"

"I'll finish the job tomorrow when you can pay me."

"Now just wait one blessed minute!"

Chauncey paused, a slight smile on his face.

"Don't I get a hot towel for this side at least?" Bert's eyes were twinkling as he stroked his smoothed cheek. The crowd of onlookers laughed. It seemed as if Bert's humour had won out and he was going to walk out with a half-shaven face, the genial crowd on his side. But Chauncey laughed the hardest, his laughter ricocheting around the room. He wiped tears from his eyes.

"Aw, sit back down now, Mr. Bert. Let no man say he leaves my shop with half a face!"

Bert eased himself back into the chair with a triumphant grin, the crowd murmuring pleasure at this morning's entertainment.

Bert called out, "What do you say, Denis Murphy? Let this countryman of yours give you a shave and a haircut and let it be on my bill!" He laughed at his own joke. Chauncey threatened to lather his mouth. The blacksmith shoved others aside to enter the shop. His huge body seemed to shrink the interior of the small cabin, as if a giant bear had entered. Who could say when or if Denis had ever had his beard trimmed? It lay across his chest like a springy dirty blond mat with particles of food caught in it, the hairs around his mouth quite greasy from the fat pork he loved to eat. He always wore his long hair tied with string into a braid halfway down his back. He crossed his powerful arms across his huge chest and said to Chauncey, "Now everyone knows you're Bert's countryman, not mine. But I allow as you're honest. What I want to know is if you can make this old reprobate look half-decent a woman might give him a glance, then by Jaysus you're a miracle maker and so maybe I'll let you work on me hair and beard a bit."

"Well now," said Chauncey slowly. "Mr. Kenyon and I might come from the same country but I'd hardly call us countrymen, seeing as I come from the South and he's from New York, so I believe. Right, Mr. Bert?"

Bert nodded, his eyes closed.

"Be that as it may, Mr. Murphy," Chauncey continued. "As for the glances of women, that may require more of a miracle than I can perform here, sir, but I can give you a decent trim for all that."

The crowd laughed uproariously.

"No! It's not me looking for the glances of women!" Denis scowled. "God, no! I meant this old reprobate here!" He clapped Bert hard on the shoulder.

I knew, as did everyone but the blacksmith, that Chauncey had deliberately misunderstood. Daniel, standing in the doorway with his father, his mouth hanging open, delighted in every sparring word. Michael reached around and clapped Daniel's mouth shut.

"You coulda caught a dozen flies, my son," he said.

Denis continued, "Your price a shilling?"

"Well," Chauncey hesitated, glancing at the blacksmith's tangled and dirty locks. "Maybe for you I might have to charge by the hour."

Denis himself laughed the loudest. "Aye, you'll do, Mr. Taylor, you'll do. You've got a bit of the Irish wit about you."

Michael looked over at me. He whispered something to Daniel who smiled and ran to me.

"Da wants to know: will you be making enough lunch we could ask C.T. as well?"

Lunch! I nodded to Michael, said my goodbyes to the women, and ran for the house, Daniel running after me to help, on his father's order. Lorna was having another one of her headaches and went to lie down while I took over. I didn't have a chance to tell her Chauncey was coming. Just as well, as events bore out.

WE SET LUNCH OUT on a plank table under the maple trees in the front yard. I had Daniel running back and forth between the kitchen and the outdoors with platters of food. Finally everyone in the McGann family was seated on the benches. Michael and Chauncey had not yet arrived. I served Paddy and Lorna and the children, but Daniel wanted to wait with me for his father and Chauncey.

"Who's that place for?" Lorna suddenly noticed I'd set an extra place.

"Oh, Michael's bringing the barber," I smiled.

"Paddy!" Lorna turned to her husband, alarmed.

"Now, let's be neighbourly. No harm done." Paddy's voice soothed. I wondered if he already knew that Lorna was due yet another child, her sixth, by late fall. She was sick every day and in a foul mood more often than not.

"Shall I go see what's holding them up?" Daniel offered.

"There they are," I said. They'd crossed the bridge and were walking up the hill.

Lorna stood up abruptly and, taking her plate, stormed off into the house. Paddy shrugged at my questioning look.

"Ah now, we're pleased you could join us today," said Paddy, extending his hand in welcome. "Do sit. I believe Oonagh's cooked enough for an army."

Chauncey sat next to Michael. They murmured apologies for being late but I was already passing them the platters of food. "Daniel has been waiting for you."

"So have you," he said to me. I blushed, glancing at Chauncey.

"Where's Lorna?" asked Michael.

"She's feeling a bit poorly," said Paddy. He leaned over his plate and took a great mouthful.

We ate hungrily, but at length we were done and I served the men big mugs of tea.

"Ah," sighed Michael. "Now that was well worth waiting for."

"Thank you," agreed Chauncey, grinning up at me where I hovered with the teapot.

"So how did the first morning go?" Paddy asked Chauncey.

"Very well, better than I expected."

Michael related the story of Bert Kenyon's half-shave and Paddy laughed.

"Congratulations," said Paddy. "I expect you'll be having a steady clientele, Mr. Taylor, and that's good for our little village too. You know, I never did get exactly where you've come from."

"Well, as you know, I was barbering in Cobourg most recently and before that in York for a few months." Chauncey paused for a sip of tea. "But yes, I've come up from the States. And you good folks I understand are from Ireland?"

Paddy accepted another cup of tea from me and took a good long sip before answering. "Gerald told me you said you'd been worried about bounty hunters coming across the line. You figure none will ride this far north?"

Chauncey sighed, "Gerald was very helpful. I appreciate you folks selling me those plots. I aim to work hard here, as I've done in Cobourg. I don't expect trouble to come north."

"My brother Gerald and I came over in 1823," Paddy said, leaning back in his chair, arms crossed. "We've done well, as you can see. We've a prosperous and peaceful village. People get along. Hard work is rewarded here. Not like the old country."

"Yes," Chauncey nodded.

"Hard where you come from too, I guess, in Virginia? I don't wonder your people have revolts down there like Nat Turner's," Paddy replied. "But bloodshed begets bloodshed. One reaps what one sows."

"Indeed," replied Chauncey, his voice deepening. "The slave masters reap what they sow. 'Whoso sheddeth man's blood, by man shall his blood be shed: for in the image of God made He man.'"

"But women!" Paddy's voice rose in indignation. "And children asleep in their beds."

My heart quickened in dismay for Chauncey. As if Paddy held him accountable for the slaughter in Virginia last year.

Chauncey muttered, "If you could know what the slave women and children suffer, Mr. McGann. If you could know what happened to black people all through the south after that rebellion." His eyes flashed as he looked around at us. "I just heard a trickle from people I know in York. Enough to know it was terrible."

Michael began talking about people not putting up with injustice, it didn't matter where you were or who. But Paddy interrupted with a speech declaring that violence would do nothing to help. Revolts such as Nat Turner's would only lead to the severe retribution Chauncey mentioned. Paddy'd be the first to declare that the conditions in the south were intolerable, but to slaughter innocent women and children asleep in their beds —

Anger surged painfully throughout my body. Whatever did Paddy mean? What did he know of violence?

I interrupted him, my voice shaking with my emotion. "How does one defend against a savage beast? A heartless oppressor? Our own brother Johnny was hanged by the English, remember, because he could not bear injustice!"

"Aw now, Oonagh," Michael put out a hand. Beside him Daniel stared at me, stricken. *Johnny hanged?* Did he not know the story? Michael dropped his hand to the table, his gaze dropped too. The men all looked down at the table, embarrassed at my outburst, but Daniel turned to his father, about to say something. Michael shook his head slightly at the boy and my anger collapsed into a sick feeling in the pit of me.

Chauncey cleared his throat. "Thank you again. I should go."

"Have more cake," Daniel pointed out the slices on a platter, wishing to keep Chauncey near. But Michael tapped his pointing hand and told him it was time to be going home themselves.

My outburst had ended the conversation, but they'd ignored what I said. I began to heap up the dishes to take inside, my face hot with humiliation, close to tears. As I reached down to take his plate, Chauncey touched my arm lightly and murmured, "Thank you." It was but an instant and then he was on his feet asking, "Can I help at all to clear this up?" He waved at the laden table. The spot on my arm where he had touched tingled.

Paddy scoffed, waving him on, "Sure and you've got a barbershop to run. Look, we have a small army of helpers here. Right, children? Help Oonagh now."

"I'll be on my way then. Thanks again." Chauncey flashed a smile right at me, flooding me so I had to turn aside, my ears burning. I hurried indoors and when I came back out he was already crossing the bridge with Daniel and Michael. I watched their retreating backs for a moment then couldn't bear it.

"Wait," I yelled and raced down the hill after them. I didn't care I looked a mad sight. Michael turned in surprise. It was him I wanted to chastise.

"Daniel," I said, quite breathless. "Hasn't your da told you about your uncle John?"

Michael gripped me hard on the arm but I flung him off. Daniel shook his head.

"Aw, Michael —" I could not continue as sorrow overwhelmed me.

Michael spoke angrily, "It does no good to hold on to past hatreds. Not here." He waved his hand about.

"Our kind brother! The least you could do is tell your son about him!"

"You don't know everything. Oonagh!" He yelled after me as I ran back up the hill. "Oonagh!"

Later, while I lay sleepless, I wondered about what he'd said. I could not drag up an image of Michael in my memory from that terrible time. Memory is a faulty guardian of the past. Where had Michael been on that day? What were his memories he chose not to share with his son? I wept to realize how little I actually remembered or knew of Johnny.

Nine

"HELLO, MISS OONAGH."

I almost fell off the log. For once I'd been resting, doing nothing but dreaming, sitting on a log in the middle of a sunlit birch glade.

Chauncey Taylor stood a few yards away.

"You scared me!"

"Beg your pardon. I thought I was making enough noise."

"You walk like an Indian hunter!"

"Well, thank you. Didn't mean to startle you."

I stood up, facing him. He leaned on a long hickory staff, a woven bag slung over his shoulder. We smiled at each other.

"What's in your bag?" I blurted, my face instantly on fire.

"Ah, it's a habit of mine to carry this here bag. I'm always thinking maybe I'll see a pretty flower I can dig up to plant at my cabin. Maybe I'll spot an unusual plant or pine cone."

"I do that too." I was pleased and surprised. "Just the other day I found a white flower, perfectly lovely with strange-looking leaves, and when I picked one, orange sap oozed from the stem. Can you believe it? Bright orange!"

"Puccoon," he said. "Some folks call it bloodroot."

"Yes!" I laughed. "That's it exactly. That's what Martha McGann told me. I showed her what I'd picked. She said it's a good dye plant."

"Yes, the Indians tell me they use it for a dye."

"I didn't dig up the plants. I just remarked on their location in the woods." I sat back down on the log. During our brief conversation Chauncey had slid to the ground and leaned back against the stout trunk of a giant birch. He now opened his bag and pulled out several twigs with leaves attached.

"See, I'm making a collection of these leaves. Not just trees, but the smaller shrubs. I want to know the names of these here plants."

"Well," I smiled, "I'm afraid I can't make no introductions myself!"

"Things pretty different where you come from too, I reckon."

"Yes," I said, suddenly shy. "No forests like this and not quite the fierce winters. It does get cold, miserable rain, but not as bitter as here."

He acknowledged my comments with a smiling nod.

I continued, afraid of awkward silence, "And how are the winters where you come from, Mr. Taylor?"

The formal "Mr. Taylor" hung in the air between us. It was the first time I'd ever addressed him by name. Except for that shameful first meeting when I'd teased him about having such a fancy name. Remembering my behaviour brought a flush to my face.

"Well," he answered slowly in a voice like melting butter. "Depends on where I decide I come from. See, could be Virginia or New York or even New Orleans, Louisiana." He grinned and snapped a twig between his long fingers.

"Most people would consider their birthplace their home, I think," I said, reaching for a twig to twirl between my own fingers.

"Birthplace, huh? Reckon? Well now, that could be a real problem." He shook his head in mock consternation. "I don't rightly know if my birthplace as was told to me was my real birthplace. If you get my meaning."

"Not really."

"Well, can you say for sure you was born where folks say you was?"

A pleasant confusion raced through me; was he playing with me?

"Mr. Taylor, sir, you have to trust what your parents tell you. I know the very bed where I was born."

"You're a fortunate young lady then, if I may say so, if knowing the very bed where one was born is a valuable thing to know. My mother had no bed. She was travelling and that's why no one was real sure just where I was born. Could have been North Carolina, could have been Virginia. I was born in a wagon on the move."

"A wagon! Oh, surely not on the move! They would have stopped for her sake, surely."

"Maybe ... maybe not." He smiled at my indignation.

"Where was your poor mam travelling to?"

"She was being moved from a plantation down in North Carolina to the place in Virginia where they claim I was born. Place in the Carolinas been sold, so slaves was sold away. Lucky sold to Virginia instead of farther south."

"So close to her time?"

"All that bumping of the cart. See, she was lucky to get a wagon ride. Mostly the others walked. That was what the owners thought of my mama, how well they thought of her. Let her have the wagon ride."

I drew in a deep breath. "Oh, very kind," I said bitterly. My heart thumped unpleasantly. "Do you really believe they were kind people to let your mam ride in the wagon?"

He muttered, "Oh, Miss Oonagh, they were kind. So kind. They had her out working the fields three weeks after. She was young, no more'n thirteen. Yeah, that's how they do down there. Now she's getting old, worn out and all, they took her out of the field. All she's got to do is the washing for the household. Maybe a bit of hoeing in the truck patch. Pretty decent of them, don't you think?" His face changed demeanour, his lip quivering. I looked away quickly to afford him privacy. I gripped the cloth of my skirt with both fists. When I dared to look back at him, he had recovered his composure but kept his face averted from mine.

I had to ask, "They made her work in the fields three weeks after her confinement?"

"Three weeks after I was born. She made a little basket and hung me up in a tree so's the snakes wouldn't get me while she was hoeing."

"Didn't you cry for her?"

"I expect I did, sure. But slave babies learn early ain't much use to cry. Matter of fact, I was a luckier baby than most. My mama got to raise me herself for the first little while. A lot of places they just take the babies right away, put them all in a house with a couple of women to nurse them. The real mamas don't hardly see them. But at Minge's place, mamas took the little sucklings right to the field with them." He rose abruptly and slapped at the leaf debris clinging to his trousers. "Best be getting back. Evening's coming on fast," he muttered. "Best you go on ahead so's no one sees us together."

I began to protest, disturbed at the implication in his words, but he gave me a stern look. I rose without another word. Slowly at first, mulling over his story, I picked my way through the trees and the lengthened shadows of late afternoon. I listened to the scuffle and crackle of his footsteps behind me, then heard nothing. I glanced back through the trees but couldn't see him at all in the dense stand of forest. I stopped and listened intently but heard only the whine of wind in the topmost pine boughs. Eerie, like a keening at a funeral. I began to run.

JUST AFTER THE NOON meal one day in the middle of July, I told Lorna McGann that I needed to gather up some bloodroot. She was lying down, as were all the children, to sleep off the heat of the day as usual, which is why I thought I could make my escape at this time.

"Are you not hot?" Lorna groaned. "Oonagh, girl, you should stay out of the sun!"

"I'll be in the forest. It's cooler there," I said reassuringly. "I won't be long. I know exactly where the plants are." She just harrumphed and put her arm over her eyes.

I took my gathering basket, walked down across the bridge and slowly past Chauncey's shop, toward the river trail. I wanted him to see me pass, to know that I was walking again in the woods. Would he follow?

"Good afternoon, Oonagh," said Bert Kenyon, who had become quite the regular at the barbershop. "Where might you be going in this heat?" He sat on the bench Chauncey had built outside by the door, fanning himself with his straw hat, wispy grey hair plastered to his forehead with sweat.

"Good afternoon, Mr. Kenyon," I murmured, nodding my head as politely as I could muster. I kept walking on. I barely had the time of day for that man and surely it was none of his business where I was going. He was a friend of the blacksmith and I knew from the look in his eyes that he had contempt for me. I could see something unpleasant in his small brown eyes, his tone verging on insult, as if I were some loose woman. Not that I'd ever heard a man speak to such a lady. But I could imagine such a tone. Bert was a loafer too, and I could not stand that in any person. I suppose Chauncey let him hang about because it was good business to have men sitting outside the shop. It looked busier, a meeting place.

At this moment the shop seemed quiet, but in the month since Chauncey had opened he'd had a stream of customers from miles around. One had to admire his ability, his business sense. I'd heard not a word against him. He seemed to be popular in the village, although never on an equal basis with others. Martha McGann had given him a tablecloth she had despaired of ever ridding of a stain — blueberry preserves. She couldn't sing his praises often enough. *How does he do it?* She asked everyone. *Isn't he amazing?* I don't know that he was amazing. He simply worked hard and stubbornly. Daniel, who found every excuse to come to the village and visit with him, told me how Chauncey had removed the blueberry stain.

"Simple, Oonagh. He used an embroidery hoop to stretch the cloth and he slowly poured boiling water through the stain. It faded right then and there. The trick is you have to pour the water from on high so it mixes properly with air. That's the trick."

I had to smile at Chauncey's talent for making the commonplace seem magical. Surely Martha McGann knew one should pour boiling water through fruit stains. Another way was to smear egg yolk over the stain to lift it. But then again, had I really known about the boiling water before Daniel told me or had it made perfect sense when I heard it?

I so wanted to befriend Chauncey myself and discover his history from his own lips, not Daniel's. Every story of Chauncey's my little nephew passed on to me, his eyes glistening, piqued my curiosity. I wanted to sift the real from the fantastical. I couldn't believe, for instance, that any child could have survived the whippings Daniel said Chauncey had received as a boy. Whippings as to leave such scars. *Like a plowed field*, whispered Daniel, his voice trembling. I tried to imagine what such scars must look like and what they meant.

I know the brutality of men. I had witnessed my brother's murder by the English. He and Adam Keane mere lads. But Daniel said Chauncey had been no more than nine or ten when he'd been whipped. For what crime? The more I mulled over this, the more I wanted Chauncey's confidence. The feeling that stole into me, I've tried to understand. I felt as if we had a common bond of suffering. As I worked long into the night at my spinning, I had Chauncey's face in my mind's eye, the way he had of smiling with those dimples. Something in me hurt to think of him like a hunted fox, travelling only in the darkness, afraid of being found out. Did he not still live in such fear? There were men who crossed the border in search of runaways like Chauncey. This was why he had chosen our little inland village.

I followed a worn path south along the riverbank. Once I glanced over my shoulder, hoping to see Chauncey following me, but saw no one. I smiled to imagine him there.

I'd marked an oak right at the spot where I had to leave the river and walk inland along a narrow deer trail leading into the forest. That was how I'd discovered the bloodroot in the spring. I'd noticed the narrow trail and wondered who'd made it. Deer or Indians? In my year in Canada I had seen only a few of these people who had travelled past our little village coming down from Rice Lake. They'd seemed polite and shy and not much inclined to stop and talk. I couldn't from that small encounter know if the entire people were like that. It was like saying all Irishmen were dirty drunkards based on Andrew Monaghan. I was careful not to make hasty judgments.

The first time I found the trail I'd followed it, unafraid that I'd become lost; it was well-worn. The path ended in a small meadow at the centre of which swamp grass grew tall and tangled around a spring. Animals, most likely deer, had left hollows where they'd lain in the grass. Lovely banks of white flowers edged this sunlit grassy haven. These were the flowers I'd described to Chauncey. Bloodroot. When I picked one, bright orange sap dripped from the cut stem. Chauncey said the natives called them puccoon. The plants would be past flowering now but I'd recognize them for their unusual and beautifully notched leaves.

I found the plants easily and took my time, careful not to dig up too many. The sun burned through the cloth on my back as I bent to the task. It was pleasant in the clearing with the birdsong and the sweet smell of the pinewoods and the grass. I lay down in the grass to ease my back for a few moments. The sky above burned a cloudless blue. I shielded my eyes from the sun and found myself staring into infinity. Where did people think Heaven was? I spread my arms out to anchor myself to the ground and closed my eyes.

I dozed but was startled awake with someone calling my name. Fear pumped through me as I sat up, looking around. There was no one, only the meadow flowers, the grasses, and the trees surrounding me. I listened for the voice to call again, and then, with a wave of relief, realized it'd been my mother's voice, the amused patience in her voice when I'd been off daydreaming again. I must have been dreaming. I rose and brushed off my skirt.

I admired my little collection, already imagining what brightly coloured yarn I would make. What colour would the orange sap of the puccoon make? Probably not such a bright orange when stained into wool. But one could hope and dream! I made my way back down the trail but long before the river I halted, all the blood sapped from my limbs. A few yards into the woods a large white sphere lay on the forest floor. A human skull? I left the trail and approached it cautiously, as if it could suddenly rear up and bite me. A skull so massive it couldn't be human unless it were a giant's. At this thought fear grew in me, for who knew what lurked in the dimness between the massive oaks and elms and maples shivering their shadows around me. Where only moments before I'd been rejoicing in the dappled shadows, the variety of leaves, the sweet scent of ripening berries, I now felt a creeping dread. But curiosity was stronger. I stopped a few feet away from the white object. It was more than a large hand span across. A twig cracked behind me. I couldn't turn to look, not to save my life. Immobile as Lot's wife. More twigs snapped. I squeezed shut my eyes and waited for the monster's blow.

"You know you can eat that."

A few yards behind me Chauncey smiled sweetly as he leaned against a massive maple. He motioned with his stick and walked forward and past me to the white thing on the forest floor.

"You scared the bejesus out of me," I managed to croak.

"You were standing so still in the forest I almost walked by you on the trail. Then I wondered what you were looking at."

"I thought it was a skull."

"It's a puffball. Just right for eating."

"Oh! A puffball, is it?" I had regained my voice and my equilibrium. Upon close inspection, I could see that it was a mushroom.

"Mind if I take it?" Chauncey asked. So saying he twisted it loose and sliced the giant fungi neatly in half. The flesh was crisp and white. "Perfect. You don't want to wait much longer to harvest this."

"How do you eat it?"

"You've eaten mushrooms before?"

"Of course, but how do you know it's good to eat?"

"Oh, my mama used to cook them up for us. We have similar ones down where I come from."

I took my chance on being nosy. "When you journeyed here, did you find these along the way to eat?"

"Oh, sure," he laughed. "Among other things like snakes and mice and juicy worms."

I couldn't tell if he was joking.

He held the carved flesh of the mushroom up to my nose. "Smell that. Good, like the earth."

I agreed. "Do you eat them raw like that?"

"Well, I have."

I reached out a finger and touched the cool whiteness of the puffball.

He murmured, "I like it the way my mama cooked it. Dip pieces in a couple of beaten eggs then roll them slices in a bit of cornmeal, a bit of salt, and fry in pork fat. Mm mm. Fit for a king." His black eyes glistened as if he were enjoying the feast. "Oh yes, that was good! Eggs! I'll have to get me some eggs." Suddenly he laughed aloud. "Ma'am, I was king of the egg thieves when I wasn't more'n five-years-old. They never caught me but once."

I thought he meant stealing eggs in the sense that we all steal from the hens. But he meant otherwise. I listened in growing dismay at his meaning.

"This was in Virginia. See, they's always some hens fly out of the coop and I was supposed to follow, see where they laid their eggs. Collect them up for the kitchen. I followed all right, but I didn't collect all the eggs. Just most of 'em. Then after dark I'd sneak out and collect the three or four I'd left for us. There was one red hen always obliged me. She hid her eggs where no one but a little shaver like me could have found them."

"You had to steal eggs? Didn't they keep enough hens to provide for everyone?"

"Well, they sold a lot of eggs to town, as a matter of fact. But corn was what they provided for us. A measure of corn on Sunday to last all week."

"Corn? Cornmeal?"

"Dry corn in the ear, Miss Oonagh. Folks would have to grind it with a hand mill after the workday for their supper and for next day's breakfast."

"What else would you eat with that?"

"Corn. That's it. Sometimes they'd throw in a bit of pork fat."

"What about vegetables? Didn't you have gardens?"

"Gardens. Oh yes. Some of the older slaves, including my mama, work the vegetable patch. But none of that's for us."

"None of it?" I had a sudden lump in my throat. "Couldn't you just take what you needed?"

He sighed deeply. "Naw. They always find out. They have someone watching that patch like a hawk. And someone always has to pay. It's the old folks, too worn out for the fieldwork, who work the vegetables. So it's them gets the floggings. No, it's an awful risk to steal even a carrot or a pea pod. You never know who's watching you and who'd tell on you just for a bit of favour themselves, you know."

"Another slave might tell on you?"

"Sometimes. The system makes people mean."

"They'd flog old people?"

"Old people, little children —"

"You said you got caught once stealing eggs. What happened?"

He was silent for a heartbeat, then smiled. "Now I declare! Miss Oonagh, you've got a particular talent for getting me to tell stories! I do believe I've taken up enough of your time."

"How old were you when they caught you?"

He turned away then faced me squarely, staring me in the eyes. He raised the mushroom to his nose and inhaled deeply. "That does smell good. Here, smell it again."

"Mr. Taylor —" I wanted to insist on his story.

He turned aside and placed the mushroom piece into his bag.

"Tell you what, Miss Oonagh. I'm going to cook up a feast this evening with this here puffball and a brook trout I caught today —"

I couldn't be rude and insist on hearing what must be an awful memory. So I went along with his change of subject. "Did you know this very mushroom was growing here, like I knew the puccoon was in the little meadow up the trail?" I showed him my little collection in the basket.

"No, can't say I did. I just happened to see you standing in the woods like you was waiting for a deer to happen by. Ever gone hunting, Miss Oonagh?"

He was teasing.

"Mr. Taylor, sure, and you know where every such mushroom resides in the woods, don't you?"

He was grinning with those dimples.

"Have you come out this afternoon in search of something in particular?"

"Well, Miss Oonagh ..." The smile in his eyes told me what he couldn't say. I smiled back at him. The unabashed joy of it. We understood each other. I wanted to rest my head against his chest then and there.

"Do you know the puccoon meadow I speak of?" I asked and ducked my eyes to the ground, to his shoes, a pair so worn I saw a toenail poking through the leather. He'd need to spend some of his hard-earned money on boots before winter. In the blink of an instant I thought this and thought of how I could be knitting him woollen stockings. I looked up quickly again, for I couldn't have him see me noticing his broken shoes. He watched me quizzically. I flushed.

He cleared his throat and turned away to pick at a dangling piece of birch bark from one of the forest giants.

"The meadow," he said. "Yes, a real nice place, isn't it, with a spring in the middle."

"Yes!" An incredible joy filled me that he knew which place I meant. "That's the place! A good place for a cabin." With those impetuous words I wanted to die and disappear into the ground. Each word I spoke to this man seemed imbued with meaning far deeper than its surface. Surely he would construe that I was inviting him to build that cabin! For us. Surely he would think me utterly forward! Much later Chauncey would assure me that he had not gained that impression from me. He'd thought I was simply making conversation. He'd been surprised and gratified that at this early stage of our acquaintance I had had such regard for him.

"I've thought the very thing," he said. "It's a lovely grassy place, good water, shelter from the winter winds, off the main trail so's one can have peace, but near enough to the village if one wanted company. Does it belong to anyone, Miss Oonagh?"

"Do you have to keep calling me that?" I blurted out. I hated the miss.

"I'm sorry, what did I say?" He stared at me with sudden bewilderment.

"Couldn't you just call me Oonagh?"

"But I did, Miss Oonagh!" His brows were raised in astonishment.

"I mean the miss. I'd prefer to be just Oonagh, if you don't mind." I was being a complete fool but I stumbled on. "I've never liked miss."

He was silent for a long while, swallowing hard and staring down at his shoes. I was afraid I had offended him.

He suddenly reached down and plucked a tiny violet-like flower from the base of a tree. He presented the flower to me and said in a low, gorgeous manner, "Oonagh it is. Call me Chauncey." His smile was a shaft of sunlight in those woods.

That afternoon in the forest he didn't have to tell me that he'd come in search of me and I didn't have to tell him that was exactly what I'd hoped he'd do. Our eyes spoke of deeper matters even as our lips spoke of cabins and meadows and the fact that the afternoon was nearly gone and that Lorna McGann would be having a fit wondering where I'd disappeared to. Chauncey strode down the path ahead of me, holding back branches that might have sprung against me. We were almost to the river when he muttered over his shoulder, "Will you share my supper with me tonight?"

I was shocked and thought perhaps I'd heard wrong. I decided to say nothing. But at the river he turned to face me. "I didn't hear your reply," he smiled.

"Pardon?"

"Let me show you how to cook up this puffball. Will you come?"

"Oh," I protested, "How can I? The children —"

"You can leave when the children are asleep, can't you? I'll do the cooking after you arrive."

"But Lorna —"

"No," he said. "Don't bring Lorna." He laughed heartily.

"I can't," I said. "I just can't." I walked swiftly up the trail toward the village.

"Who's to stop you?" he called after me. "Where's the harm?"

You've brought this upon yourself, I chastised myself as I tried to hurry away from him. *All men are the same. You're friendly and they take it wrongly!* The more I considered his invitation the angrier I became and the faster I walked until I was almost running.

"Wait, Oonagh. Wait!"

I couldn't stop but did slow my pace. The afternoon had worn away into a small sliver before the dusk. The river water jostled with all the colours of the sunset, orange pink green black. He caught my arm.

"It's only a meal, Oonagh."

"Lorna and Paddy would —"

"Ah, I thought you were a grown woman with her own mind. Beg your pardon." He backed away, shrugging his shoulders and spreading his hands out in defeat.

Now I was angry. His voice full of feigned regret! I drew myself up tall. He was still a head and shoulders taller. "I'll have you know, Mr. Taylor, sir, that I'm not in the habit of visiting bachelor men in their quarters after dark. You insult me!" With that I whirled, my skirt flying, and strode away in righteous indignation.

To my astonishment Chauncey let out a roar of laughter. I turned in his direction and spat on the ground. "How dare you!" I yelled. "You insult me more. I thought you were a friend. I thought you were decent!"

He drew closer but I backed away. I shook my finger at him, my words spewing out. "Do you really expect a decent woman to visit you at night, just like that? How dare you?"

He advanced, his hands spread as if to show he was weaponless.

"Oonagh, it's not like that."

"Oh?"

"Come now."

I saw the sudden uncertainty in his eyes. As I continued to glare at him he stopped talking and stared at me with naked fear, his eyes widening.

"Aw, great Moses," he muttered. "I'm sorry. I won't bother you again. I just thought — please, Miss Oonagh, don't make trouble for me."

Trouble? Then I realized he'd got me all wrong! It was my turn to apologize. "All I mean, Chauncey, is that people keep an eye out. I can't visit you at night. People would talk and it wouldn't be nice what they'd say. Even if we were a courting couple and the wedding date set, folks like to talk nasty. They'd be counting the months for our first child." I touched his sleeve and I knew exactly why I was saying such bold words to him. I wanted to erase the awful fear I'd seen suddenly spring into his eyes. I wanted him to say, okay then Oonagh, girl, let's get married and really get them folks talking.

"I didn't mean nothing by it, Miss Oonagh. I'm just being friendly, like you said, sociable. Thought you'd like a taste of that there puffball. That's all." The way he stood with his shoulders slouched and the slight slur in his words — I went cold all over.

"Stop it, Chauncey."

"I surely will, ma'am. I ain't never going to bother you again."

"Chauncey, please!"

"What did I do now, Miss Oonagh?" He really bowed his head now and scratched at the earth with one shoe.

"God damn it." I heard myself swear almost as if I were in a dream. "God damn it. Don't call me Miss Oonagh!"

"Sorry, miss. Oh, sorry again, ma'am."

I could have hit him. "I want you to bother me," I heard myself declare.

He straightened up his posture, looked me full in the eye, and burst out laughing. For the first time, I witnessed the laughter Daniel had described to me, Chauncey in the full bloom of it. He fell onto the ground and rocked himself. *My stomach*, he groaned, and laughed some more.

"I really must go now," I said loudly. "Do you not see how the sun is down?"

He sprang to his feet in one fluid motion.

We stared at each other.

Then I remembered. "Daniel is coming tomorrow. He said you two were going fishing."

"Yes." Chauncey grinned at me. "Oonagh." I felt a slight shift in the universe. "It'll be a right proper row when you get back to the McGanns. Best get going." So saying he reached for my shoulders, turned me about on the trail, and gave me a little shove.

I RAN UP THE river trail. The sun had disappeared behind the hills in the west. Lorna gave me a dirty look when I entered the kitchen.

"We thought you'd got lost," she said.

"I went farther than I'd expected," I murmured. I set the basket down in a corner and got to work. The children raced around, the baby wailed in its cradle. "I'm sorry," I said. Lorna was mashing a mound of old potatoes we'd cooked the night before. I began to slice a couple of new onions. We were making potato cakes, the thing to do with the old sprouty potatoes.

"A few minutes more and I'd have got the men to go looking for you."

"I fell asleep in the sun after I finished gathering roots. My back hurt so I lay in the grass to rest it."

"You fell asleep!" She peered into my face and nodded. "I dare say. Your face is all burnt. You'd better put some tallow on that or you'll be peeling."

My face was burning, now that she mentioned it. Sting of the sun's heat. So I hadn't told a lie after all, I really had fallen asleep out there in the meadow. No wonder the afternoon had slipped away.

"You know, Lorna, what woke me up? Me mother's voice. She was calling me."

"Aw, no!" Her eyes went round with worry. "Pray for her. She wants you to pray for her."

"Do you think so?" I was amazed at her belief.

"If your poor mam has called to you, she's in need of your prayers. Oh, tonight, Oonagh, you must light a candle just for her and pray. You must."

What could Lorna possibly think my poor mother needed my prayers for? Was she in trouble in Heaven? After all these years was my poor mam still in purgatory? I didn't believe this for a minute, but the teachings of childhood have a powerful hold. My mother's voice had awakened me. But she had not called my name as if she were in need, but with a note of amusement, as if once again she had found her lazy girl daydreaming. Lorna was a religious and superstitious woman, careful never to disturb God or the fairies. She was sure fairies came over from Ireland with every boat.

I had no reply to Lorna's admonition to pray. Indeed, sometimes I wished I had her simple belief. If only I could close my eyes and murmur to a benevolent God who heard me, a sweet and loving Mother of God who would intercede for us poor sinners. But if Lorna believed that Mam was calling out for prayers, for intercession from us still alive on earth, did she believe Mam was suffering still? Why would God want that?

All evening as I went about my tasks I thought about my mother and the possibility that her soul had cried out to me. I tried to comprehend what Lorna would envision as my mother's soul needing my prayers. Was she some invisible being floating above or beside us? Where was Heaven in that vast sky? I wished there were someone to whom I could voice my doubts. But I wasn't that brave then.

When the children were snug in their beds and Paddy had gone outside for a final smoke, Lorna called me from the kitchen where I had just covered up a bowl of bread dough to rise overnight.

"Come, Oonagh," she called.

I followed the sound of her voice into the tiny parlour. She had lit candles in front of the image of the Holy Virgin she had placed on a high shelf. "Come light a candle," she beckoned. In her hand was a slender white candle made especially for such purposes. I wanted to back out of the room but she had caught me, her eyes glowing in the candlelight. "Come." She reached out to me and I went forward, a heavy grief in my throat.

I DIDN'T GO TO Chauncey that night as he'd asked. But I lay in my bed mulling over the words we'd exchanged. What were his beliefs? Would he have said that my mother's voice in my dream meant she needed my prayers? I wept to think of my mother in pain, to remember the words Lorna had whispered over and over, her own litany, her own intercession on behalf of my mam. I didn't believe it, but the thought of my mother still suffering, hurt as if I did believe it. I wished I had the daring to slip out of the house, to run down the path and across the bridge in the darkness to Chauncey's cabin on the edge of the village. I imagined our conversation.

> *Why, Oonagh Corcoran, you've come after all.*
> *I couldn't miss your supper. Are you a good cook?*
> *Indeed I am. Here, have a plateful.*
> *Thank you.*

And then a long silence while we ate his delicious supper. I would ask him if he believed in ghosts, in restless souls, in God and hell and purgatory. I would ask him about his own mother. We would by now be sitting on the grass by the river and watching the moonlight flicker on the water. This was as far as I could get in my dreaming. I wanted to know much about Chauncey, but I didn't want to invent him at all.

Ten

THE NEXT DAY I was out in the yard, up to my elbows in soapy water, washing baby clothes when Daniel came running around the corner.

"You never walk, do you?" I smiled as he slid to a halt.

"Oonagh, can you come fishing with us?" he blurted out.

"Do I look like I have the time for fishing? Go on with you. Catch me one pretty brook trout."

"C.T. says to tell you that the supper was fine, but he didn't have salt." My nephew spewed out the words then halted, unsure of himself.

"What?" I paused scrubbing to stare at him.

"Well, that's what he wanted me to tell you," he said sheepishly.

"Tell me again," I ordered, frowning. "And slow down."

"The supper was fine, but lacked salt." He looked triumphant. He'd got it right. "The supper was fine, but lacked salt," he repeated and grinned. "What does it mean?"

"It means what it says," I said sharply, hiding the excitement the words had sprung in me. "Tell him the store has a goodly supply of salt. He should get him some." Daniel nodded. "Get going now," I said and dabbed his nose with a small puff of soapsuds. "Get going before I put you to work." He hurried off and I returned to scrubbing away fiercely on the stained clothes. How cheeky of Chauncey to get Daniel to deliver a message — then I thought of the perfect response.

"Daniel, wait. Come back!"

I ran after him, wiping my dripping arms on my apron as I ran. Although it was still early in the day the heat was already quite oppressive, sweat trickling down my temples. "Now then. Tell him: 'And she became a pillar of salt.'" I laughed at his bewilderment.

"I don't understand? What's this about salt?" He frowned.

"You don't need to understand! Just repeat after me," I ordered. "'And she became a pillar of salt.'"

He did as I asked, a frown on his brow, then he asked, "What's a pillar of salt anyway?"

I laughed so much at his quizzical expression. "That's from the Bible. Don't you know? Lot's wife?"

He shook his head.

"Ah, you little heathen!" I cried and rubbed my wet hands over his hair. "Now go go go!" and I gave him a little shove on the back.

Leaning over the washtub I smiled to imagine Chauncey's face when Daniel delivered the message. What would he make of it? How would he interpret it? A man who could quote the Bible as he did that day to Paddy. A pillar of salt, a woman turned to salt for contemplating the loss of her home, a woman who disobeyed God's commandment. But what I meant had nothing to do with Lot's wife. The more I thought about it, the more I felt embarrassed at the boldness of my message. Would he even understand?

THE NEXT SATURDAY I took advantage of the cool morning to weed in the garden behind the house. Paddy had taken his family to Cobourg for a few days to visit Lorna's ailing mother. In my solitude I enjoyed pretending that the garden I worked in was mine. Daniel caught me singing at the top of my voice.

He squatted down in the next row and asked, "Oonagh, will you go fishing with me?"

"Is Chauncey too busy?" I asked, knowing that he most certainly was on a Saturday. Daniel hung his head and poked a twig into the earth.

"So go on your own, then. You know the good spots, don't you?"

My hands were encrusted with earth, fingertips green with weed juice. Every time I drew another handful of weeds from between the cabbage plants, I raked the damp earth loose with my fingers, relishing the feel of it.

"I know the best spot," Daniel agreed. "But it's better when someone else is along."

"Oh, you get lonely, do you?"

"Well, Mr. Goodwood saw a bear down that way last week."

"Oh sure, and it's better with two people along," I said.

"I'm not afraid of bears."

"Tell you what. You help me finish up the weeding and I'll go fishing with you."

He beamed at me.

I shoved a hoe into his hands. "The beets," I pointed out the rows.

He worked carefully, turning over the soil, now and then leaning down to pull out the larger weeds.

"Can you hill up the rest of the potatoes?" I asked him when he leaned on the hoe and surveyed the finished beets. He groaned. I threw a small clod of earth at him for he looked so woebegone, as if I would keep him weeding forever.

"Come on! Or we won't have the time for fishing. I'll go make us a lunch to take."

From the window I saw him working quickly to hill up what I hadn't got to. Then he arched his back and slung the hoe over his shoulder.

I met him at the door with the lunch basket. "Now let's go fishing."

He cast his eye glumly up to the heavens and shrugged. Yes, no doubt the sun was already too high and the fish would have sought the deep water, but he didn't openly complain. We set off, walking down the river path, mostly in silence. Birds sang all around us and small unseen creatures rustled in the underbrush. Now and then Daniel smiled up at me and I was increasingly glad I'd decided to accompany him. Then Daniel said "Here," rather authoritatively. "This is the best spot."

We slid down the embankment to where a creek entered the river, creating a small estuary of sorts. The spot he headed for was up the creek along a narrow path to where dark cedars overhung the water and where a huge boulder jutted out of the bank into the sunlight, a natural partial dam impeding the flow of water and creating a deep pool, half-dappled in shade. In this pool several big fish lurked, he declared. They'd tried a few times, he and Chauncey, to catch these fish. Their speckled shapes slipped along in the brown water, avoiding the lures. At this time of the day, with the sun soaring to its zenith, the fish would be slumbering in the darkest depths. Maybe we wouldn't even see them.

"So this is where you and Chauncey come." This place, well-hidden from the path along the main river, took my breath away with its beauty and its solitude. A perfect spot for bathing. With no one around, it would be paradise.

"Sometimes. See, if it rains, over there's a sort of cave." He pointed to the embankment just beyond the boulder where the roots of a giant cedar had been exposed by the run of water, their tangled web created the roof of a cave.

"Ah," I said and sat down on the boulder. Daniel handed me a line and hook to dangle into the water. I dropped the hook into the water and sat back, gazing about.

"Don't you want a worm on that hook?" Daniel asked.

"Oh," I said, rather absentmindedly. "No, no. It's fine." In truth, paying scant attention to Daniel, I was imagining Chauncey here and what he would say and where he would sit. What would I do should he come upon me suddenly as I bathed.

"Do you think a fish will take your empty hook?" persisted Daniel.

His voice penetrated my daydreaming and I exclaimed, "Oh! You mean I should have a worm. Can you put one on for me?"

I could do many things, including wringing the neck of a hen destined for the roasting spit, but I hated baiting hooks with fragile squirmy worms. Daniel sighed and took over with an air of superiority.

WE FISHED FOR ABOUT an hour in that spot. Daniel asked me questions about Ireland. What about fishing in Ireland? Had I ever gone out by myself in a boat on the sea? Just the currach to get to the island where Aunt Margaret had lived. And the boat to Galway. Had I ever been out on the sea in a storm? No, indeed, no. Da had been much too careful to be caught in a storm. But then, yes, the storms on the way to Canada. I didn't wish to talk about it now. We were silent for several minutes and I stared into the dazzling water, full of my own thoughts. Then I looked over at Daniel and saw his crestfallen face.

"If you like fishing, Daniel, it's because it's in your blood. And if you like the sea, that too is in your blood. Your grandda is from the Claddagh, fisherfolk. Has your da told you this?"

"No," he said. "He never tells me stories of the old country."

"Do you pester him for stories like you pester me?" I smiled.

"Oonagh, I think my da must have been very unhappy in Ireland. He has nothing good to say about it."

"Oh, but I'm sure he misses it. Misses our Da and Liam and Mona and Lizzie. It's been so long now with no word from them."

"I'm sure they're all fine," he said. "Da says Grandda should come to Canada."

"He won't," I said. "Not with the cholera. They're packing people off like herring in barrels in those ships."

"You and Mairi are very lucky, aren't you?" he said cheerfully.

"How so?" I drew my line through the water slowly.

"You missed the sickness."

"True," I sighed. "Da's right not to come now."

He leaned over to peer at me, a bright smile on his face. "Just think, Oonagh. By the time the others come over, you'll have your own sheep farm. Your own animals and everything."

"Maybe."

"Maybe? Of course you will."

I grinned and, leaning down, splashed some water at Daniel.

"Hey!" He splashed me back. By the time we ended our game, we were knee-deep in the water. Any fish that might have been in the pond were long gone. We were sopping wet.

"Might as well go in!" he shouted, tugging off his wet clothes and flinging them up on the boulder. Naked, he leaped into the water like a little frog. "Come on, Oonagh." He urged me in, never realizing for a moment that as a woman, swimming in a river might be an unseemly thing for me to do. I slipped off my sopping clothes and threw them up to the boulder. Clad only in my undergarments, I plunged in and shrieked with the sudden cold. Daniel laughed at me but before he could figure out what I was doing I dove below the surface, aiming for his skinny brown legs. He was balanced on a submerged rock. He yelled as I gripped his ankles and tumbled him into the water.

He emerged sputtering water and laughter. I floated on my back, my white shift ballooning about me, a slight current edging me toward the boulder. I floated up the pond, the back of my head in the water, my eyes closed against the glare of the sun.

"Did you learn to float in the sea?" Daniel paddled near.

"The sea? Oh my, no. It's too cold. There's a small lake up in the hills behind my da's place. A wee lake, but at the very top of the hills, so high up that a body can look over and see another village far away across the sea below."

I held up one hand with the fingers spread and with the other I indicated a place on the tip of my thumb. "Our home was here, on this piece of land. These are all fingers of land with the sea in between. This little lake up in the hills above our house: here. You couldn't see the house from there. I taught myself to float like this in that little lake. Just below it they used to cut turf. You had to be really careful going up there; the ground's boggy in spots. You could get stuck. A stone wall goes all the way up the hills and so I used to walk on that. But to get to the lake itself, I'd have to leave the wall and jump from solid ground to solid ground —"

"How could you tell what was solid?" he interrupted.

"Well." I narrowed my gaze up at the brilliant sky framed by the green of the trees. Not a cloud. The sun-warmed surface of the pool as I floated felt delicious on my arms as I waved them back and forth.

"Go on! How could you tell it wasn't quicksand?" he demanded, paddling beside me, splashing my face with his efforts.

"You'd step where a boulder poked out or on the hummocks the cows left when they cut through the turf with their hooves. They made little islands of the turf. But I did sink my feet into a bog a few times."

"Did you sink right down?"

"Oh, no, no. But that little lake was a gem. I thought I had discovered it! Then one day there was Colum, sitting, smoking a pipe. All of eleven he was!"

"Smoking a pipe!" he laughed. "I can smoke a pipe."

I unfastened my hair from its braid and swished my head back and forth.

"Your hair looks like black water snakes," Daniel remarked. I wished for a moment he was gone so that I could slip out of my garments altogether and feel the water slide over my skin as I did, a young girl up at the lake. I closed my eyes.

Daniel said, "How do you sleep on your back like that in the water?"

He was standing waist deep nearer the shore, clasping his arms about him.

"You don't know how to float? You were just swimming."

He shook his head. "Not on my back."

"Let's get warmed up a bit, then I'll teach you." We climbed onto the boulder and into the blessed hot sun. "Look away now, Daniel. I'm going to change."

He stretched face down on the boulder, hiding his head in his arms while I changed into the damp dress and hung up my dripping garments.

"Watch you don't burn in that sun."

"I like the sun on my bare skin," Daniel said.

"Lucky boy. It's been an age since I was bare under the sun."

"You never!" he laughed.

"How would you know? How do you think I swam at that little lake? I was younger than you are now."

He snorted at the thought.

I stretched out on the boulder with an arm over my face against the sun, my hair spread out to dry. The sun's heat caught in the smooth rock gave it a quality of aliveness like a warm body. I sighed with the pleasure of that warmth on my back and my legs. I inched up the dress until the sun's warmth was full on my thighs and then breathed a deep sigh of happiness.

"Talk," I murmured. "Don't let me fall asleep or I'll burn."

"What shall I say?"

"Tell me about Chauncey." I smiled.

"He can read," he said.

This drove all sleep out of me. I sat up, my hair trickling water down my back.

"Read? What can he read?"

"Everything," he said proudly. "He has books. I've seen them."

"Has he read to you?"

"He let me read to him. He wanted to see how well I could read."

"You read well?" I lay back down, shading my face again. A great shame came over me, for I couldn't read. But Chauncey could. And Daniel.

"He gave me a portion of the Bible to read."

"The Bible is it?"

"Yes. He has his own Bible and he made me read a little piece."

"Do you remember what it was?"

"It was about who was blessed."

"Ah ..." I said, feeling a tangle of emotions.

"I remember: 'Blessed are they that mourn, for they shall be comforted.'" Daniel recited softly. "It made me think of Mam, when she lost the babbies."

"I like those verses," for I knew them; my mother had taught me them. "But what does that mean — to be blessed — and how should they find comfort?"

"I don't know," he said truthfully.

"'Blessed are the meek, for they shall inherit the earth.' I wonder at that one too!"

"Oh, you know it!" he said.

"'Blessed are the pure in heart, for they shall see God.'"

"Right, Oonagh! Do you know all of it?"

"'Ye are the light of the world. A city that is set on a hill cannot be hid.'"

"I thought you couldn't read!" He was astonished.

A man cleared his throat behind us and we both almost rolled down the boulder. I sat up hurriedly, pulling my skirt down.

"Chauncey!" Daniel yelled. "We haven't caught one single fish!"

My heart pounding loud in my ears, I stood up too quickly, becoming dizzy. "Well now you're here, Mr. Taylor, I'd best be off." I couldn't look at him for the salacious thoughts I'd had earlier.

"Oh now, why? I'm not poison!" he protested.

"I was just keeping our Daniel company till you came."

"Oh, Oonagh! You don't have to go at all!" Daniel cried.

"Now how would you know what I need to do or not?" I chucked his cheek.

"The McGanns aren't home!" he pointed out.

"Oonagh, stay," Chauncey said. "If no one's needing you at home."

"Oonagh, you can't go. Your clothes are wet!" Daniel pointed to where my undergarments were still dripping. "And we haven't eaten," he laughed, pointing to our basket hung up in the cool shade.

"How was the water?" laughed Chauncey.

"Paradise!" I smiled.

Daniel sank back down to his haunches. He knew I wasn't going anywhere.

CHAUNCEY BUSIED HIMSELF BAITING his hook and setting his line in just the right spot. Daniel leaned over his shoulder, expecting a fish to leap out of the water now that Chauncey was here. I pretended to be intent on my own line too, but I watched Chauncey from the corner of my eye. We sat in silence. A welcome breeze sighed in the trees, dashing shadows over the water.

"Where's your hat, young man?" Chauncey suddenly said to Daniel.

"Over there," he gestured to where it hung on a twig.

"Not doing you much good there, is it? Go get it."

Daniel jumped to do what Chauncey requested, as if the man were his father or elder brother. I smiled at Chauncey's calm authority over the boy.

"Daniel tells me you can read," I said brightly.

"He says you can't," he replied, keeping his gaze at the water. His blunt statement startled me; I was instantly defensive.

"Are slaves given schooling then?" I muttered.

"Not exactly. It's forbidden."

"I can understand that."

"You can, can you?"

"Oh, yes," I said softly. "To read is a gift, a power."

"I heard you earlier as I came up," he said. "Where did you learn those Bible verses?"

"My mother was a learned woman," I said. "She knew many things by heart. Did you know that, Daniel?" I looked over my shoulder. Daniel stood rooted to the ground listening to us. He looked guilty, as well he should have been, telling Chauncey and me tales about each other. "Well, come on. You've got your hat."

"Where's your hat, Oonagh?" Daniel said pointedly. "You'll get burnt red like a beet."

"Here now," said Chauncey. "Here's the trick. This is how we do down south." He drew his large white kerchief out of his pocket, assuring me that it was clean, and squatting beside me proceeded to tie it around my head. I tipped forward as his fingers drew my wet ropes of hair over one shoulder. His fingers grazed the nape of my neck as he tied the cloth and I rested my forehead against his chest. It was but for a moment. I took in his scent and closed my eyes against a surge of longing. He tapped my head.

"There you are," Chauncey said. "I've got my own hat on." He clapped his hand on the top of his head.

"No you don't!" Daniel shouted with laughter as Chauncey continued to grope around at the top of his head.

"Well, well, I'll be. I coulda swore I had me a hat."

"You're sitting on it!" Daniel whooped, for Chauncey's poor straw hat was crushed underneath him.

He pulled it out with great feigned surprise. I smiled, shaking my head. He shook the hat and pounded his fist into it to uncrease it.

"How'd you like this hat?" he asked.

"It's a lovely hat."

"I made it myself."

I was suitably impressed with his handiwork. It was a fine hat, if a bit worse for being sat upon.

After a silence between us I said, "Daniel says you have books. You let him read you some of the Bible."

"Yes, a bit of the Sermon on the Mount."

"Are you a religious man?"

He was silent for such a long stretch of time that I felt compelled to apologize for the question. "It's none of my business; sorry for asking."

"No," he said. "It's a good question. I always have trouble finding a clear answer. But I'll tell you. Right in here" — he pointed at his chest, his heart — "I want to believe in a God who is loving and just and who would see the least of the sparrows fall and stretch out his hand to shelter it. But here" — he pointed to his head, "I know there is no such God at all."

I took in a sharp startled breath. I looked first at Daniel who squatted beside us taking in every word and then at Chauncey.

He continued, staring into the water, unmindful of my excited gaze. "I'm sorry, Oonagh, to say such a thing. It must sound terrible to you —"

"Not at all!" I interrupted. "I don't think there's a God, either." He turned to see the joy on my face.

So began our conversation. He described how the slave owner on the plantation in Virginia where he'd been raised would gather all the slaves on Sunday afternoons. A Methodist minister from town, himself an owner of ten slaves — a "turkey vulture of a pious Methodist preacher man" — would read them passages from the Good Book. The little children were drilled in those verses.

His voice rang out, "Luke twelve, verse forty-seven: 'That servant, which knew his lord's will, and prepared not himself, neither did according to his will, shall be beaten with many stripes.' Ephesians six, verse five: 'Servants, be obedient to them that are your masters according to the flesh, with fear and trembling, in singleness of your heart, as unto Christ.'"

"Yep, we had to stand out there in the hot sun and shout back these words until we got them right. You got 'em right, you got your corn portion. I asked my mama what those words meant and she said it meant I had to be good and do what I was told. It wasn't until I was in New Orleans and learned to read for myself that I went back into the Bible and studied those verses for the meaning."

"Who taught you to read? Why did you go to New Orleans?" I'd been leaning on my hands gazing at him as he spoke and now shifted into a more comfortable position on the boulder facing him, cross-legged, my skirt tucked under.

He laughed, "Getting ready to set for a spell?"

"Well first: how did you get to New Orleans?"

He told me how he'd get into trouble as a little boy, being wild and wilful, so the master sent him off to a sheep farmer to get broke.

"Get broke?" I interrupted.

He nodded, "Yeah, you know how they break horses?"

"You got whupped, right?" Daniel broke in.

Chauncey stretched his arms high, "Are we ever going to catch a fish today?"

Daniel pulled up his empty line and shrugged. "They're all gone."

"You know," Chauncey said wisely. "All the fish are snoozing over there in the shade. I bet if you was to dangle a juicy worm right there under the cedar roots, you might wake 'em up."

"You think so?" Daniel said, eyeing us both. I don't think Chauncey fooled our Daniel one bit, but the boy moved obligingly farther down the pool and out of earshot. We watched him in a silence that grew until we both drew in breath at the same moment.

"So where was I?" he said softly, leaning slightly toward me.

"You'd been sent to a sheep farmer to get broke." Just repeating that raised gooseflesh on my arms.

"Oh yes. Farmer Haines. He was a bitter and brutal man. It didn't take him long to break me into a hard-working boy who kept his mouth shut. I was there for two years and learned everything there was to know about sheep. Then one day they brought me back to the plantation, stood me up in a line of children, very young to half-grown like me, and out come Miss Constance with her daddy, walking up and down, looking us over. She pointed at me and said, 'That one will do.' The master said she had a good eye, must be she was her papa's daughter after all. Could she pick any others might be good enough for New Orleans? And that's how I got to go there. I was lucky, you could say. I had it pretty easy for four years down there. She taught me to read, I learned to barber. I learned a lot of things."

"Did they ever whip you?"

"The master was usually upriver at his other plantations. Sometimes I got in a fix with Miss Constance for staying out too late barbering down at the waterfront hotels. She'd pretended to beat me, only using a feather duster instead of a whip. Said she figured I was striped enough already." This last he said so low I wasn't sure I heard right. He glanced sideways at me, quizzically.

"Whew, the sun's hot today," he muttered.

"Just how old was this Miss Constance?" I imagined a girl not much older than he.

"Late twenties by then, I figure."

"And you?"

"I started to New Orleans, I guess I was about fourteen. I come back to Virginia four years later." Chauncey turned to look at Daniel slouched against a fallen tree, his feet in the water. "No nibbles?"

Daniel splashed his way back to us, slipping on stones, beaming as if he'd been redeemed. "No fish!"

Before he got to us I said so only Chauncey could hear, "Chauncey Taylor, I like talking with you. Why don't we meet more often, walk in the woods?"

"Hmm," he said. "Sounds good. Right now I'm going to swim." He splashed into the water and grabbed Daniel as he came up, spinning him high before letting him drop with a mighty splash. They slapped at the water like a pair of seals. Daniel yelled for me to come swimming again, "Teach me how to float!" I declined, instead laying out lunch in the shade. Chauncey commenced teaching the boy. I didn't wait for them. When they saw me eating they rushed out, dripping water deliberately all over me like great shaggy dogs, admonishing me to save them a morsel at least.

Chauncey sat in his dripping clothes and when I handed him a hunk of bread with chicken I told him he could at least remove his shirt and lay it over the rock to dry. It'll dry on me, he said. Nice and cool. His tone told me I could mind my own business and I shut up, feeling foolish. Who was I to tell him what to do? A guilty voice inside me admitted I'd really wanted to see the scars Daniel had described. As we ate we talked, our conversation like spinning yarn from various strands of wool. Our talking must have made him drowsy, for Daniel was the first to stretch out, full and contented. I too lay down on the flat boulder to rest. Chauncey lay under a tree, his hat covering his face. Somewhere in the forest a woodpecker knocked on a tree. The wilderness hummed with bees and cicadas. I closed my eyes and mulled over what Chauncey had related.

I NEXT OPENED MY eyes to see Chauncey peering down at me, a finger to his lips for silence. He'd nudged me awake. He pointed at

Daniel asleep in the sun, his arms flung over his head. I rose and gathered up my petticoat, which was dry now, and laid it gently over the boy so that he wouldn't be burnt, although the lengthening shadows of the maples on the west bank would reach him shortly.

Chauncey inclined his head, motioning for me to follow. Without a word, we left Daniel asleep and walked into the coolness under the trees. For several minutes we were both lost in our own thoughts, Chauncey directing our steps to where a path cut into the forest, walking side by side until the forest path narrowed and Chauncey stepped aside to let me lead.

"You said you'd like a walk in the woods, didn't you," he murmured as I brushed past him. Although I could hear him directly behind me, I couldn't refrain from glancing back several times just to make sure. After we'd walked a few minutes, the path entered a tiny glade where a giant tree had fallen years ago, opening up the forest floor to meadow grasses and flowers, daisies in particular.

"Let's sit here." So saying, Chauncey sat at the foot of another enormous tree and patted the ground next to him. I sat beside him, tucking my legs underneath my skirt.

"Have you been here before?" I asked. He nodded and took a deep breath of that perfumed air.

"And you say," he said slowly, "that there is no God. Just look around you."

I looked at him in alarm, for I'd thought we'd had a meeting of minds. I looked around at the beauty of the place. We'd spoken for a couple of hours at the river about our beliefs or lack of them. Chauncey had just told me how the most pious southerners could be the most brutal toward their slaves, justifying their actions with Bible verses. The same woman who talked about Christ's mercy and *suffer the little children to come unto me* would beat a small slave girl about the head with a block of wood for falling asleep minding the baby in the night. It was this that set him to questioning whether God existed. He'd concluded that God was made up by men to explain and justify their actions in the world.

I said, "All this beauty doesn't prove God exists. Just because we don't know how all this came about doesn't mean that God must therefore exist, does it? I can't prove to you that God doesn't exist, but then I can't prove to you that the elves don't exist either, can I? Lorna really believes in the little people, that they've come here with us from Ireland. I've never seen any and I doubt she has but she still believes in them. I'd call that superstition but it's her belief. So why isn't God a superstition? When something good happens people say, 'Thank God,' and when something bad happens they pray for God's mercy. Look now how everyone's in the churches praying for God's mercy with the cholera. If God can take it away, why does He visit us with it in the first place? Why does He need us to beg for His mercy? None of this makes sense unless God is just like Lorna's little people, the fairies and elves, born out of superstition and ignorance."

"Well said, and so sternly. But what if I was to say, Oonagh girl, you're just angry with God and so you reject Him."

We gazed at each other and I saw the method in his questioning. He really wanted to know my mind and wanted me to know it as well.

"If I really believed in God, how could I dare be disappointed in Him? How could I dare to be angry?"

Chauncey shrugged. "Maybe God tests us today as he did Job."

"I reject Job's god! But my rejection would mean nothing, for why would the Supreme Being, who has created all this, even notice my existence?" I waved my hand at the flowers, the sun shining through into this little spot in the forest darkness. "Isn't that a lot of arrogance and selfishness on the part of religious people to think the Almighty would be caring for their trifling wants and needs? In such a world as this? And if He was so almighty powerful why would He make His creation so flawed in the first place? Make a creature like Man who causes such suffering to his fellow man? Just so God can watch poor souls scurry about like ants disturbed by His Almighty foot!"

"Ah," he said, smiling. "You blasphemous woman! Once you learn to read the Bible, your questions will be returned to you a hundred fold!"

"No!" I cried. "Bible or no. There's more awe in observing the earth, believing in no god at all. Look up at the stars at night and wonder if there are other worlds as marvellous. The earth is a wondrous mystery. I don't need an explanation that some god made it all."

"Strong opinions."

"You haven't heard the half of them!" I laughed. "I keep them to myself mostly. They'd tar and feather me out of the village if I told them what I really think!"

"Goodness, girl, you're shaking like a leaf. Are you cold?"

I was shaking, but it wasn't with cold. It was the excitement of saying to another human being all the thoughts I'd kept stuffed inside me. I couldn't stop shaking and I could feel tears rising. Chauncey wrapped his arms around me and pulled me close against him.

"There now. Hush," he murmured and swept his hand over my hair, pushing it back from my face. "There now." He rocked me and after a while my shaking stopped and I began to feel ashamed of my emotion.

I pulled away slightly. He let me go.

"Sorry," I muttered.

"Nothin' to be sorry for."

We sat close together, not touching for some time before he broke the silence. "I want to tell you something important. If it wasn't for some fine religious folks helped me on my way north, I doubt I'd be here talking to you on this beautiful day." He held up his hand to stay me. "Nothing's simple." He scraped up a handful of earth. "Look. What is it?"

"Earth," I said.

"Now take a good look. What's in my hand?" He held the earth out for my inspection. I leaned closer, feeling immensely foolish. Then I saw what he wanted me to see, the grains of earth, sand and small pebbles and sticks and leaf mould. Chauncey flung it away, then stretched behind and picked a couple of daisies. "No two alike, I'd venture." He presented them to me for inspection. "Just take a good look at how intricate a simple daisy is."

"You said you weren't a religious man! Have I offended you?"

"No, you mistake me. I'm not a religious man. I don't believe in the Christian God. But I do know life is complicated; I don't have the answers. I'm not as sure of things as you seem to be. I know, though, that my mama takes great comfort in her faith, and if it weren't for God Almighty she might be dead already just from losing heart. And there was folks when I crossed the river in Pennsylvania who took care of me and helped me heal, sheltered me, gave me new clothes they'd made and fed me and passed me on up the road when the coast was clear, and they was mighty religious Christians."

"Ah, but was it their Christian religion telling them to help you? What about the others reading the same Bible and using the whip?" I protested. "I don't think it's religion or God that makes people just or kind, Chauncey! Didn't anyone help you at all who wasn't religious?"

He laughed and slapped his thigh. "I didn't have deep discussions with everyone I met on the way! But I'm sure more'n a few was helping me out of just plain human sympathy." He paused and then muttered, "And their righteous anger at slavery."

"Ah hah! Human sympathy! Righteous anger at slavery! That's it exactly. I don't need God or a priest or minister telling me I need to love my neighbour. It's not God or religion fills people with righteous anger against slavery, is it? I'm not a believer but I wouldn't want to hurt anyone and I'd help anyone who needed it. I sure don't need a Holy Bible to tell me what's wrong or right! Some of the people in the Bible are terrible. They had slaves. Who was Hagar? Sarah beat her and Abraham agreed to cast her and her child out into the desert. He'd have killed his own son in obedience to God. This is the story of God's mercy!"

Once again Chauncey reached for me. He pulled me close against his chest. "Do you always tremble like a leaf when you're speaking your mind?"

He was right. I was shuddering again, as if plunged into freezing water. "Hush now, no more talking," he ordered and patted my back as if I were a six-month-old. I let him, leaning my head against his warm chest, feeling exhausted and tearful.

"Trouble is, Oonagh child, you carrying a load of hate. It's makin' you shake and shiver."

I shook my head but he continued to stroke my hair. "Oh yes," he murmured. "I recognize it. Let's just rest now, be quiet for a while. Listen to the wind up there."

So we stretched out on the grass, my head against his chest, his arms holding me close against his side. I knew then for certain that whatever was good and gracious and loving in the universe had brought us together and whether that was God or not I believed in the power of this love. Chauncey had seen right into that hidden centre of me. His strength of character was such that after all he'd gone through he knew hate was the corrosive weapon of ignorance. He was finer and stronger than that. The most powerful force for good in the world is not religion but love. The Bible says that God is Love, but just maybe it's the other way around.

That afternoon we talked no more. We listened to the wind high in the pines and oaks and beeches. The air was still mellow, the grasses sweet in the hot sun, the crickets soothing in their chorus. My head on his chest, his arms around me, I listened as Chauncey's breathing slowed. He fell asleep. I too must have slept until Daniel's frantic cries through the woods startled us awake. We ran, fearing he'd been hurt and found him prancing about on the boulder at the creek, wearing my petticoats. He laughed hysterically when we ran up. "I thought that would fetch you!" Pointing dramatically at the sun shining low through the trees, he said, "You've been gone a long time."

Eleven

THAT SHINING DAY BY the river, when Chauncey said he knew there was no God, I felt the joy of a thousand summers enter me. I may offend some with these thoughts but I am not ashamed of them. Since I began thinking for myself as a young girl, I'd doubted the existence of a Supreme Being, but always in secret, in the black depths of my heart, for whom could I trust with such blasphemous thoughts? I couldn't confess them to a priest; I no longer believed in the authority of such men. Could I speak to Mairi, who would probably collapse with shock? Mairi didn't spend much time on her knees, but every evening without fail she and Josie mumbled the rosary, taking turns, just as my mam and da had, and theirs before them. I'd grown up feeling alone, often frightened at the bold rebelliousness brewing in my mind. Even in my friendship with Colum I'd never dared voice my thoughts of God. I'd never been completely free with anyone, afraid of being discovered "godless." Now I lived in the household of Lorna McGann, a pious woman who insisted on the household gathering each evening for prayers. I dutifully murmured my share of Hail Marys and Our Fathers. As I muttered the words I no longer really heard, I often dreamed about evenings in my own little cabin, sitting by the hearth, knitting or spinning, relishing the crackle of the fire. I sometimes tried to imagine a man sitting opposite me, but until I began to speak to Chauncey, that man in my daydreams had no face, not even Colum's.

ONE AFTERNOON NEAR THE end of summer, Chauncey and I walked in our bloodroot meadow. We'd left Daniel down by the big river watching our fishing lines. We had told him we wanted more roots, but the look he gave us told me he understood far more than I'd thought him capable. I felt a twinge of guilt until he grinned and blew me a kiss.

"Tell me what you do in the evenings," I asked Chauncey. He stood several paces away from me in waist-high grass.

"I sleep," he laughed.

"No, before you go to bed," I insisted.

He walked away from me, toward where the spring had formed a small pool. Frequently we found fresh deer tracks here and we determined the deer preferred this watering place to the swiftly flowing river.

"Sleep. I love to sleep. Never get enough," he said.

"I don't believe you!" I laughed. "You just don't seem like the sleeping type."

"Oh?" He quirked one eyebrow.

What I really wanted to hear was that he read books at night, because that was what I envisioned him doing.

"You have books."

"I have a Bible." He hesitated, looking away from me. When he spoke next, he spoke to the trees and the grass. "And I have a book of verse."

"Poetry?"

"Yes."

"Can you teach me to read?"

He reached into the voluminous pocket of his trousers and produced a slim volume bound in dark brown leather. My spirit took flight.

"Can I touch it?" I moved quickly through the grass, my hand outstretched like a greedy child.

"Are your hands clean?"

I wiped them hurriedly on my skirt, then held them out for inspection. Chauncey placed the little book with leaves as delicate as moth wings in my hands. Carefully I turned page after page. The print seemed impossibly small, the letters too crowded to distinguish. Tears blurred my sight. "What a lovely thing," I breathed. "And you can read this? Where did you get it?" I handed the book back to him.

He smiled. "They never missed it in the master's library in New Orleans. So many books, mostly only taken down for dusting. Miss Constance was the one taught me to read. Give me a Bible for my own. She was breaking the law, you know. But this little book I took is special."

"Will you read it to me?"

He smoothed his hand over the leather cover and laughed. "It'll take us some time to read through these," he said. "But we can start with one of my favourites."

His voice rang out, echoing in the woods, and soon I realized that he was not really reading but reciting. "'Let me not to the marriage of true minds / Admit impediments; love is not love —'"

"Wait," I said. "Which word says love?"

He showed me as I leaned upon his warm arm, breathing in the scent of him. Chauncey was the cleanest man, a smell about him of soap and shaving lather and scents from bottles as well as his own good smell. He said, "Pay attention now. Watch my mouth when I form the word. L — O — V. You don't pronounce the E. See? Love. Watch ..." I watched. His lips were so finely shaped I couldn't watch them shape sounds without wanting to touch. I reached out my fingers. Our reading lesson was over for the day.

POOR DANIEL. HE TELLS me now how he would deliberately call out our names loudly when he knew it was time to go home. He was afraid, he says, to go looking for us in the woods or meadow for fear he might surprise us. As well he might. We were glad when he came to the village, for somehow he gave us the opportunity to meet without the worry of tongues wagging. But Daniel didn't come to the village as often as we wanted to meet and we figured out ways to get together. We planned our days as generals plan battles. Each time we met we arranged our next chance encounter.

Come to the store tomorrow at ten and I'll be there.

Like as not I'd come to the store with one of Lorna's children on my hip and so we met and talked about the children and their health and Lorna's health.

Be crossing the bridge on Monday at three. I'll be delivering laundry to Martha McGann.

And sure enough at three on Monday, I'd saunter slowly toward the bridge, my pace quickening when I saw him approaching. We would meet on the bridge and pause for a few magical moments before he went on to his delivery and I on to whatever errand in the village I had contrived. We had many such planned encounters. Fleeting moments. We were sufficiently discreet, we remained undiscovered.

Then one day I suggested Chauncey come up to the house and ask for me at the front door. We could come out into the open with our affections and let the world know we were a courting couple. He advised against this. He cautioned that not all men had the liberal heart of my brother Michael, that many would be angry.

"Angry? Because I've chosen a barber and not a blacksmith?"

"You know what I mean, Oonagh. Confound it. I am black."

"Well," I said. "I'm what's called black Irish. And I'm not white but speckled." With that I turned away, but Chauncey caught my arm.

"What?" I asked, unable to keep the anger out of my voice.

"Where the sun hasn't kissed you," he murmured, "you're white as fresh-fallen snow."

"But not as cold." At this I wrenched free and raced back up to the village from our meeting place in the woods. I swore never to speak to him again, sure his affection for me was merely skin deep since that seemed to be the barrier to our open avowal of love. How naive and innocent I was, and how right he was in his fear for us. But then, as I ran crying up the trail, I was certain he didn't love me enough to tell the world. A whole week went by before once again we made eye contact at the store as he was entering and I leaving. Just that look. And once again we were meeting on the bridge and walking the woods on our forays for herbs and roots.

LATE INTO SEPTEMBER I lay awake one night long in the darkness. I had turned over in the bed so many times it was a wonder it hadn't collapsed under me with all its creaking and groaning. Every time I turned I imagined Chauncey's face, his eyes. I remembered my conversations with him and imagined new ones. I longed to ask him more about his past, about his family. The season was passing so quickly and winter would be upon us and no more Daniel coming to go fishing, no more secret walks in the woods. Although we spoke of many things in our swift encounters, we hadn't returned to the weighty issues we had begun to discuss on the riverbank. I longed for more depth to what we said to each other, for our conversation to be truly meaningful and not just idle speech. I wanted to tell him about my brother John.

Truth was I couldn't sleep for imagining living with Chauncey in his little cabin, lovely evenings by the hearth, he reading to me from his poetry book while I knitted for our baby. My limbs melted at the thought. Later, baby asleep, Chauncey and I would lie in bed under blankets I had woven. I would rest my head on his shoulder.

Whenever I came to this point in my daydreaming, impatience flooded me and I wanted to scream at the pain of not being with him.

I rose that night and stood by the window peering out. The moon hung low in the west, shedding abundant light, making visible every tree, every shrub. Beyond the trees moonlight glittered on the river. Leaning far to the right of the window frame, I could make out the dark shape of Chauncey's cabin across the river at the edge of the village. And a light in his window. Burning a candle so late? Or so early? Silent as a ghost I wrapped a shawl around me, crossed the children's room, and slipped down the stairs. Once outside I raced in my bare feet across the grass stiff with an early frost, down to the bridge, and along the river's edge. No one in any of the houses above could see me. As I passed the Allens' place their dog gave a few sharp barks then fell quiet.

At Chauncey's door I almost lost courage. The candle in the window was guttering and I wondered again at its purpose. I knocked so gently a mouse would not have heard it. No sound from within. I lifted the latch and entered. This was the first time I'd come into Chauncey's cabin and my heart pounded so fiercely I was near fainting. Chauncey lay in his bed on his back with an arm under his head for a pillow. He was snoring softly, and at that sound I panicked, wondering what I was doing, coming into a man's room half-dressed in the dead of night. Fear constricted my breathing. Suddenly he sat up and stared at me. Darkness closed in. I would have fallen to the floor if he hadn't reached me first.

"Are you unwell?" he whispered. He held me against him, asking, "Are you ill? Oonagh! Say something. What's happened?"

"I couldn't sleep," I managed to say.

By now he had helped me to the bed.

"Your feet are freezing!" He began rubbing my feet between his warm hands. I almost fainted again, with embarrassment.

"Oh, they're dirty!" I protested. In answer he reached for a cloth hanging on the wall and proceeded to dry my feet.

"Do you go barefoot in the winter, too?" he asked, grinning. The candle guttering on the windowsill began to go out, throwing chaotic shadows.

"Do you always burn a candle all night?"

"You see it from your room?"

"I couldn't sleep. I looked out and saw it."

"I wondered if you'd see it from that distance."

"But you were asleep. A waste of a candle."

"Ah no, not a waste at all. For here you are." He stroked my hair back from my forehead.

"You lit it for me?" I asked, quite surprised.

"Come now, tell me why you couldn't sleep." He climbed over me onto the bed and in one swift movement had me wrapped up cozily in his arms under the quilt. The candle went out and we lay in darkness with a strip of moonlight gleaming through the window and across the bed.

I know it is generally the man who asks a woman to marry, but the words spilled out of me as he pressed me closer, the heat of him warm through the thin nightgown all down the length of me. I whispered into the crook of his neck, "Let's get married. Right away."

For answer, he began kissing me. Before I could stop him he'd removed his nightshirt. In the dark he kept kissing me, his hands everywhere on me he could reach under my clothes and I did not stop him. No one had talked to me about what happens between a man and a woman. I'd asked Mairi after she married Josie to tell me about it but she'd declined with great shouts of laughter at my curiosity. Now I'd entered this mysterious place. A small voice in me exulted. With each movement of his lips on mine, the taste of his tongue caressing my lips, the tip insisting on entry, my own desire doubled and redoubled until I was pressing myself upwards to him, longing for what I didn't know to happen. Here I was in the arms of a man whose very scent made me swoon. All caution fled and left me in this place where only touch and taste and smell mattered. He drew up my nightgown and I helped him, raising my arms like a child. He laughed and flung the gown to the floor. His lips brushed across my breasts. Caressing his back I felt his scars for the first time. He paused for a moment, kneeling over me, and drew my hands from his back to his front and I felt his swollen hardness.

"Oonagh," he breathed. I withdrew my hands swiftly as if I'd touched a burning brand. Fear lurched into me. In all our meetings in the woods we'd never loved beyond lingering kisses and caresses.

I rolled away from him, pulling the quilt to me to shield myself from his eyes that even in the darkness had seen everything already. The moonlight was enough for me to see his eyes and the expression on his face. I dared not look below his face.

"Oonagh," he held out his arms. "Oonagh, come now."

"Let's marry first."

"Oh," he groaned. "Yes, yes, let's. I agree."

Once again he'd surprised me. Instead of being angry, he was quite the opposite.

He folded his arms across his chest and he laughed from deep inside his chest. "Woman, you just about done me in."

I didn't know much about men and thought maybe once a man was excited like that and not fulfilled he'd be in pain. Chagrined, I moved toward him, meaning to comfort him somehow, but he only laughed again and put out his hand to stop me getting closer.

"If you want us to be married first, don't come any closer. No telling what'll happen if you do. Besides," he dropped his voice to a whisper, "you better put some clothes on or you'll catch your death. What you mean walking around here in that undressed state, girl? Don't you know you in a man's house?" His voice rippled in joyous laughter as he teased me. When I was dressed and he had his night-shirt safely back on, I hugged him tightly.

"Will you really marry me?" I pushed my nose against his neck, breathing in.

"We could get married right now, this very minute."

"No," I hesitated. "No, we need witnesses, a priest."

"You want a priest?"

"Well, how do folks get married where you come from?"

He was silent for a shade too long as I looked up into his face. He kissed me. Anyone who has ever loved will understand how we were unable to stop touching each other. I wanted to climb right inside him somehow and never leave.

"Someday," he murmured, his lips sliding along my forehead, temples, and around to the nape of my neck, "I'll tell you how the black folks at home get married and what happens to the families. I want to tell you about my family, my little mama, my sister Sadie. My brothers. But right now you got to go, quickly, before some soul sees you here. It's just about morning." With that, he withdrew from me.

His words chilled my heart like a sudden sharp winter wind on a mild October day. His tone told me his stories wouldn't be joyful.

"We could have a minister," I said. "There's a Methodist comes here once a month."

"No Catholic priest?"

That was the last thing I wanted. I shook my head and reached for him again, pressing as close as I could. No two people fit together as well as we did. His arms completely encircled me. I fit my head against his shoulder when we stood.

"A Methodist. That'll be all right, won't it?"

"For two people don't believe in God ..." he muttered.

"We need some kind of minister to make it lawful, don't we? Mairi would want us to have a priest. But can't we just make our vows in front of witnesses?"

"Well, we could just jump over a broom."

"Jump over a broom?"

"Yeah. That's what folks back home do to get married. Even some poor white folks down there do it like that."

"Jump over a broom?" I repeated. This seemed familiar. Where had I heard of this? "A broom? An ordinary broom?"

"Any kind of broom. Don't matter, long as it's a broom."

"What does it mean? Why a broom? And do both people jump in the same direction, same time, or jump toward each other?"

"Listen. Roosters' crowing. You must go now."

"Here," I said, reaching for his right hand with mine. He clasped it firmly. The room was growing light with bleak pre-dawn. Filled with the urgency of the moment, I reached with my left hand for his left hand, making a loop over the right hands clasped.

"You see how we're connected now. This is how my people get betrothed. We're betrothed now. We belong to each other. Almost as good as married." We gripped each other tightly until my fingers ached. "Nothing and no one can ever tear us asunder." I stared at him.

I'd never seen his eyes more serious. "Go now. Go down by the river so no one sees you."

ON THE FIRST SUNDAY afternoon in October, I asked Chauncey, "What is your earliest memory?"

He'd taken me to a place he knew, a high hill overlooking the valley below, a far horizon on all sides. Below us in several directions, smoke billowed from land-clearing fires. Chauncey pointed to the southeast at the smoke spiralling from the chimneys of our own village. We couldn't see the river for the forest but Chauncey had climbed here once at dawn and had been able to see the route of the river by the white coil of mist that hovered above the trees.

"My earliest memory?" he repeated.

"Yes. The first thing you remember."

We sat high on a pink granite boulder still warm from the noon-day sun. The air was mild and if not for the yellow and russet tingeing the green forest spread below, we could have believed that it was spring or early summer.

Chauncey held my hand and stroked with one finger the lines on my palm. He sighed and suddenly smiled at me, "No," he said. "You tell first. What's your earliest memory?"

I shook my head. He always found ways to evade my questions. "I asked you first."

"If you tell me your memory, I'll come up with something, I promise." He squeezed my hand.

"Well," I began. "The very first thing is just a little glimpse. I see my granny, Mam's mam. It's her wake. She's lying on the table and some-one has lifted me up to see her. I don't recognize her. She's shrunken and tiny. The person holding me says, 'Say goodbye to Granny.' That's what I remember. I told Mam about this memory. She said I wasn't even four."

"What else?"

"It's your turn," I protested.

"Just one more," he said. "What else can you remember?"

For a long moment I watched a pair of hawks circling above the trees. I pointed them out silently to Chauncey and he nodded.

Then I knew. "When my baby brother Liam was born. That's the next thing I remember after my granny's wake."

"Were you at the birth?"

"I just remember how he looked lying in the bed next to Mam. He was shrieking, all red-faced and wrinkled. I thought he was awfully ugly but I never told my poor mam so, she looked so pleased to see him!"

We both laughed. He put his arm around me, drawing me closer. I rested my head against his shoulder and waited. In all fairness it was his turn.

"Death and birth," he murmured. "You have a fine memory."

I knocked my head against his shoulder. "Go on," I insisted. "It's your turn."

My head rose and fell as he breathed deeply. He wrapped his other arm around me so that I was completely in his arms. He took a long time finding his words. His arms tightened slowly around me. I turned my face against his chest and tears stung in my eyes. When he finally spoke, his voice was low and rumbling against my ear on his chest. "I'm trying to sort through the memories. I don't think you really want to hear this, Oonagh love."

"Yes, I do."

Once again he took a very deep breath. "The very earliest: some-one lifted me from my mother's side and ..." He stopped. "It's best not to bring it up. It isn't for your ears."

"I'm not a child, Chauncey. I want to know you."

"You do. Indeed." His voice was bitter and stung me to my very being. I raised my head from his chest in dismay but he drew my head back and stroked the hair from my cheek. "Shh," he said. "Listen. I must have been three or four, like you. I slept every night with my mother, with her body curled around me like a blanket. We had straw to sleep on. This was before my sister and brothers were born. I was her first. One night someone lifts me away from my mama and I can hear her crying, 'No, no.' I'm tossed into a corner of the shack and the man — a white man — tells me to shut up and stay there. My mother is pleading with this man. 'No, no.' I watch and I think he's killing her. But I can't move because I'm terrified he'll kill me too. He finally leaves her lying there on the straw shivering and crying and goes out. I still can't go to her because I'm completely frozen. She calls my name, tells me fetch a dipper of water. Now that takes me some time. Must've had to go to the well. It's dark. How did I get that dipper of water? I just remember being terrified, the night so dark. But when I come back, she's sitting up, smiling at me. She's not dying at all. She drinks the dipper of water and tells me to lie down quietly again and go to sleep. I'm shaking and shivering and crying. She curls herself around me once more and shushes me with a soft song she makes up as she sings, something about the stars in the sky and the yellow dawn."

I trembled with the shock of this memory related in such a quiet, casual tone.

"The thing is," he chuckled, "Mama told me years later that that man was my sister's father. I asked her, well then, who's my father? I knew it wasn't the same man. She'd never say. Who fathered my brothers? She got real sad at me for asking. Course I knew it was the master himself. But think since they were his sons he'd feed and clothe them better? No, nothing much to wear at all the first years 'cept what Mama stitched together, and you know, it can get cold down there all the same. No shoes."

"How awful," I whispered.

"That's how it is," he muttered. "The worst is for women. Now you'll despise me because I don't even know who my father was."

I assured him most certainly not.

"That's why I don't like to talk about the past," he spoke over my protestations. "You'll stop loving me when you really know me."

"Never," I whispered. "How could I? That's not your fault."

"Nor my mama's, poor thing."

"Couldn't she have told someone?"

I was still that naive, that unknowing.

Chauncey let out a great huff of disbelief. "That white man," he said grimly, "was her owner, the very man who'd bought us and brought her to Virginia at my birth. She couldn't refuse him. By law she's his property to do with as he likes. Remember I told you how she birthed me in a wagon on her way?" I nodded as he continued, "Well, I reckon my father — if I can give the man such a title — was her former owner or some other white man back in North Carolina. See, if I was purely African, I'd be much blacker than this." He leaned his arm against mine and drew back his sleeve.

I drew back my own sleeve for comparison. "You're still pretty dark," and I stroked the skin of his wrist. I leaned forward to kiss it but Chauncey drew down his sleeve. I glanced up at him; he was gazing far away.

"I seen some really black, black people down in Louisiana. Boy, when I first saw them men working down on the docks, those backs and shoulders glistening sweaty black, I felt a great longing to be like them. Black as the most fertile earth. Black as blackest night, no moon, only stars. Yeah. That's when I realized even my own mama must've had white devil blood in her. Them slave owners treat you worse than livestock but they sure do love to breed the women. You know, my mama couldn't have been very old when she had me. She might have been thirteen, but I figure she wasn't much older than twelve when he done it to her, the man that took her first. Hell, I reckon he had daughters that age."

At his bitter words, I wondered that he could possibly love me, a woman whose skin he'd described once as white as snow where the sun hadn't touched. My colour must fill him with disgust. Every time he looked at me did he not remember the white men who had so abused his mother, who'd fathered him and then sold him and his mother, completely uncaring?

"How can you even look at me with love?" I murmured.

"What?" he said.

"White skin must be an abomination to you."

He was still for a moment. Then he exploded into laughter like a fire igniting suddenly. It was frightful to hear him, laughter without mirth, a parody of laughter. He roared and I brimmed with tears, a flood topping a riverbank. I tried to move away from him but he clung to me quite fiercely. The sound of his voice raged all around us. He wasn't laughing, he was yelling, sound without words, an inarticulate howling. Then the sound of his howling shaped itself into words, *Oh Oonagh. Oonagh.* Like a mourning dove. He was rocking me back and forth as if it were me that needed the comforting — but it was himself weeping.

A huge boil had been lanced in him. Such grief flowed. He talked to me of his sister, Sadie, whom he plainly adored, and his little mama, as he referred to her. She was old before her time. She was only thirteen years older than Chauncey but she'd been used hard all her days and then they'd set her to the gardening and the washing of laundry instead of fieldwork. She couldn't have any more babies after her last son, Seth, was born, as she miscarried every time. The master accused her of taking pennyroyal to abort the babies, and maybe she did. Each time she miscarried they flogged her until she was so scarred up she walked a little crooked. The master gave up on breeding her, her value diminished. Then he'd sold her little boys south. She'd gone crazy, tried to take a whip to the master and they'd flogged her really bad and flogged Chauncey for coming to her defence. This was three years ago now. If it hadn't been for his mama and the consequences for her and Sadie, he'd have killed the master and as many of that family as he could in revenge. But instead his mama told him better to escape and try to get Sadie free too. The same thing happened to his mother would happen to Sadie. She'd be about sixteen now, he reckoned. *Same age as my sister Mona*, I thought.

When he'd made his escape, Sadie had been working in the owner's house in the kitchen. Yes, that owner's eye would be on her in a lecherous manner all too soon if not already.

"But you say she's his daughter!" I cried.

"They're worse than beasts, these men. They deliberately make these babies and so increase their property by sons and daughters who remain slaves. There was an owner in our area in Virginia who hired a white man to breed all his slave women. See, mixed-breed girls, if they're good-looking, fetch a big price in the brothels, especially down in New Orleans. At least animals make babies honestly ..."

I was stricken silent.

"I'm saving up enough money to buy them. Bring them up north here." Chauncey smiled at me. "I reckon my mama's price won't be too high, but Sadie's be costly."

"You can buy them?" I was shocked. My next thought was that if he attempted such a thing surely he'd be captured himself. "They won't sell to you, they'll catch you!"

"No, I'll get some white man to go down and do it. I've been thinking maybe even your brother Michael. He's a good man."

"Yes." Excitement leaped in me. "Michael would do it. Surely we can save enough money soon." I hugged him fiercely and kissed the dimple in his cheek. I would have to work even harder now that I knew this. I'd earn more money. We'd have to get me a loom. "Chauncey, there's hope!"

"Hope," he sighed.

"Have you ever built a loom?"

"And my brothers. Where they are, I don't know. They're little fellows still, the oldest is about your Daniel's age. They got sold off to a dealer bound for Georgia. It's pretty bad in the far south."

"What would they be sold for, such little boys?"

He shrugged and picked up a stone. "Fieldwork. Stables. Mostly fieldwork."

"That's Seth and ...?"

He looked at me and smiled a queer smile. "The older she called Daniel because she said she wanted him to be strong-minded like Daniel in the Bible."

"Daniel," I breathed, cold prickles all over me.

"The youngest is Seth just because she liked the sound of it. Gentle, she said, like a soft breeze."

"What did she name you?" I said slyly. Would he tell me now?

He grinned. "The master's mother opened the Good Book and with her eyes closed pointed to a place on a page. Her finger landed on Nebuchadnezzar, king of Babylon. Well, that wouldn't do, would it? A king, yet! So she closed the Bible, reopened it, closed her eyes shut, turned the pages, and pointed again. This time her finger landed on the word kingdom. So then those folks actually considered calling me King, since it seemed the Lord was guiding that woman's hand so. But she said that she should try this once more and see. This time her finger landed on Abimelech. So she gave up. They called me Sam." He laughed, that sound without mirth, and slapped his knee. "Sammy. God I hated that name from the moment I knew it. Sameee! I can hear them screeching it across the yard, across the fields."

"Is that what your mama called you too?"

His smile softened. He picked up another stone and began rubbing the stones between his fingers. "She called me her sunshine. Shine she called me —" He bit off what he'd been going to say.

"Go on," I nudged him.

"She gave me a name handed down in the family. But that's secret."

"You can't tell me?"

"Maybe when we have our firstborn son," he smiled, that smile creating a warm swoon in me. "Heck, she called me lots of things, not always so pretty depending on what I was doing at the time!" He laughed again and tossed the pebbles away. He waved at the western horizon. "That sun's dipping down." He leaped up and reached down to pull me to my feet.

"But wait," I evaded his hand. "Tell me about your escape. How did you do it? How did you manage?"

"Come," he said, his hand stretched for mine. "That sun'll be down before we get to the river for sure."

"Tell me as we walk along," I begged him, clasping his hand and rising to my feet. "I need to know."

"All in good time," he replied.

We descended to the valley floor in silence, an outward silence, for certainly my own brain was seething in remembrance of what Chauncey had just related, full of the images I imagined of what his poor mother had gone through. And what of his sister, Sadie? I determined to speak to Michael soon about what we could do to help. The dusk was fast falling, the forest dark when we parted on the riverbank a mile or so below the village. I saw in Chauncey's eyes that his mind too had not been silent. But he wouldn't countenance another word from me, just pushed me on my way.

Twelve

NOW THAT WE WERE betrothed and our marriage was to take place after harvest, I spent as many nights as I could down in Chauncey's cabin, sneaking out of the house after everyone was well asleep. Chauncey kept his candle burning in the window for me. During these hours he taught me to read, using his Bible and the book of verse he'd taken from the house in New Orleans. I asked him to tell me about Miss Constance, for she had inscribed the Bible she gave to him with: *To Sammy, for being so good, Miss C.* He told me she fancied herself Chauncey's mistress when they were in New Orleans. She'd taught him to read and taught him that he'd much prefer being his own free man. But he wouldn't elaborate any more, no matter how I questioned. He shut right up, getting a little angry that I persisted.

One evening I dared to tell him I felt envious of Miss Constance and he stared at me in great bewilderment. "How could you?" he asked. "A silly, spoiled, vain, lazy, wretched woman! Of all things, Oonagh! A slave owner!"

"But she taught you to read! That was good, wasn't it?"

He stared at me, a deep crease between his eyes. Then he scowled. "She had her reasons for doing that, believe me. She really was the worst sort, Oonagh. You want to know about her? She taught me to read so that I'd read to her when she was too lazy to read for herself. She made me recite endless love poetry; I had to whisper it in her ear.

She made me brush her hair for hours, rub her feet, scratch her back and — you want to hear more about Constance? She made me pleasure her. Know what that is? Huh?" He turned and spat into the fire. "That's what I think of her!" His vehemence and his story frightened me. He remained brooding and silent the rest of the evening. I slipped away, leaving him on his bed, head buried in his arms.

A few evenings later I finally saw a candle glowing again in his window, the signal that all was clear. Our reunion was sweet. We did not speak of our last meeting. We made ready for my reading lesson.

A slip of paper dropped out of the Bible as I lifted the book down from the shelf. I retrieved it and handed it to Chauncey.

"You see where I keep this paper? Right here in Exodus thirteen. See? When the children of Israel came out of bondage in Egypt. Verse twenty-one: 'And the Lord went before them by day in a pillar of cloud, to lead them the way; and by night in a pillar of fire, to give them light.' I figure the North Star is our pillar of fire." He showed me that written on the paper was a list of people and towns. "Guard that closely. Don't lose this. Pillar of cloud by day." Most on the list were people he hadn't met. A white man in New Orleans had given him these names, said they were people sympathetic to the plight of slaves and willing to help fugitives. "I memorized the list like a poem and then when I landed in York I wrote it all down. I never come across these people myself but they might help in the future. Now these last three names I added myself, white folks in Pennsylvania. This Mrs. Esther Lewis and her daughters, I stayed with them for the winter. She healed me up pretty good. By the time I got to her place —"

"Wait," I interrupted. "She healed you up? Tell me from the beginning. How did you escape in the first place?"

"I'll have to write an account of my life," he smiled.

"Yes," I agreed. "After we're married I'll sit in that corner spinning and you'll sit over by the window writing your account. That's a splendid idea!"

OFTEN WHEN I ASKED him to tell me about his journey, he would find ways to evade the telling. I reminded him that he'd related stories to Daniel with little difficulty, so why was it so hard to talk to me? Ah, but he told Daniel the adventurous bits he knew a young boy would enjoy. With me, only the truth would suffice and the truth was difficult.

"All right," I said one night. We were lying together under a blanket for the evening was chilly. "Suppose I ask you specific questions and you answer best you can. Let's move backwards. How did you cross into Canada?"

"Ferry across the Niagara River."

"Shame! I believe you told Daniel you came across Lake Ontario! That you thought you'd been betrayed, that it was the ocean and you were being shipped south again. Until someone drew you up the water and said taste it, it's sweet lake water."

"Ah." He laughed suddenly, from the belly, and I admonished him to be quieter. Suppose someone was passing? They'd find us out.

"Find what out?" he said. "That we snuggling here like a couple of hot cats? Mmm, honey, what was you asking?"

"How did you get across to Canada?"

"Ferry cross Niagara River. Then a boat across the lake to York." He nuzzled my ear and once again any talk about his past was lost in the warmth of our present.

ONE NIGHT I DREW his shirt up slowly, kissing him as I went up his chest. I made him turn and I inspected his back closely in the dim candlelight, my fingertips tracing each scar. This was no plowed field but a ravaged countryside. I pressed my lips between his shoulder blades and wept. His body quivered. He reached around and drew me into his arms and we lay for some time, quiet beneath the quilt. Then he began, taking a deep breath.

"I already told you about the boys being sold and my mama taking a whip to the master. I jumped in to stop him kicking her on the ground. He had us both whipped."

He told me how he was hung in a shed and whipped over several days. When they were done with him, they laid him in an empty cabin to heal on his own amidst the summer heat and the flies. His mama lay near him. Sadie tended them in the darkness before dawn. In the day they lay half-conscious, waiting for Sadie. She told them no one else was supposed to enter that tiny cabin lest the overseer or one of the other slaves spying would see and report them for a whipping themselves.

By the light of a candle she'd stolen from the kitchen, Sadie picked the maggots from his back, hundreds and hundreds swarming like flystrike on a sheep. She washed his wounds and their mother's as carefully as she could. She went out to the back garden in the dark and cut a whole armful of comfrey leaves to make poultices, which she carefully laid across the worst of the deep lacerations. Finally, only a couple of hours before she needed to go back to work in the kitchen, she gently laid down the rough sacking the cook had sneaked for her, covering their bodies, hoping to keep the flies off while she was gone.

SEVERAL NIGHTS LATER CHAUNCEY opened his eyes to see Sadie peering into his face in the glow of a candle. Someone else said, "Sit up now, up," as hands under his armpits slowly raised him. "There you go, honey, there you go." He sat in a wash of pain. A voice murmured, "Maybe he can't go yet." He heard his mama's voice saying, *He can't go yet.*

He tried turning his head and found that he could. His mama was sitting right beside him. *Mama.* He began to cry but she hushed him. She looked up and again said, "He can't go yet, do you think?"

He looked up too to see old Peter's grizzled face looking at him earnestly. "Son, think you can walk?"

He closed his eyes in a wave of nausea.

"Wanna lay down?" Mama, again.

No, tell me, what, tell me what. He thought he said. They understood his sounds. *Shh, now.*

Young Ben told him the plan they'd worked out. He could leave now, still badly wounded. No one would be checking for another week or so and when they did he'd be miles away tracking north. *How?* His head cleared as he managed to look around at Mama, Sadie, Peter, Ben.

Ben whispered, "Can't go to Norfolk. They'd be checking every boat. You hafta walk."

Old Peter said they'd get him on a mule, head straight north of here. Peter's brother, who lived on the banks of the Chick, was waiting to take him across the river. He was to follow it up, steering clear of Richmond, and find the road north to Washington, travelling only by night.

Everything happened disjointed, a dream. Suddenly Ben was hoisting him up again and hurrying him out, Mama touching him on the cheek once by the doorway. She shook her head when he tried to speak and made him go. Holding on to Sadie's arm, he inched his way in a darkness so profound he had to feel ahead with his toes. Then voices whispered round him as several hands lifted him, another pulling him astride a mule. In the dark the animal was shitting with nervousness. Chauncey held on tight to Ben's skinny waist. He heard nothing now but his own breathing and the clink and scrape of the mule's shoes on stones. Bushes scraped his legs on either side. His shirt stuck to his wounds and every step of the mule sent slivers of pain deep into him. How did the boy know where to go? He felt Ben's hands suddenly, grabbing his and holding them tightly against his chest. *Hang on. Stay awake.* They rode through such a stillness, not even noises of frogs or crickets, he thought he was likely dead after all.

A VOICE MUTTERED, "OPEN your mouth. Come on, open." He opened his mouth and a thick wooden spoon dribbled warm broth in. "Ah, now that's better. Open again. Son, don't you move from this spot. I'll come get ye when it's time." And then waves of sleep. He awoke to see a rat eyeing him speculatively. Daylight beamed in from a small square hole in the wall. A hen outside was shrieking her jubilation at laying an egg. He heard voices in the distance. He hissed at the rat. It scampered away.

He was lying on his belly in a very tiny hut. He raised his head and was rewarded with wave after wave of headache. Nothing was going to work right. He slipped back under.

"Boy?"

He opened his eyes to a candle glow.

"Boy? Wake up now."

"Sadie?"

A woman's low laughter. "I ain't Sadie. Here, some more soup. Come on, sit up. You leaving soon. You hafta eat some."

And then an argument over his head and he realized he'd been sleeping again. "You going to get us all killed!" The other voice: "But the boy can't go yet. He can't even stay awake, how's he supposed to walk on by himself?" And the first voice: "He sure can't stay here no more. They going to start looking for him any day now!" A silence in which he managed to sit up. He looked around. A single candle and two worried looking faces, a man and a woman. They stared at him.

His voice came out thick, his mouth dry. "Appreciate what you done. I gotta go now." He tried to rise but his left knee buckled painfully. The woman reached out to steady him. When he stood up his head touched the bark-slab roof.

Turned out he'd been at Peter's brother's little hidey-hole in the woods for two full days. They came from the plantation at night to bring him food. Old Fred, a much older version of Peter, had inspected his wounds the first night and brought his wife the next to help dress them. She fed him more soup. His energy returned.

Chauncey thanked the worried couple for their care. The old woman tied a small sack of ground corn to the rope holding up his pants. The old man led him out into the night through woods and brush and then across a wide open pasture in which shapes lowed softly as they passed. The inky sky above was punctured with stars. The old man stopped him for a moment to ask if he knew how to tell north. Chauncey pointed out the North Star and Fred grunted with satisfaction. "Keep walking that way. By morning find a good place to lay up. If you keep heading straight north, in two, maybe three nights, seeing as you're still moving kinda slow, you're going to come to a big river. Follow it up, sorta west, until it gets smaller all of a sudden. A cabin on the bank right about there belongs to a freeman named Thomas: my wife's brother. He'll help you cross."

CHAUNCEY TRAVELLED FOR WEEKS like this, good souls guiding him, telling him who to trust, who to avoid, what landmarks to watch for. In continuing pain, he walked too slowly through the nights and slept fitfully through the days, concealed in thickets. Once, when the clouds concealed the stars for several rainy nights, he discovered that he'd been walking in circles. East of Fredericksburg, a woman in a tiny boat rowed him across the Potomac, depositing him on the Maryland bank with the admonition to stay away from the river and keep heading north to Baltimore, avoiding Washington. He thought he was keeping due north as he circled around swamps and dense brush, forded streams, and once a large river, floating himself across by clinging to a log. One night he was surprised to smell the sea so close. He realized he must have been heading more easterly. It had to be the Chesapeake, but just where he had no idea. He avoided farms and people, and reached the shore just as dawn lit the sky. All he'd eaten for three days were some corn kernels he practically cracked his teeth on. He sat on the deserted beach wondering how far he was from Baltimore. The gold and orange of the impending dawn shot up out of low-lying clouds and leaked down into the shimmering grey waters. The dark shapes were islands out there and what must be the eastern shores of Maryland. That much he could figure out. But the Chesapeake is broad; he still didn't know where he was. If he could just find himself a little boat he could row his way up the bay.

Once he began thinking like that, it was impossible to consider walking again. The nights were turning colder. He'd been to Baltimore before with the master and he remembered the indented coastline. At the rate he'd been going, he'd be walking all winter. His wounds still festered on his back. Sometimes his shirt became stuck to his wounds and he had to lie down in a creek to loosen it. They weren't healing up.

The beaches stretched south in a smooth expanse; to the north was a point of land. Weariness sank through all his muscles. The sun was risen; he had to find a spot to hole up in. He walked north, rounded the point, and startled two small children busily digging clams. He gasped and they yelped, leaping backwards. Chauncey scrambled up the bank and headed for a thick grove of trees right in the middle of a large corn field. He flung himself in the undergrowth. No one was following. It then struck him that the two children were black. Would they betray him? He was too tired, too hungry, for good judgement and now in searing pain as the worst of his festering wounds burst open. He crawled deeper into the underbrush and curled up.

IN HIS SLEEP HE heard a twig crack by his head and he was instantly, terrifyingly awake, his body frozen as an ice block; he waited for the blow, unable to move a muscle.

"Hmm, thought for a bit there you was dead," a man's voice whispered close to his ear. "If you alive, sit up. Ain't safe here. Patrols all over the place tonight."

It was almost dark. The man continued, "You stay here they going to get you. You careless, boy: cut a sure path through this corn. We been looking out for you."

At this Chauncey felt blood rushing back into his limbs. He sat up. A short stocky black man squatted next to Chauncey. "All right, we have us a live one. We going to wait here till it's good and dark. No more talking. When I say so, follow me quick as you can."

Ten minutes later, the dusk deepened, they raced back down the way Chauncey had run in the morning. Just before the shore the man turned north onto a well-worn path along the bluff. Chauncey's feet began to drag, his chest to burn. The man leaped down into a ravine; Chauncey almost fell trying to keep up. He thought, *what if this is a trap*, just before he was propelled into the pitch black of a cabin. He heard movements and whispering. He stood still by the door, his hands outstretched defensively. Something heavy scraped across the plank floor, then someone lit a candle to reveal a trap door in the floor and a candle flickering in a cellar.

The man beckoned him forward. Chauncey lowered himself down. He would not be able to stand up once the trap door closed. Another face smiled at him from a corner of the cramped space. The man warned him that once the trap door was shut he wasn't to make a sound, no talking at all. He pointed out a pipe that led out of the wall. "That there leads out for air and it's hid under a bush, but if you talk, someone passing by could hear you. My wife'll let you know when you can come out for a stretch. Won't be long. I've got to arrange things for you."

His wife handed down a large hunk of bread and a bowl of chowder. Chauncey took them gratefully, smiling up at her beaming face. Beside her he recognized the small faces of the children he'd startled on the beach and he nodded at them. They smiled dazzling smiles. The man waved at them. "They told me where you was. My lookouts. Eat up now, we got to close this. If you need to, use a bucket over there." Chauncey followed his pointing finger and saw the wooden bucket against the stone wall. The other man in the cellar just smiled and shrugged.

"Come on now, Sam, eat up quick."

Chauncey began spooning up the warm soup until he realized that the man had said his name. He looked up, startled, but the man had been waiting for his reaction and chuckled. "My boy, we been looking out for you for weeks. Figured maybe you might head this way, but you been slow. There's bills out for you, describing and naming you. Got a reward posted: $150. You must be valuable. Best you avoid Baltimore. Finish up and I'm going to shut this. We'll talk more tomorrow."

Chauncey handed up the emptied bowl and the trap door slid into place. A heavy piece of furniture was shoved onto it. The darkness was that of the tomb and for a few moments all the air left his lungs and he couldn't draw in fresh. Then a hand touched his arm and the other man's voice very close to his ear whispered, "Come on now, just lay down and don't worry. Taylor's going to get us on our way as soon as he can." The man drew him down on a pallet and a blanket slid up over his shoulder. "There you go." The man stretched out next to him and gradually Chauncey could feel the heat from the stranger's body, a welcome heat in the damp chill of that cellar.

He wanted to ask a lot of questions but when he whispered, "Just where is this place?" the man shushed him. Above them in the cabin footsteps shuffled back and forth across the floor and then the rustling and creaking of the bed that he realized was right overhead and then silence. But Chauncey had slept all day. How could he sleep now? Out of the dark the man's voice, barely a whisper, "Faith, boy."

CHAUNCEY STOPPED THE STORY and I hugged him close, wanting to hear more. But he murmured, "Oonagh, we got a lifetime for the rest of the story. Honey, you got to get back to the house." He kissed me, and this time, before dawn came, before I had to run back up to the McGann's, we came to know each other, as it says in the Bible. As I hurried across the grass in the dark pre-dawn, I exulted at the thought that I carried his seed within me. How wonderfully strange.

Thirteen

NOT MANY TASKS ARE smellier than that of washing wool fleeces. Behind me on pole racks a number of fleeces dried, bleaching white in the October sun. I'd meant to have finished washing these a long time before this but there was always so much work to do in Lorna McGann's household, with the children, laundry, gardening, harvesting the garden. I had only a little time in the evenings for my own work. A number of the people who'd given me their fleeces to spin were hinting that they required their finished yarn and soon. "Before you know it winter will be upon us all." Why did the fleeces in this country have to be so dirty? Of course I knew the answer. With months of fiercely cold winter, people often had their sheep in lean-tos where they lay in their own filth. Then there was the ever-present possibility of sheep getting into a patch of burnt-over forest. Burrs and seeds created hopeless cotting.

Back home in Connemara, the fleeces were much less likely to get so soiled. I envisioned the stony hills rising green above the sea, the white sheep scattered, cropping the grass between the boulders. Mam in the corner of the cottage spinning the yarn that helped to make our living, the air thick with the odour of greasy wool. That smell always brought me back to my childhood helping Mam with the wool washing and picking. Mam spun raw wool without washing it first. Easier to handle, but, more importantly, the greasy wool repelled water, which is what Mam wanted when knitting the jerseys she was known for. Many a fisherman was glad he wore one of her thick wool jerseys when a storm blew. But I doubt Mam had to use wool as filthy and cotted as what I was given here.

Gently I squeezed the rinse water from the wool and laid the dripping fleece over another pole. There was enough drying now to give me plenty of work in the next few evenings, picking over the wool, carding it, spinning. With luck and good weather I might even have some skeins dyed before the end of October. Before the wedding. My wedding. I grinned and picked up another dirty fleece.

Chauncey and I had decided to keep our wedding secret until a few days beforehand. Only Daniel knew. We had decided to wait until after the harvest so that everyone who wanted to attend could come. It had been so difficult not to burst out with my happiness when I saw Mairi or Michael. Mairi had asked me why I was so happy these days.

"Goodness, Oonagh. If I didn't know better, I'd say you were in love!" So Mairi had said just yesterday when she had come to collect my spun wool. She was going to be weaving blankets on her loom. A room upstairs in Mairi's new house had been allotted just for the loom and I had looked forward to weaving there in winter when Lorna McGann didn't need me, but that was before Chauncey and I had decided to get married. Now I would get my own loom.

"Lorna says you're in such a good mood these days she's half-afraid of you!" Mairi had laughed. Her fingers assessed the skeins of yarn I'd spun.

"Do you suppose we'll ever get Liam and the others over here?" I changed the subject. In truth I was afraid of Mairi's opposition because we'd be getting the Methodist preacher instead of the Catholic priest. Chauncey was still bent on going to Peterborough to speak to the Catholic priest, but I knew he'd refuse to wed us. The Methodist came through here regularly. In fact, people were talking of building a Methodist church in the village, an indication of how much the place had grown and how much it had become more Protestant than Catholic, more Scots and English than Irish.

Mairi packed the skeins she was taking into a basket. "Michael doesn't believe they will ever come," she said softly.

Because I'd been thinking about our wedding plans and whom we could get to perform the ceremony, I looked at her in alarm for I thought she meant someone coming to the wedding itself.

"Who won't come?" I asked, my fingers busy with picking out vegetation from more wool.

"For goodness sakes, Oonagh! You yourself just asked the question. You must be in love! Who is it?" Mairi grabbed me by the shoulders and smiled into my face. "Tell me now."

I shrugged, smiling back.

"How do you like that yarn?" I nodded my head toward another pile of skeins. "I've got some flax as well. And more coming if only Paddy and the boys would get to it."

"Next year Josie says we can plant a small field of flax."

"Come here now, Mairi, give me a hug."

"Ah," said Mairi, obliging me with a swift embrace. "You are in love and I'll be sure to find out who."

LORNA CALLED FROM THE house. A man was standing on the back porch with her. I shaded my eyes to see who. "Come. Take a rest. See who's come to visit."

My heart dropped. Andrew Monaghan. He stepped off the porch and strolled across the grass to me. I wiped my hands on my apron. *What was he doing here?* I'd been so relieved last spring when he'd announced that he was going to stay in Cobourg and work in the construction taking place in the vicinity.

"Oonagh, my girl, you're looking very fine."

I flushed. He reached out a hand but I evaded it and walked past him toward Lorna, saying, "Lorna, shall we have a pot of tea for Andrew?"

I saw by Lorna's expression that my action — rude, I admit — had not been overlooked. But I couldn't give Andrew the slightest notion that I welcomed his advances and compliments.

"Well, so. Oonagh, guess who we saw in Cobourg a few days ago."
Andrew continued with his cajoling voice. I didn't want to guess.
I didn't want to face this man much less have to talk to him. But I
forced myself to turn and smile and be pleasant.

"I could never guess," I murmured.

Life had been good to Andrew. His work all summer had given him
muscle and bulk, and his skin glowed with a rich tan. His thinning hair
was bleached from the sun, his beard glistening golden. I could see in
his brown eyes how marvellous he thought he was, what a prize for any
woman. He leaned close and murmured, "Colum O'Leary himself."

The name pierced into the pit of me.

"Oh, indeed." I determined not to show any emotion. "Is he
coming here? Did he have news of home?"

"No, he's not coming, but here's a letter for your family." Andrew
grinned, reaching into his pocket. "Would you like to see?"

"Of course!" Automatically I reached for the packet Andrew held.

"Ah. No. Sorry. It says here: 'Michael Corcoran.' I'll have to take
it to old Mihal himself. Besides, you can't read, can you?" Andrew
held the letter high over my head. He was teasing, yes, but there
was a flicker of animosity beneath the light, teasing inflections of
his voice.

A corresponding hatred flared into me. "I could read that letter,"
I muttered. "But please, do take it to Michael." I turned and left
Andrew and Lorna at the porch and returned to my wool washing.

"Ah, come now, Oonagh Corcoran. You never could take a joke,
could ya?" Andrew followed me across the yard to the washing tubs.
"Have you really learned to read?"

I refused to say another word and concentrated on the wool.

"God! How can you stand to work with that filthy stuff? Smells
vile! Oonagh, I'm talking to you! Give me a moment, will you!"
Andrew's voice had lost its humour. He glared at me.

I lifted a hank of fleece and waved it around at him, spraying dirty
brown water perilously close to where he stood. "This'll make a nice
pair of mitts, or a vest, don't you think?"

He backed out of range. "Filthy stuff."

"Yes, isn't it magic? From this, your lovely wool jersey!"

"Listen. I'll be back for the harvest celebration. You'll be dancing with me." He folded his brawny arms across his chest, a small sneer lifting his lips in a parody of a smile.

"Oh?" I raised my brows ironically. "Really. Why me?"

"Yes," he said. "You know I've picked you out for me." Leaning closer to me so that I smelled his pungency and felt his breath on my cheek, he whispered, "You'll dance with me. And one of these days you'll marry me."

I laughed out loud, startling him. "No, Andrew. I'll never marry you."

He turned about and strode across the grass to where Lorna had emerged from the house with a tea tray. "You will," his parting shot.

He sat on the porch with Lorna. I could practically feel his gaze boring a hole in my back turned to the house. Finally, after some time, all the fleeces I'd been soaking were rinsed and hanging to dry and I had no more excuse. I had to face him. But when I did, to my relief Andrew had gone.

What was in the letter? I hadn't lied about reading it. Chauncey had taught me enough over the summer that I could read anything that Liam might have written.

Much later at night, when I lay in the darkness of my room, it occurred to me that I hadn't given Colum O'Leary another thought since Andrew had mentioned him. This realization filled me with a curious dismay. Could my heart be so fickle as to so displace thoroughly one love with another? Was a new love then the death of the old? Could this ever happen with my love for Chauncey? His for me? It seemed a long time before sleep overtook me.

THE DAY AFTER ANDREW'S visit, Michael came to the village to see me. I'd only expected to see him when everyone gathered at the McGanns' house for the harvest supper and dance. I'd imagined I'd have enough patience to wait until then to find out the contents of the letter from home. But when I heard one of Lorna's little girls chiming, "Unca Michael is here," I quickly covered the bread I was kneading with a clean cloth and ran to greet him.

"Oonagh," he smiled, and instantly in his eyes I saw something was wrong.

"Is it Da?" I cried, touching his sleeve with my floury hands.

"Da is well," he muttered.

"Well, then?" My heart sank. *Lizzie?*

"Everyone's well. Come. Can you walk by the river for a few moments?" He held my arm. Because he wouldn't look at me directly, I suddenly wondered if Daniel had told him my little secret. In fact, I was sure of it because he held my arm so tightly and his face, usually so kindly and full of fun, was now grim as winter.

"Goodness, Michael." I pulled my arm from his grip. He was startled at this and flashed a glance at me. Fear sank into me, for his eyes were full of tears. By now we were walking along the path away from the village, on the east side of the river. This trail was not well-worn, but it led to a lovely spot where the river, freed at last from the mill's wheels, flowed swiftly, parting around a small wooded island.

"This is far enough. What's the matter?" I pulled on his arm and indicated an old fallen tree trunk. We sat and he pulled out the letter Andrew had brought.

"Both Lizzie and Mona are emigrating."

"Wonderful!" I clapped my hands. "When are they coming?"

"They're not." He hung his head. "Not here, anyways."

"Not here? Where?" I couldn't believe what I was hearing.

I reached for the letter but Michael held it up out of my reach and read: "'Mona has wed Jeremy Malley, the pipes player from Galway. They have decided on New South Wales where he has two brothers. They will take Lizzie with them.'"

"No!" I could not contain my anguish. "No, Michael! No. Why can't they come here?"

"I don't know," my brother said wretchedly. "I knew you'd take it hard. I doubt our Mairi has stopped crying since I read the letter to her this morning."

I was awash in tears as if I'd heard they were all dead.

"Still," Michael murmured. "I told Mairi and I'll tell you the same. We should be celebrating for them, not mourning. Our little Mona is married and from what I hear to one of the finest pipes players in all Ireland. That we should celebrate. All are going off in good health to a new country. I'm sure New South Wales is a fine place, after all."

"Jeremy Malley is a fine player." A fresh fall of tears began.

"Do you want to hear the rest of this letter?"

I nodded but Michael remained quiet until I calmed my tears and wiped my face on my sleeve.

He read from the beginning: "'We are all well and have much news to tell you. Firstly, Da is well again. He had been a bit ill for a while but Mrs. Keane has been helping the girls to look after him. She has promised to look after him when the girls go. Mona has wed Jeremy Malley, the pipes player from Galway. They have decided on New South Wales where he has two brothers. They will take Lizzie with them. We have heard that things is very good in New South Wales and the climate warmer than in Canada. By the time you receive this letter they will be on the high seas. Pray for them.'" Michael's voice broke, his mouth fighting for control over his emotions.

He didn't resist as I took the letter from him. Liam's writing was not easy to read, but I managed: "'Da and I will stay on here in the village. We have had to give up the place —' Oh, Michael!" Tears filled my eyes now. Poor Da. What of the loom? Mam's table? Our little home? Michael reached for the letter again and I gave it to him.

He read, "'— and are living in a room at Mrs. Keane's. Jem has given me work at his shebeen —'"

"We knew it! You should have seen him with Libby Harrington at Mairi's wedding! Dancing and dancing! Do you remember Jem's daughter, little Libby? Don't be surprised to hear of their wedding sometime soon!"

"Wedding," Michael grunted.

I was pierced with the thought once again that he'd heard of my own intentions. "Even as little ones they liked each other. Libby would hang onto his and her brother Niall's hands and swing." I glanced at Michael.

Michael sighed and continued, "'I am taking Niall's place for he has decided to go to sea. We have not heard yet just where he has gone. He has promised to send us word. Mrs. Keane wants me to send you her love and to tell you she prays for each of you every night. Da sends you his love. He wants more news of Oonagh. Has she found a husband yet? Your loving brother, Liam.'"

My heart pounded. At the very least he must comment on how well I'd read what I did. Surely he'd wonder where on earth I'd learned. Maybe this would be a good time to tell him about Chauncey and me. I waited, staring off across the little river and thought again of my sisters and of my da with no home. I couldn't look at Michael now.

"Can you get away soon and see Mairi? She's heartbroken," was all he said. He rose and in silence we walked back to the McGanns.

I DIDN'T SEE MAIRI until the afternoon of the harvest supper, two weeks later. Even if I'd been inclined to go see her, I really didn't have the time. We at the McGanns were extremely busy preparing for the special gathering of our neighbours and kinfolk, and I for one was anticipating the evening as the occasion of the announcement of my betrothal. Although the women would all bring dishes, Lorna McGann felt the need to prepare an enormous amount of food. As the wife of the miller she felt expected to provide delicious baked goods in variety. For three days straight the oven was in constant use until the larder could contain not another bread loaf or cake.

On the Friday evening before the gathering, Chauncey came by with a string of fresh fish and slung over his shoulder a newly woven basket covered with a clean cloth.

"What's in there?" Lorna asked, reaching for the basket.

"It's for you. Can you use them?" he asked, giving her the basket.

"Apples! My word, where did you get them?"

"Taste them," he laughed, and with a small knife he sliced one open. "They're small but very good."

He popped a little piece into little Deborah McGann's mouth and the child wrinkled up her nose. The apple was crisp and sweet. He gave me one just before Lorna covered the basket up again, declaring that these apples were too good to be baked into anything. They were to be served fresh.

"Put them in the cellar, Oonagh, would you?"

"Mind, don't forget them there!" Chauncey cautioned. As if we could forget such a delicious treat.

"Where did you find them?" Lorna asked him again. I was already halfway down the cellar stairs and I paused to hear his answer.

"Oh," he laughed. "Quite a piece southwest of here, actually. I found them on my way back from Peterborough. I circled well south and came upon some folks that had this little orchard by the side of their house; they let me pick a basket."

"You went to Peterborough? Don't tell me you're thinking of moving there, are you, Chauncey? You wouldn't leave us, would you?" Lorna's voice was full of a teasing jocularity, which I suddenly hated because it sounded to me entirely insincere. Lorna did not normally speak with such a tone. She wouldn't have cared if Chauncey fell off the face of the earth. He murmured something and she gave a great peal of laughter. She was flirting with him! Then my heart quickened, for the man she was flirting with was mine. I was so sure of that I could afford to smile. I thought of Paddy, Lorna's husband, who was himself a good strong man but surely no prize, not one like my Chauncey. Her Paddy had no sense of humour and folks often had to repeat their jokes for him before he would finally laugh half-heartedly, as if he still didn't quite understand. He was not slow-witted. But a sense of humour is not given to all of us. In comparison, my Chauncey was greatly gifted. Of course Lorna would flirt with him. Who wouldn't want to see his smile? I kept an ear to the murmur of voices upstairs.

I placed the apples on a shelf. The cellar smelled of the earth even though it was well-lined with stone. The floor too had been lined with stone. Not too many houses could boast of such a fine-built cellar that would keep foods unspoiled. Paddy McGann and Gerald had done very well since coming to Canada. Their houses testified to the fruits of hard labour and good luck. Mairi and Josie's cellar on the other hand, though built of stone, had an earthen floor. Chauncey and I would have to build an entirely new house as his little cabin didn't have a cellar but was built up upon four cornerstones.

When I returned upstairs, Chauncey was gone.

"Where did he go?"

Lorna frowned. "What do you mean?"

"Well, I thought he'd stay a bit." I said, dismayed. I felt cheated. It had been several days I hadn't seen Chauncey. I'd wanted to ask him about his trip to Peterborough.

"Goodness, Oonagh. The man has more to do than chat with the womenfolk, don't you think?"

"Did he say anything about Peterborough?" Dismay loosened my tongue.

Lorna raised her brow at me. "I don't pry into people's business, much less a nigger's. Oonagh, I'm surprised at you!"

At her use of "nigger" my stomach lurched. That word. It's as if someone spits into your face. Was that how she saw Chauncey? I looked away to hide my anger. A thousand hot words threatened to spill from my lips. I almost told her that I was about to marry "that nigger," that all I longed for was to sleep at his side the rest of my nights. I longed to bear his children and suspected I carried the beginnings of his child beneath my heart. I had not told Chauncey yet. But I wished for it, a beautiful baby. I held back every nasty word and instead mumbled something about fetching some fresh water and grabbed up the water pails.

I ran to the side of the house to see that Chauncey had already crossed the bridge. I willed him to glance back up to where I stood in the dusk, and to my relief he did. He waved. I waved back, joyfully, taking no heed that others might be watching. The next day we would announce our wedding plans. Everyone else be damned.

BY NOON ON SATURDAY, families were already making their way into the village and settling themselves on the meadow between the McGanns' house and the river. A place had been established where any carts or wagons could be drawn up and the livestock, oxen or horses, hobbled or tied. Most people in our parts, however, did not own a horse or even a pair of oxen, and some of those fortunate to do so started out before dawn, making the rounds of neighbouring homesteads to help bring the families in. Other people had simply walked from their farms, each family member carrying the food and blankets they would need for the picnic. Some farmers would be bringing in a few bushels of corn for a husking competition. Winners would be given a sack of meal. This was an opportunity for the farmers to get some corn husked easily before taking it to the mill and for some folks without a corn crop to obtain cornmeal.

I doubt I'd slept more than a couple of hours the night before. I kept rising to look out the window toward Chauncey's cabin, hoping for a candle flame, wrestling with the temptation to run down there across the frost-stiffened grass in my bare feet. No candle flame meant not to come. What had he accomplished in Peterborough? Even if the priest denied us, and well he might — Chauncey not being Catholic and I not a faithful one — our wedding would go forward. We'd simply jump the broom as Chauncey had described. We'd gather the folks around and declare before witnesses that we promised love and faithfulness to each other. Sleepless, I rehearsed the words we should say.

With this long busy day ahead, Lorna calling for my help, I'd had no time to think about the evening and dancing under the stars. Only once in a while a pleasurable little picture would enter my mind, an image of Chauncey and me holding hands and everyone gathered around laughing and saying, *Well wasn't it about time, Oonagh.*

"Oonagh!"

I looked up from the cooking to see Mairi smiling at me, her little one snug in her arms.

"I've been meaning to come and see you. I've had no time!" I rose from the fire and threw my arms around her and the baby both.

"Watch out!" she grunted as I hugged her hard. "Watch me babbies!"

"Babbies?" I reached to take the little one from her and Mairi repeated, significantly, "Yes. Babbies."

I held the baby in my arms and stared at my sister. She patted her stomach gently and smiled, nodding, and suddenly her eyes were full of tears.

"So soon, Mairi?" I leaned forward and kissed her cheek.

"Oh, Oonagh! We'll never be seeing the girls again!" And she was sobbing, covering her face with her shawl. The baby in my arms stared at her mother, her lips quivering. Then all three of us were crying.

"Ah now," Lorna bustled in and bent to my task at the fire. "If you're going to be weeping, the two of you, making the babby cry too, go on somewheres else." She tasted the beans and pronounced them perfect. "It's not a funeral, you know. Nobody's died. Those sisters of yours will do fine. Paddy says it's not half as bitter a winter in New South Wales as it is here."

How could we continue crying with Lorna's sharp eyes and sharper tongue? She meant well. She rubbed Mairi's back and shushed the baby still wailing in my arms. Then Lorna smiled and said, shoving us out the door, "Go on now, go for a walk."

THE MEADOW HAD BEEN transformed with several tripods erected with large spits for the roasting of venison and pork, and families were settling down in a large circle around a bonfire. Little children scurried to the woods along the river to fetch dry wood. The pile of wood grew faster than it could be burnt. Some bigger boys were marching into the meadow carrying great logs across their shoulders.

"Come, let's go this way," my sister suggested and she tugged on my arm. She seemed recovered from her grief. We walked toward the river and took the same path Michael and I had taken earlier. Above us the maples and oaks flamed in their autumnal glory against a clear sky blue as it only is in October. The air was scented with the woodsmoke and the spicy smell of the dry poplar leaves crunching underfoot.

"Do you know for certain?" I asked her when we were finally seated by the river. "Couldn't you and Josie wait, for goodness sake?"

"Men," she shrugged. As if I should know.

The sunlight was surprisingly warm, although with such clear weather there was sure to be a hard frost tonight. Boys raced by us from time to time, whooping and crashing through the brush in pursuit of each other. My sister pointed out a family arriving by canoe, a slender craft heavy in the water with so many people aboard. Several other watercraft were pulled up on the muddy shore.

I looked at my sister's face carefully to see if she was truly pleased to be expecting so soon. I asked her again, "Mairi, are you certain?"

"I know for certain you're a fool," she said. My heart jarred.

"Well maybe," I tried to smile. "But are you pleased?"

"I thought you had more sense, Oonagh. I thought you were the smart one."

"What are you talking about?" I asked her, though I'd guessed.

"Even Denis Murphy would be better. How could you do this? To be telling that wee Daniel ahead of me or Michael!"

I stood up and walked to the edge of the riverbank. Below my feet the deep water swirled around a submerged log. The afternoon sunlight penetrated the depths and showered gold on a small school of minnows swaying in the current. Behind me Mairi was insisting that I answer her, that I come back and sit beside her and tell her that our Daniel had got it all wrong.

When I gained enough mastery over my feelings that I could remain calm and gentle as I wished to be, I turned to her, arms folded. A shiver began in the nape of my neck and then, even as I heard myself speak calmly, I felt a violent tremor take me over, as if the afternoon had suddenly fallen very cold.

"Mairi, I thought you would surely be glad for my happiness."

"Happiness!" she sputtered. "Happiness!" The baby had fallen asleep, but at Mairi's loud voice it startled awake, flinging its little hands out. Mairi quickly put it to breast, wrapping up its hands into the blanket. I took that time to reach her side and swiftly bent to hug her close.

"Yes," I murmured against her hair. "I'm so very happy. We will be married in three weeks, before any snow falls. We want to announce our betrothal this evening before everyone and invite all to celebrate with us." I wanted to tell her then that I thought I too was with child and so we should doubly celebrate. But the words would not come out.

My sister was silent. The baby nursed noisily, and suddenly at that little sound I wanted to weep. Why couldn't my sister rejoice with me?

"Chauncey is a good and kind man, Mairi. You know he is. You know he is hard-working and charitable. He truly cares for me. Look how our Daniel loves him. A child knows. That's what Jesus said, 'Out of the mouths of babes and sucklings.'"

"What will people say?" she muttered, not looking up at me.

"That I'm a fortunate woman." I waited for her response, and when none came I became angry. "I don't really care what people say. He's a far better man than many I could name in these parts."

"Shhh!" she admonished me. She was rocking the baby and glancing up at me; I felt pity for her fear.

"I'm not asking your permission, or Michael's, for that matter. This is my decision. But I'd like your blessing. I'd like you to share in my joy."

"I've not had anything to do with that man," she murmured, and brushed her lips across the baby's cheek.

"Chauncey," I said. "His name is Chauncey Taylor."

"Chauncey," she said. Suddenly she flashed her eyes up at me in a big smile. "It's just like you, Oonagh girl, to get yourself a man with a name like Chauncey instead of some simple Tom or John or Mick."

"Or Paddy," I laughed.

"Or Bob."

"What did Michael say?" I asked.

"I don't know. He left too quickly after he read Liam's letter. I was upset about the girls, and then Daniel saying that so sudden-like about you and Chauncey. I thought he was fooling, only then I realized, how could a young one like him know? But Michael had already left and taken Daniel with him, and I haven't seen him since. I don't know if he quite believed the boy or understood."

So Michael had already known when he brought me Liam's letter. She told me then how Daniel had let slip my little secret and how upset the boy was at himself. She said she'd been unable to sleep well since, worrying about our sisters and brother Liam and Da, and then worrying about me. She said again, "What will people say?"

"Why should you worry about what people say? Who are these people that you should worry?"

"Well, we have to live here, after all."

"Did you worry back home when people would say I was a witch or a Druid or a pagan?"

"They said that?"

I had to laugh at how large and astonished her eyes grew at my words. "Did you never hear that silly gossip? I'm sure it was Bridie O'Rourke herself who spread the stories."

"Never! You're making it up."

"No, I swear —"

"No, don't swear!" Mairi flung her hand up to stop my oath-taking. "Josie never mentioned a thing to me. And he would've if people were going around saying you were a pagan. Honestly, Oonagh, sometimes you aggravate me so."

"I just want to know why other people's opinions matter so much to you. How about my own good opinion? Doesn't that count with you?"

"It does. Of course it does. And I want your happiness. But are you sure it's with this one, this — man?"

"Were you sure Josie would be the one?"

"Ah, it's not the same, Oonagh!"

"Why not?" I stood back from her and folded my arms. She couldn't meet my gaze. "Why ever not?" I repeated.

"I think you're courting trouble."

I laughed at that. "Oh Mairi, Mairi," I said, patting my stomach. "It's too late. I am in trouble." I laughed as she flung a hand up to cover her mouth. "Oh Mairi, please! Be happy for me, for us!"

But she only stared at me with those stricken eyes welling up, struck dumb at the notion that I was pregnant too. Tears rolled down her cheeks.

"If you and Michael stand with us and wish us all the best, no one will oppose it. Please, please, Mairi. Stand with us tonight and wish us happiness in front of everyone. No one will dare say a word against us. Michael is well-respected here and —"

She interrupted me as she stood up.

"Have you told Michael yet?"

"He likes Chauncey, I know he does. And respects him!"

"But have you spoken to him yet?"

I had to admit I hadn't. The moment had not risen.

"You must speak to him before you make your announcement. Maybe he will stand with you."

"And you?"

Once again she flashed me the barest of little smiles and turned away.

"Mairi?"

She strode up the path back toward the village. I ran after her. "Mairi! Please!"

She turned around on the trail. "You look a fright. Go quickly and do your hair up properly. I'll not have my baby sister looking like spindrift in front of all these people." She turned her cheek for me to kiss and immediately my heart was light and floating.

Fourteen

A NUMBER OF WOMEN had gathered on the McGanns' porch where we had a good view of the activities on the field below. A huge pine had been hauled up for the wood-chopping competition. Two men at a time chopped furiously at either end to beat each other in cutting through the log. Mairi had called me out from the kitchen to see, for Chauncey was pitted against a man I had never seen before and the other man was winning. But then the other man was twice Chauncey's size, with arm muscles on him the size of barrels. Everyone gathered around whooping and hollering and cheering for either Chauncey or Red, as that massive red-bearded man was aptly called. Although the air was not warm, sweat poured off both men as if it were the hottest summer day. They'd removed their coats and rolled up their sleeves.

"Cool them down!" someone shouted and a bucket of water splashed across their backs. Both men yelped with the chill as everyone roared, then they resumed their competition with renewed vigour. I was laughing along with everyone else. Then I saw Daniel at the edge of the crowd trying to push his way in. Without thinking, I dashed off the porch and flew down the hill.

I wormed my way into the crowd until I stood right behind him craning his neck to see. I clapped a hand hard on his bony shoulder. He cringed when he saw it was me. I shouted in his ear above the noise of the merrymakers. "Where's your father?"

"He's still coming in Will's wagon."

I was too excited to be angry at him. He'd meant us no harm. "I doubt he's going to win!" I laughed, meaning Chauncey.

Chauncey was now playing up to the laughter of the crowd. Everyone knew the other man had superior strength. Red was almost through his section of the log while Chauncey still had a good half of the log to go. So Chauncey put his axe down for a moment and with great exaggeration wiped his face on one sleeve and then the other. He yanked out his shirttails and wiped some more. Then he begged for more water to be thrown on him and was promptly obliged, whereupon he yelled and began trembling as if greatly cold. Then, as if he just remembered what he was supposed to be doing, he began hacking at the log again, shouting out great heave-hoes with each strike of the axe. Within minutes Red had chopped through the final inches of wood and shoved the round of log away with one mighty kick and whoop of triumph. Chauncey sank to the ground, the very picture of dejection for one little minute, and the crowd groaned with him. Then he leaped up, and as if he were the master of ceremonies, threw his hand out toward Red, declaring him the winner. Everyone cheered. That big man, Red, a stranger to me, came up to Chauncey and made a big show of checking the size of Chauncey's arm muscles. Then he grabbed up Chauncey's axe and finished Chauncey's work. Chauncey stood next to him, arms crossed, as if he was observing very closely how the job should be done. Every once in a while he would look up at the crowd and give a huge wink. The crowd loved it. It was as if Chauncey and Red had worked out this humorous act together beforehand. We found out later that Red was newly off the boat from Scotland. He had just come into our part of the country seeking his fortune as a blacksmith, an occupation that explained his huge size and wonderful strength. I liked him immediately and later wished he'd been our blacksmith instead of Denis Murphy. Red Macbeth had a decency missing in Denis.

I drew Daniel away from the noisy throng and beckoned him

to listen closely. "I can't get close to Chauncey in this crowd. So you must tell him yourself. You must tell him that your da knows about our betrothal. Tell him he needs to ask Michael to stand with us tonight when we announce it. Can you remember this, Daniel? It's very important."

He hung his head in shame. "I'm sorry. I didn't mean to tell."

"Oh, shush," I said. "No time for that. Can you remember what I just told you?" I shook his shoulder a little impatiently. "Pay attention. It's important. Tell Chauncey he must talk to Michael right away when Michael gets here. Take him to your da. There!" I pointed out Will Larkin's wagon pulling up, overloaded with people, children scrambling to jump out. Then I ducked down behind him so Michael wouldn't see me and gave him a little push.

"Go on! For goodness sake's. Go get Chauncey." Then I was away, dashing across the grass back up to the McGanns' house.

CHAUNCEY AND DANIEL APPROACHED Michael. I tried to gauge by the set of the men's shoulders, by their hand gestures as they spoke, just how the conversation was progressing. Around me women were chatting, babies were laughing or wailing. Mairi was showing off her baby daughter to an admiring group. It wasn't often that the women in the outlying farms were able to get together and see each other's new babies or handiwork, and everyone was taking full advantage of the mild autumn afternoon to catch up on the gossip.

"Now there's a brawny good fellow if I've seen one," laughed Emily Cotterage, the woman from farther up the river. "Look at the muscles on that one!"

Everyone knew Emily, having come from the United States, could be quite forward, but here in the group of women such forwardness was greeted with shouts of laughter. She had pointed out Red Macbeth down below on the meadow. The man was now in the process of showing the crowd his prowess in hurling a huge cedar log. He'd rolled up his sleeves well above his elbows, displaying the pelts of red hair on his arms that corresponded with the heavy red hair of his head and beard. Perhaps it was simply the slant of the late afternoon sun, but his hair seemed to glow like fire.

"There you go, Oonagh! There's the man for you at last!" Martha McGann joined in the merriment. "A red bear."

"Good gracious," giggled Emily. "I'll wager there's enough of that red wool you could shear him, Oonagh. Weave a blanket!" The women shrieked with laughter. Startled babies cried.

"Oh, stop, stop," Lorna cried, clutching her big belly. "You'll make me pee meself!"

Mairi glanced at me but I couldn't take my eyes from the scene below in the meadow. Mairi nudged my arm but I paid no attention. If I ignored them all, maybe they would leave me be.

Emily squatted in front of me and grinned into my face. "You're trying to ignore us. Well, we know a good match when we see one."

"What?" I smiled back. "Whatever are you on about?"

"One of these days, Oonagh Corcoran, you'll see. And I'll wager it'll be that red giant down there will up and put you in his pocket."

I turned to Mairi but she only shrugged and smiled. Emily said slyly, "Well? Don't you think he's a likely-looking man?"

"Oh, likely! Aw, he's beautiful," I said, winking at Mairi, thinking of Chauncey.

"The red giant?" Emily said, astonished. "Beautiful?" She pointed a finger toward the meadow. "The red giant?"

"What about him?" I decided to play dumb. "Is there something wrong with him?"

"You know what I think, Oonagh Corcoran," said Emily, standing up straight with her hands on her hips. "I do believe either you're being deliberately daft or else you really want to be a nun. Eh? What do you say?" She turned her merry eyes around at the group of women. "Is the girl daft or what?"

"Well, you'll all see tonight," I blurted to Mairi's sharp intake of breath. Everyone paused and looked at us. Then Emily swiftly took up the cue.

"Ah," she said. "You have some news for us!"

"Emily, is that not your boy they're about to toss in the river?" I pointed toward the bridge and as soon as Emily was occupied in trying to locate her small son in the crowd, I winked at everyone else. "Where?" cried Emily. "I don't see him!" She took off running for the bridge at full tilt as the women left behind on the veranda giggled at my ruse. Below in the meadow, Chauncey and Michael had disappeared in the crowd.

SOMEONE CALLED MY NAME. I looked up from serving bowls of hot stew to a long plank table full of youngsters. Almost all had brought their own bowls, but here and there a hungry wee face looked woebegone until I mercifully brought forth an extra bowl. Amid great shouts of laughter their parents were now engaged in shucking corn and the children swivelled now and then to catch sight of their parents in the contest.

"Oonagh!"

I looked around, trying to determine the male owner of the voice calling my name. Then I saw him, Andrew Monaghan, waving from the riverbank. He had just disembarked from a large canoe and was striding up the grassy field in the deepening dusk. How could I avoid him? He'd already seen me notice him. I bent to wipe gravy off a small girl's face.

"There now, love. Have you had enough?"

The small girl nodded shyly.

"Go on with your brother. Mind you stay close by." The child slipped off the rough bench and ran to where her slightly older brother was sauntering toward the corn shucking. One pile of corn already heaped up golden, next to it a pile of dry husks. Now everyone was starting in on Will Larkin's load. Even from here I could hear the merriment at Will's expense. They were teasing him for his lack of a spouse to help him with the harvesting and shucking of corn.

"Why," someone shouted, "you've brought your entire harvest for us to shuck!"

Maybe if I didn't meet Andrew's eyes, he would leave me alone. I looked for him again quickly and saw that he had disappeared. Smiling, I bent to help another little child with his supper. A few moments later someone clapped his hard hands over my eyes.

"Guess who," Andrew whispered, his mouth much too close to my ear.

"The devil himself," I muttered, standing completely still, although I wanted to scream and hit at his smelly hands pressed on my face. "Let me go."

"Ah, not till you say my real name, though I won't deny the other either."

"Andrew Monaghan, I'm in the middle of feeding these children." He took his hands away. I resisted the urge to scrub at my face.

"Don't forget," he grinned. "You're dancing with me tonight."

"If I have time."

He pointed a finger at me and then chucked me like a small child under the chin. "You will, I promise you."

The children at the table giggled.

"Now what are you laughing at?" I said to the children, reaching down and wiping yet another little mouth. I refused to listen to Andrew any more, although he kept on talking for a few moments more. Then feeling foolish, no doubt, at my lack of attention, he strode away.

CURSED LUCK THAT MONAGHAN had shown up! His unwarranted possessiveness frightened me. Just who did he think he was? Why did he think he had any right to me at all? I'd so hoped that he'd have found another woman down in the communities on the Front. But no. He'd come back to pester me. All I could hope for now was that Michael would indeed agree to support Chauncey and me in our decision, thus warding off any interference from men like Andrew. Or Denis Murphy. The thought of these men made me sick.

SO MANY PEOPLE HAD come from miles around in our district and from as far away as Belleville and Cobourg, family and friends come to celebrate the harvest. Down on the Front, close to Lake Ontario, that great inland sea, farmers were able to produce more than their families could ever use in a year. But here on the frontier, where men pushed hard at the edges of an endless forest, a good livelihood was not easy. It was Paddy McGann who had first organized these harvest celebrations. Lorna had explained to me that in their years on the river they had seen many a settler's family go hungry because they hadn't enough corn to last them. Perhaps the weather had been too dry or the land too rocky. Paddy had early decided that there must be a way to ensure that people survived, body, soul, and self-respect intact. As the miller, he knew quite well who in the area had had bountiful crops and who was struggling. At first he had organized the harvest supper and had a priest for services. As the years went by, more people came into the district who were not Catholic and Paddy, out of respect for them, decided to hold the religious mass on a separate day. On the day and evening of the harvest festival he wanted nothing to separate neighbours. Then several years ago he had suggested a corn-shucking contest with sacks of ground meal going to the victors. If the victor was someone who didn't need such a sack, the meal could always be given to a needy family, a widow with children perhaps. It must be said that in spite of Paddy's growing success in this country, he never forgot the hunger of his childhood in Connemara, and as much as he could help in a situation where children were hungry, he would.

THE SUNSET THAT EVENING was a marvel to behold and in the clear cold air the shrill voices of the children hushed as they left their running games and drew closer to the huge bonfire. Against the line of hills in the northwest, the sun threw up its own bonfire, the flames licking up past the tremendous forest and colouring the vast sky overhead. Long streamers of cloud that one hadn't really noticed earlier now took on the flames of the dying sun and many gasped to look up and behold the sight. "Keep watching," I heard one boy say to his mother. "It's always changing!" The now orange light fell upon the faces turned up to watch the sky. And then a few minutes later the orange of the clouds faded to a grey-white and soon stars gleamed here and there. The bonfire the merrymakers had made now came into its own strength. More and more people came across the darkened grass to sit on a blanket nearby or to gather where the dancing was going to take place. We could smell the frost in the air, the nip at the nose of the coming cold weather. But tonight we would dance and sing and eat well and give our thanks for the bountiful harvest.

THE FIDDLERS WERE TUNING up. The first person to dance was the Scotsman, Red Macbeth, who danced merrily around the circle of people watching until several others leaped up to join him in the jig. Then came the call for a set and couples formed a line. I looked for Chauncey. But too late. The set had formed and away went the couples to the music of a jig. People were clapping. Another set was forming. Someone grabbed my hand and pulled me toward the dancing. Andrew Monaghan. He grinned at my startled face.

"Come now, Oonagh, let's see you smile."

We danced up the line and took our turns and bows. Andrew's grip on my hands hurt. I tried to smile at him, at the people we were dancing with. But all the time I was looking for Chauncey. Perhaps he was still talking with my brother. I couldn't see Michael.

To my relief the dance ended and I dropped Andrew's hand. He reached to clasp it again but I managed to evade him.

"I have to do something, Andrew. Find another partner, will you?"

"Oonagh!" he protested.

"Oh," I exclaimed, grabbing hold of a young woman I vaguely knew. "Betty! Do you know Andrew Monaghan?" I practically shoved Betty Stenson right into his arms. "He came over on the ship with us. Andrew, Betty Stenson. Her family has a farm about three miles up the river."

What could he do but be polite? He smiled at her and bowed from the waist. Her face coloured and she smiled behind a hand. She was one of those young women whom time had passed by. For one reason or another — I never did find out her story — she had not married and now she was closer to thirty than twenty. She lived with her parents and several younger siblings on the homestead, worked often as not as hard as a plow horse, pulling stumps with the men. But tonight with Andrew Monaghan smiling down at her, she could feel the stirrings of hope. He did look very good this night, hair and beard neatly trimmed, clean clothes, polished boots. He took her hand and gave me a sideways grin as if to say, you win this round but just you wait. I made my escape.

The music continued. When a fiddler needed a rest, another sprang to take his place. There were several fiddles, tin whistles, and a couple of bohruns to liven up our evening. I wanted to find Chauncey and drag him into the dancing. He had told me he enjoyed dancing and was pretty good. But I couldn't find him. I began to wonder if he had gone to his cabin. Then I saw Michael. I ran to him, my heart pounding with suspense.

"Where is Chauncey?" I demanded.

"Wait now. Calm yourself," he muttered, glancing around. He took my arm and led me away from the crowd.

"Where is he?" I said loudly.

"Don't make such a spectacle of yourself." My brother's hand tightened on my arm until I winced.

"Let me go!" I muttered. "What is the matter?"

"Oonagh! There you are!" Chauncey's voice from behind, cheerful and even boisterous. I turned with great happiness to see him striding down from the McGann house, his arms laden with the basket of apples. I looked back at Michael questioningly. Why had he taken me aside; had he been about to say something to me?

"I was looking everywhere for you!" I smiled at Chauncey.

"She was about to go crazy!" Michael laughed. He was still holding my arm but now he patted my shoulder.

"I'm just going to put this basket down by the bonfire. Wait right there, will you?" With that Chauncey continued on his way with the apples. Near the fire he was accosted by several small children eager for an apple.

Michael leaned close to me. "What I wanted to say to you was that you should be aware of people's reactions when you announce your betrothal. Not everyone will be as welcoming as I am." I turned to see him smiling at me and finally heard the essence of what he had said. He was welcoming! I threw my arms around him and hugged him as I doubt I'd ever hugged him before.

"God, woman. You'll strangle me!" he hugged me.

"Did you ever do the Corcoran crush, Michael?" I asked. I was fighting tears.

"We need at least three of us," he said. "Where's that sister of ours?"

Chauncey was weaving his way back to us through the crowd. The firelight glistened on his smiling face and I was gratified to see how many people stopped him for a word or two. A man clapped him on the shoulder. I felt at that moment very confident of the outcome of the evening. I moved to meet him. Michael followed.

I DREW CHAUNCEY FORWARD into the light of the fire and into the dancing. By now so many couples were up, it was a little confusing. The music poured into the night and the flames bounced against the darkness and our shadows leaped against the wall of night like a whole other populace dancing there in the shadows. Every time I had to leave Chauncey and face another partner, even if just for a curtsey or a hand, my eyes searched for his. What a long line we had to traverse before we faced each other again! But this was where the man was to swing his lady partner. His hands slid around my waist and effortlessly he swung me up and off my feet and everyone around laughed as my skirts flew. He plunked me back on my feet and we were both laughing so hard we did not notice Andrew Monaghan until he had placed his hand on Chauncey's shoulder and wrenched him around. The crowd fell back in a ripple around us.

"Keep your filthy hands off my woman."

. I charged around Chauncey and confronted Andrew myself.

I didn't consider that Andrew had probably been drinking and that drink made him a vicious man. "How dare you!" I yelled into his face. At that moment the music stopped and my voice rang into the sudden quiet. The crowd watched in silence. Andrew's face was red with anger and he raised a threatening fist.

"How dare you," I said again more quietly. "I have never been nor will I ever be your woman! Apologize to Chauncey."

He slapped me so hard I fell to the ground, the taste of blood in my mouth where a tooth gouged my inner cheek. I heard a roar as Chauncey leaped past me and drove his fist into Andrew's face. And another roar as the crowd surged forward. Someone pulled me to my feet and dragged me away from the melee, but I yanked back, furious and anxious. I wanted Chauncey to come away with me. Michael shoved into the crowd and I shook off the hands that held me back. Someone yelled at me, "Come away now, you fool!" But I wouldn't listen. I clawed and shoved my way back to the centre of the crowd, and when people saw that it was me pounding on their backsides, they were quick to part and let me through. Afterward people told me I was screeching like a banshee the whole time, but I wasn't aware of that. All I knew was that if I didn't get right in there, Chauncey was either going to be terribly hurt or he would hurt someone. Either way this wasn't the way I wanted our engagement announcement to be. But I would announce it, by God, for all to know.

It was Red Macbeth who picked me up and flung me over his shoulder like a sack of meal. "Come on now," he said, his big arms restraining me. "You canna go in there. Not a pretty sight." But I saw, I saw. Several men, among them the blacksmith Denis Murphy, and Andrew Monaghan, his face a bleeding mess, held Chauncey with his arms behind his back. My brother Michael was himself held by the Salter brothers, the same men who had built Chauncey's cabin. Everyone was yelling. Except for Chauncey, who was glaring at Andrew.

"Put me down!" I yelled at Red and hit him on his back as hard as I could. In reply he slapped my bottom and told me to behave.

He was going to deposit me up at the McGann house and if I knew what was good for me that was where I would stay until this mess was cleaned up and sorted out. I kept on pummelling his back and ordering him to put me down. I heard the crowds roar again and again and I was so afraid that my Chauncey was being beaten by those cowards.

"He's my betrothed!" I yelled at Red. "Chauncey and I are to be married! Please set me down!"

"Oh, well now. Why didn't you say so?" That big man immediately plunked me down on my feet and I almost fell from the force. "He's your fiancé, is he?" Red's eyes shone. He was silent a minute, staring at me. I turned to run back to the fray but he snaked out a big hand to stop me. "Tell you what. Know how to ride a horse?"

I nodded, mystified.

"Okay," he grinned. "I'm your horse. You get up on my shoulders and we'll ride right into that crowd and you can tell the whole damn lot of them what you just told me. I'll keep you safe."

Mairi screamed at me from the McGanns' porch. "You get up here right now!"

"Sometimes a man'll have a bit too much to drink and he don't think as straight as he should. Now that's young Monaghan there. I reckon he don't know you're already engaged."

"He's a liar!" I was perched up high on Red's shoulders, his big warm palms gripping my knees through my skirts. Red marched back into the crowd, carrying me on his shoulders as if I were a small child instead of a rather tall woman. He shouted, "Make way, move aside!" People fell away from us, greatly startled at the sight.

In the centre of the crowd Chauncey was slumped on the ground and Michael still held back. Andrew, restrained by several men, including Paddy McGann, was still trying to kick at Chauncey's head. I almost fainted. With me still on his shoulders, Red calmly walked up to Andrew and grabbed him at his collar.

"You'll quit this now!" he thundered into Andrew's face. My brother dashed across to Chauncey and lifted his head from the ground.

An eerie silence fell over the people. I realized they were all agape at the sight of me up on Red's shoulders. I was holding on to Red's thick hair, my feet gripping his sides.

He tapped me on one knee. "Now tell them," he ordered.

"Chauncey and I are betrothed!" I saw the open mouths, the gasps of astonishment, but heard only my voice and its struggle to keep from breaking. "Chauncey and I will be wed in two weeks. Please come join in our celebration."

The crowd sounded like a wind rising in the pine trees. Then Paddy stepped up and speaking in a loud voice he said, "There'll be a wedding in two weeks. Congratulations, Oonagh and Chauncey! Let's give them a hand! And then let's celebrate the harvest. Come on, folks!" He began the clapping. There was sporadic clapping and some whistling. I slid to the ground in a blackness for I was sure my Chauncey had been killed. Michael was holding his head and someone had brought a basin of water and a wash rag. Finally Red let me go and I knelt at Chauncey's side, tears streaming down my face. The crowd began to move away, but I watched no one but Chauncey.

"Is he —?"

"He'll be fine," said Michael. "He'll come around."

Michael had caught a few bruises himself.

"Such cowards!" I cried.

"Ach no," Red muttered. "Drunken idiots. Here, let me lift him up. I'll take him to his cabin."

"Let me get the wagon," said Michael.

"No, man. He's light as a feather. He's lighter than you are, Oonagh lass," Red teased as he hoisted Chauncey up into his arms and cradled him there like a baby. Then off he went. A good number of people followed along. I ran ahead to open the door and ready the bed. By the time they arrived at the cabin, Chauncey had come to and was joking with Red about having had a bit too much to drink. I was probably the only person there who knew he'd not had a drop.

Fifteen

LORNA COULDN'T ABIDE THE sight of me after "that scandalous per-
formance" of mine, as she described it, the evening of the harvest
dance. The morning after the whole terrible incident she confronted
me in the kitchen as I was kneading bread. She was shocked that I
would have allowed myself to be carried by that big brute of a Scotsman into that brawl. And then to declare so brazenly that I would
be married to — here her voice dipped and she hissed — *that nigger*.
I turned my back on her, on the bread dough half-made and washed
my hands clean. She yelled at me but I ignored her and marched
straight up to my room. I packed my belongings, and leaving them
neatly tied on the bed, went to find Paddy at the mill. He was busy
with the last of the grain to be milled before winter froze the giant
mill wheel. Already ice rimed the edges of the river in the mornings.
Soon, all too soon, a deep silence would descend over the village with
winter's smothering snow. As I hurried over the bridge, my angry
mind relived Lorna's hateful sneer.

Paddy was in conversation with a settler from north of the village
who was waiting for his flour. When he saw me he motioned for me
to wait in the little alcove that served as his office and there I waited
for what seemed hours until the flour was done and the farmer
on his way. Paddy came in, his face grim, and I could see Lorna
had already persuaded him to dismiss me. He said he was sorry but
after all the wedding was in a scant few weeks. I would've moved to

Chauncey's anyway. He wished us much happiness but had I considered everything? Life would not be easy with Chauncey as my husband, what with the way that people regarded the black fugitives from the States.

"Oh?" I raised my brow. "And how is that? I've noticed only a great respect for him since he's come. I thought people here sympathize with those who've managed to escape to their freedom. Slavery is a vile institution. Don't you believe so?"

"No disputing that." Poor Paddy was clearly uncomfortable. "But Oonagh, think! To marry outside of your own people — now the priests may have a word or two about that."

"I don't care what the priests or anyone may say about Chauncey. You know as well as I that he is a finer man than Andrew Monaghan."

"That's where you go getting yourself in trouble, Oonagh. Measure your words. Andrew had his cap set for you and he's disappointed, I dare say. But he's not a bad man."

"He's a drunk and a bully. He always was and so's his da back home. Used to beat the women in the family. I swore I'd never marry one of that lot," I spoke contemptuously. Poor nervous Paddy. He gestured for me to keep my voice down, a gesture that enraged me.

"I'll go then to my sister's. Can you help me with my belongings? I'd ask Josie but he left for Cobourg this morning with a load."

"Of course. Are you ready to go now?"

MAIRI WAS CROSS WITH me and spoke only when necessary. Josie spoke not at all. He avoided me completely when he returned. Andrew had been one of his best friends since they were boys and Josie took the incident as a personal affront. It was too much to hope that he would take my side in this and see that Andrew's behaviour had been inexcusable.

I was not idle while at Mairi's. We placed my spinning wheel upstairs next to her new loom, a very fine one, in the larger of the two rooms just under the sloping roof, and I worked all day. When a rain swept in, I welcomed the sound — like a thousand horses galloping overhead on the roof. A window in the gable end afforded light and a view when I wearied of the pattern slowly taking shape in front of me. Through the window in the little bedroom where I slept, I watched the breezes take the last flaming leaves off a sugar maple that Josie had left undisturbed when he cleared the space for the house. Mairi had persuaded him the tree would provide welcome shade in the hot days of August and so it had. Mairi had tapped it for its sweet sap this past spring and been pleasantly surprised at the quantity of sugar she was able to produce from a single tree. It was a true giant and I loved to rest my eyes from the weaving by staring out into its tangle of bare branches with the odd bird perched there, feathers fluffed against the cold, waiting for leaves and the nesting season all over again.

The western window in the loom room stared straight into a high hill barren of trees and littered with boulders. At the summit the men had left one giant oak standing as a sad and ineffective sentinel. This late into the fall its leaves, still clinging to the many branches, were a golden brown. It would take at least four of us to encircle it. Whenever I gazed upon that oak, I felt melancholy. There remained on the hillside giant stumps waiting to be uprooted. Why had the men levelled all the trees on this hillside? It was too steep and stony for farming.

I WAS AT THE loom trying to finish up a blanket for Martha McGann, when I heard a rustle at the window. I looked up to see the sky full of snow. The first real snowfall of the season touches me with excitement and more than a little twinge of fear. It's true that those with sleighs can get about more easily and rivers are easier to cross when frozen. Many people in our area used the Indian shoes made of twigs and rawhide to help them walk over the deep snow. Although the snow was beautiful, it did create great hardship for many people. One hoped that the winter would not linger past the provisions one had put up and that the animals would find enough to eat browsing in the woods. It was not uncommon to see both man and beast emerge from the dying days of winter gaunt and ill-nourished. On the other hand people more fortunate who had warm homes and plenty of provisions and firewood often enjoyed the winter more than the summer. No insects. Winter was a respite from those stinging devils, though cluster flies and spiders living in the logs and rafters still managed to plague us through the winter. People in the towns welcomed the snow for breathtaking sleigh rides. Fewer people in our remote area had such conveyances; most relied on the Indian shoe or else walked with difficulty when the snow became deep. But there was more time to visit family and neighbours. Although idleness was hardly the rule of our lives, it seems to me that winter provided much more occasion for merriment.

I'd been hoping the snow would stay away until after our wedding. We'd been fortunate that any snow sprinkled since September had melted almost as soon as the sun was up the next day. But this snowfall was here to stay.

"Oonagh, it's snowing!" Mairi called up the stairs and I called back that I had seen it.

"Come down for a bit," she called again. "I want to see what the baby thinks of it."

Mairi had the baby all bundled up warmly so that only her eyes were visible, shining as she stared at our excited faces. We hurried out into the snow whirling down almost soundlessly, huge snowflakes circling around our upturned faces. The baby squirmed in Mairi's arms and startled with surprise as a cold flake landed on her nose. Mairi, completely enchanted by her baby, couldn't take her eyes off the little face. The wool blanket was soon sparkling with snowflakes and water drops. At that moment I knew all would be well between Mairi and me, for she looked up and gave me her sweet, loving smile. Then she leaned back over the baby who was gurgling her funny noises.

"It's hardly cold, even," Mairi sighed and kissed the baby's face.

I looked up into that dark grey sky with thousands of white flakes falling. After a few moments it was dizzying to contemplate. The snow wet my face and hair. I knew my hair must look like Mairi's, white with snow. This is what we'll look like when we're old, I thought.

"Ah, snow maidens!" called out a cheerful voice. Chauncey stood at the edge of the clearing with another man I didn't know.

"Oh," exclaimed Mairi, and she raced for the cabin and disappeared inside. I knew exactly why she'd fled like that, for the interior of the cabin was less than tidy, with heaps of washed wool waiting to be picked sitting right on the plank floor near the fireplace. Josie was away on a trip to Cobourg, so we'd let our household habits be a little lax. Mairi had spent the entire morning picking wool while I'd been upstairs at the loom. I knew she was rushing about sweeping up the litter and gathering the wool into baskets. Chauncey and his companion wouldn't have known that, so I hastened across the yard to assure them that my sister was indeed quite happy to welcome them to her home.

Chauncey took up my hands in his and spoke as if he hadn't noticed Mairi's flight indoors, "How good to see you."

We hadn't seen each other for the past two weeks, not since that terrible evening of the harvest celebration. But not once had I doubted he would come for me and that we would be married. Michael had stopped in last week and told us that Chauncey's business had fallen right off and that he'd felt hostility, especially from Denis.

Chauncey turned to the man with him and introduced him as Reverend Gordon, a travelling Methodist minister.

"Reverend Gordon has kindly consented to marry us next week at my house in the village." Chauncey smiled down at me, still gripping my hands. I understood his eyes asking if I still wanted to marry him after all the trouble we'd had. His face was bruised.

"Oh, thank you!" I smiled at the minister. I asked them to please enter as I was sure they could do with some hot tea and a bite to eat.

In the few minutes we'd remained outside in the snowfall, my sister had worked wonders indoors. All the wool had disappeared into neat baskets shoved under the table near the window. The litter from the picking had been swept up. A new log was already snapping on the fire and a kettle of water swung over on the hook. Mairi came forward as we entered and asked the men to please come in and if they would like some tea. It would be ready soon. I handed them a corn broom at the door to brush snow off their boots.

Reverend Gordon travelled a wide area in his work and so we asked him what Peterborough, Ottawa, Montreal, and York were like and we heard the smallest details in vivid colours. Then Chauncey, with a sidelong glance at me, asked him to tell us what he thought of Niagara Falls.

"Ah, me," Reverend Gordon sighed. "Now there is a place beyond words. Truly, beyond words." He actually stopped talking and took a good long sip of his tea. I gulped my tea to keep from laughing. Mairi was enthralled. She waited for him to continue, her mouth open in a smile. I nudged her foot next to mine where we sat on the settle and startled her back to herself.

"Reverend Gordon, sir, have you indeed been to see the Falls?" she asked.

"Ah, Mrs. McGann. Indeed I have. And the very best time to go, may I say, is in winter, for it is then that the awesome power of the Lord is visible."

"How so?" asked Chauncey. Once again he caught my eye in that sidelong way of his and joy bubbled in the pit of my belly. I don't know now what was so profoundly humorous about Reverend Gordon, but both Chauncey and I had to choke back our hilarity several times during the visit. Perhaps we were just so relieved to see each other again and in good health. But the Reverend was oblivious to our mood and described at length how in winter the falls froze solid, huge columns and pillars of ice.

"However does the Lord do that, freeze such a huge rushing flow of water?" he smiled at us, his voice trembling slightly. "You must be sure and travel there someday," he concluded. "The Falls are a mighty work of God and humbling to the most arrogant of men. No one who looks upon that enormous flow of water rushing over the cliffs and disappearing in a thunderous deluge in the mists below can ever doubt the might of God."

"Well then, certainly, Oonagh, you and I will go. Soon, too, perhaps even this winter. It would do us both good to witness such a mighty work of God." Chauncey smiled innocently at me.

"Yes, go in the winter. You must be very careful not to walk too close to the gorge for all the ground is icy." Then the minister downed his tea all at once and declined Mairi's quick offer of another cup.

"No, my dear. Thank you kindly, but I really must be off. I was just passing through your little village and Chauncey waylaid me like a highwayman and said I must promise to perform his wedding next week. I agreed. Of course I hadn't realized that you would be Irish. Are you not Catholic?"

"Chauncey isn't," I said quickly.

"Perhaps you'd consider joining our church then, my dear." He peered kindly at me under heavy lowering white brows. Those brows reminded me of my own Da for an instant and I was swept with a sudden chill.

"Ooh," I exclaimed. "Is there not a draft under that door still, Mairi? Did you feel it, sir?"

"Oh, drafts!" he laughed. "I haven't sat in a cabin yet that doesn't have drafts coming from every corner."

"We will see you on Saturday next?" I asked.

He smiled and nodded. "No fear. I will be here on Friday evening. Chauncey tells me you plan to have the wedding at his cabin."

"If that's all right."

"God is everywhere," he interrupted me. "I could perform a wedding in the middle of the woods and be assured of holy ground." His voice trembled with a deep emotion. He had a long mournful face with large blue eyes that contrasted with the white shock of his brows and hair, and his face was worn with deep creases. For all that, he couldn't have been much older than our brother Michael, but a man old before his time, thin and gaunt.

After agreeing on what time we would come to the village on Saturday, Chauncey and Reverend Gordon took their leave of us. Chauncey promised to go by Michael's and inform them of our plans for Saturday. They waved to us just before the forest and the veil of snow still falling gently hid them from view.

Mairi shut the door and ordered me to fetch some rags from the barrel upstairs to stuff under the door to block the fine snow sifting in. Before shutting the door for the night I hurried out into the darkening evening and carried in several armloads of wood. The small creek nearby where Mairi got the water was still flowing freely and I filled both water buckets. Then I shut the door firmly against the cold and stuffed the rags into the crack under the door.

"There!" I turned to see Mairi rolling some potatoes out of the hot ashes.

"Let's eat," she smiled.

Later in the night Mairi, the baby, and I snuggled together in the bed. The baby slumbered while we talked together softly. The darkness loosened our tongues in such a way that we spoke of things we never could in the light of day. Mairi spoke about our mother and how she missed our sisters and wondered how they were. Were Liam and Da all right and in good health? She spoke about how even though I'd be living in the village again, closer by far than New South Wales, she'd miss me terribly because I was marrying. I told her I'd felt the same when she wed Josie, that I was losing my sister. She hugged me and we both shed a few silly tears, for weren't we both there, close in the dark and loving sisters still? I thought but didn't say, *how nice it was when Josie was away.* But of course soon enough I'd be gone and Mairi would be left alone when he was away like this. I told Mairi she should think of staying with Chauncey and me whenever Josie had to go to Cobourg. No, she'd replied. It was good that Josie had obtained such employment for the winter at least. She was perfectly fine here alone.

"I will pray every day for you and Chauncey and your happiness," she said suddenly, after a long silence in which I'd thought she'd fallen asleep..

"Thank you, love. We'll visit often. You bring your babbies to town and I'll come visit with mine." I couldn't help giggling at the thought.

"Oonagh, I never spoke with you about what happens between a man and a woman. But I suppose — are you really with child?"

"I believe so," I smiled. "A June babby, I think."

"Goodness me," she exclaimed, counting on her fingers. "An early babby." She suddenly giggled.

"Where's Father Christopher when I finally need confession!" I laughed.

We were silent for a few moments, listening to the fire crackle. Then Mairi murmured, "I'll be end of May." Her hand reached for mine across the sleeping baby between us.

Mairi's breathing slowed, deepening into sleep. The baby snuffled slightly and I soothed her. Soon this will be me and Chauncey with our child slumbering sweetly between us. With this blissful thought, I fell asleep.

THE BABY SUCKLED LOUDLY — Mairi had fallen asleep again. I watched as the baby sucked and patted Mairi's breast with one tiny fist. The daylight in the room was still very dim. The baby sank back, peacefully sated and fast asleep. I gazed upon them both and the longing for my own little one grew and grew within me until it was a pain centred in my breast. We three curled into a warm nest of quilts and blankets, but I could feel the chill of the air on my cheek. I blew a breath experimentally, and sure enough I could see it. The water would be frozen in the pails and perhaps the fire out. Not completely out I hoped. I hated having to make a fire anew when most of the embers had burnt out like stars in the morning sky.

I didn't feel like getting out of our warm nest. Yes, we'd stuffed rags under the door, but there were several other places I'd noted last night that could use better chinking. And although it was indeed pleasant to have clear windows, the chill was easily felt through the glass. This was the coldest night yet, the ushering in of winter to be sure. Mairi was deeply asleep.

I slipped from the bed and felt the shock of the cold floor on my bare feet. I quickly pulled on my stockings. The cold was intolerable. One of us should have awakened during the night and replenished the fire, but we'd been so warm and comfortable and tired after the day's work. I had set a pile of kindling by the fireplace. I prayed for a small ember left in that pile of ashes.

Even though Mairi had been careful to bank the fire last night, I was shocked at how few embers remained. By now shaking with the cold, I worked as quickly as my numb fingers would allow to kindle a new fire. Finally life blew into the remaining embers, and with a small bit of dry wood shavings to start, the flames ignited. I laid a few more sticks on the blaze and sat back on my heels, shaking with cold.

"Oh, good, Oonagh, good. Now come get warmed up," my sister ordered. I turned to see her smiling at me from the bed. She held open the covers as I dashed across and dove into the bed. She shrieked as I pressed my frozen toes to her warm legs. The baby gurgled up with laughter too, as if she understood that we were two sisters who would miss each other terribly when apart, as soon we would be.

"Who makes the fire in the morning when I'm not here?" I demanded.

"We take turns. Sometimes I make it and then sometimes I make it."

"You mean Josie makes it," I corrected.

"No! I make it." She pealed with laughter at my face. "Aw, Oonagh, you're always too serious."

"Does Josie do anything around here for you?"

"You know he does. Leave him alone. I don't know why you don't like each other," she said sadly.

"He took you away from us," I smiled.

"Am I supposed to think ill of Chauncey because he's taking you from us?"

"Ah, you've got me. Now I'm hoping you'll think the world of him, as I do, for the happiness he's giving me."

"And babbies?" she said, grinning at me.

"Wee boys and girls with his lovely dimples."

"Ah, go on. You're just mush," Mairi scoffed and hit me slightly on the side of the head. "Why don't you tell me what you want to get done today instead. Look how the day is fast fading as we slumber here like lazy cows."

"Speak for yourself, sister dear. I'm no cow. Not yet!"

The morning was spent cozying up in the bed. I'd replenish the fire and scamper right back into the delicious warmth of the blankets. If we'd had animals to care for we would have been up to see to them. Or if Josie were home. But as long as the house still felt so chilled, we stayed in bed and talked. After all, we had only today and tomorrow left in which to be the sisters we'd been growing up in our parents' home in Connemara.

By midmorning though we had to rise reluctantly and get to work. I wanted to finish the blanket for Martha. She'd already paid me for it in fleeces, which Mairi was spinning.

"Go on," said Mairi. "Don't worry about anything else but that blanket."

So I set to work in the chill room upstairs, wearing fingerless gloves as well as my coat. A bit of warm air came up through the hole left in the floorboards. We'd placed the loom right over it to help keep the weaver warm. At noon Mairi brought me a bowl of hot broth and left me to my work again. I was rewarded after the long day's work to know that I had indeed finished the blanket and could go to my wedding day unencumbered. If I didn't finish, I'd have had to travel back to Mairi's to finish the work.

"Don't rush," Mairi had said when she brought me a cup of tea late in the afternoon. "I'd love to have you come back and stay with me for a while."

"Oh, sure you would. But would Josie? And Chauncey would have a thing or two to say about it. I'll finish it in time."

She kissed the top of my head and left me again. How glad I was that she was not angry with me anymore. How lucky we were that we'd be still living close to each other. As I worked, I daydreamed of the room in the house Chauncey and I would build where I could have my loom; I'd weave such gorgeous blankets and cloth that I would be renowned even to Belleville and maybe York.

THE SUN WAS GOING down when I stood up and stretched to ease my cramped muscles. I looked out of the window at the hillside, its stumps and boulders concealed in snow. One look and I hurried downstairs. Grabbing up a shawl to cover my head, I rushed outside. At the very top of the hill the giant oak had sent a flurry of its golden leaves scattered across the snowy slope, as if some rich man had generously flung a big bag of gold coins. Mairi was calling me but I stood there a few silent moments. Maybe this would be the only time in my life when all these would come together: an early snow in late October when the oak still carried its load of deep golden brown leaves; sunlight low over the rim of the hill casting its peculiarly yellow light, a wind that had shaken the leaves down over the clean untouched snow, and me, the woman seeing this. I wanted to call Mairi out, but before she would've had time to come stand beside me the light would've changed, yellow dimmed to grey, the gold gone. I watched alone.

Sixteen

ALTHOUGH I HAD INVITED all at the harvest celebration to attend our wedding, I expected only my family to come and, even so, that Josie would arrange to be doing something else that day. I would not mind. All I wanted was to be wed peacefully, with those present wishing us joy and a long life together. This was all I hoped for. So I was happily surprised when it was Josie himself early on Saturday morning who awoke the household with a great shout of a song. I dressed hurriedly and made up the bed that Mairi had set up for me in the upstairs room. Mairi was now singing loudly with Josie and my heart beat just that much faster for the wedding song they were singing. I had to sit suddenly for my eyes swam with tears.

"Where's that sleepy bride anyway?" Josie shouted up the stairs.

"I'm coming," I called back. What could possibly have wrought this change in the man? Maybe Mairi had managed to make him see that all would be well. Or maybe he was just relieved that I'd be out of his home soon.

I gathered up my belongings and the bundle of new blanket I'd made for Martha McGann. Then I trod carefully down the narrow stairs. Josie took up my bundles and my spinning wheel and went out to place them in the wagon he'd brought home last night from the store. Mairi placed a bowl of porridge, steaming hot, in my hands.

"Eat now," she said.

She had cut up slices of apple into the oatmeal as it cooked, a rare treat. Josie had brought back a basket of apples from the Front yesterday to our great delight.

"When did you cook this? I didn't hear you up at all," I asked.

"Josie cooked it," she said triumphantly, glad to show me that her man could do things around the place.

"Well he must've been up for hours already. That anxious to get rid of me, is he?" I laughed.

Mairi's happiness fled at my rash words; I was immediately sorry for my sharp tongue. She turned away without a word to attend to the baby. I ate my porridge in silence. But presently she turned her smiling face to me again. She gathered the baby up in her arms and presented her to me.

"Hold her for a minute, will you?"

I loved holding that little child in my arms. Her bright eyes in that small face peered up at me and when I smiled, she smiled, and when I shaped my mouth in an "O," she did likewise. I touched my nose to hers until she giggled, such a delightful sound. I didn't notice what Mairi was doing until she stood in front of me and said, "Now then, this is yours."

She had draped over her arms the lovely lacy shawl of white and cream-coloured wool that she had worn at her own wedding over Mam's special dress.

"The dress would be too small, I thought. You're much bigger than Mam ever was, or me."

"Yes," I agreed. I hadn't asked Mairi about the dress for I knew she wanted to keep it and I knew it would take some work to fit it for me. Besides, my good grey wool gown was hardly worn. And I hadn't dared to ask about the shawl, for it was a very lovely piece of work, one of our Mam's finest, and I knew it was Mairi's treasure. Still, I'd been hoping that she'd lend it to me for two reasons: I wanted to wear something of my Mam's, to feel her close to me on such an important day of my life, and it was a beauty of a shawl that would dress up any gown.

Mairi carefully laid the shawl over my hair and shoulders.

"Ah, indeed. I do see our Mam in you," she smiled. "This sets off your eyes. You have very lovely eyes, Oonagh. Do you know that?"

"Thank you, Mairi. So much. This will come back to you for her wedding some day," I smiled down at the baby falling asleep in my arms.

"Oh, heavens. Let her be little for a long while yet."

Mairi kissed my cheek and I whispered, "I'm sorry."

Of course she understood my apology. She leaned forward and kissed my other cheek. Then she eased the baby from my arms into hers and whispered back, "Now go get your own little one, will you!"

THE DAY COULD NOT have been lovelier for the time of year, a good omen. Much of the snow on the track had melted, but under the leafless trees deep snow still lay in patches striped with blue shadows. The dry air was cold but not bitter, and as the wagon crushed over them a slight breeze lifted the spicy odours of the fallen leaves on the track. The blue sky glowed, but it was still very early in the day, and as we topped a rise, off to the west a large bank of dark clouds towered like an ominous mountain range. Maybe by evening we'd have more snow.

AS WE DROVE DOWN into the village, I was surprised to see many wagons and carts parked by the store and even a rather fancy carriage. Horses were tied up at every spot, even to trees down along the river. The inn was full of people.

"Well, Oonagh, looks like you'll be having a big wedding!" laughed Mairi.

"Oh, surely not! They're here for something else."

"No. Look at Chauncey's cabin!"

The front was festooned with bright paper streamers and some-one had gathered pine boughs for the doorstep. Mairi pointed out the small crowd in the sunlight. She pointed out a small group of

Indians who stood aside, probably Chauncey's Indian friends whom
he'd come to know in his wanderings in the woods.

But my heart almost stopped at the sight of the men lounging
in front of Grills Emporium and Inn. Andrew Monaghan and his
brothers, Denis Murphy, even Bert, that creepy little man whom
Chauncey had tolerated for too long. Why had they come? Then a
horrible presentiment came over me and I whispered to Mairi,
"Where's Chauncey? What have they done?"

Someone yelled, "The bride's here!" and the door of the barbershop burst open with our Daniel first out, followed closely by Michael
and Jane, all smiling widely. Still no Chauncey, but at the sight of
my family I relaxed. Daniel climbed into the wagon and grabbed
up my bundles before I could say hello. He stopped just long enough
to peck my cheek, his eyes shining. Michael reached up to help me
down.

"Glad to see you survived the trip in this contraption!" he said,
patting the wooden boards of the wagon.

"Every tooth in my head has rattled loose," groaned Mairi.

"How's the little one?" Jane reached out to take the baby.

I asked Michael in a low voice whether the men present were there
to make trouble. No, he assured me. Every last one of them had patted
Chauncey on the back in congratulations. Denis had even bought him
a whiskey last night at the store.

I wanted to tell my brother that Chauncey didn't drink. The men
were all talking and laughing, watching us.

"Were you there too?"

"Paddy told me about it when I arrived this morning. He seemed
pleased."

"What about Andrew?" I said into Michael's ear.

"The same. He shook Chauncey's hand in front of everyone and
said, 'Patience is a poultice for all wounds.' He said it in Irish, you
know the proverb. Then everyone tried to translate it for Chauncey.
That's the best meaning, don't you think?"

"But what did he mean by it?"

Michael shrugged, "He probably doesn't know himself. He probably meant something like what Mam used to tell us when we fell and got hurt, remember? 'By the time you marry, your pain will be forgotten.'"

"No," I said. "No. I don't like the sound of it."

"Come now, Oonagh. The minister is waiting on you at the cabin. Chauncey will stay at the shop and Daniel will run and get him when you're ready." Michael drew me to Chauncey's cabin where Mairi and the others had already gone. I threw a glance over my shoulder at the men clustered outside Grills and caught Andrew's eyes. He smiled and bowed slightly. I was not comforted at all by that smile.

"Michael," I said, tugging on my brother's sleeve. "Please do watch out for Andrew. He's not here for any friendly purpose."

"You'd think differently if you'd been here last night. They had a regular celebration, with music and drink and good cheer. You're worrying needlessly. Men are here from Cobourg, Colbourne, Port Hope, and even Belleville because they wish Chauncey and you well. They all like Chauncey; they've sat under his razor! So relax now. Stop worrying. It'll make lines in your brow you don't need." He kissed me on both cheeks and hurried me into the cabin.

MAIRI AND JANE HAD drawn a curtain around the bed in the corner and made me sit there behind it, out of view. I hadn't seen that curtain before, but I didn't want to betray the fact that I'd been in Chauncey's house, so I kept quiet. Soon people began shuffling into the cabin and I wondered if all those men outside planned to come in. How could they all fit? I tried to distinguish the loud bantering voices. Tears sprang to my eyes. Perhaps all would be well. Would Lorna or Martha McGann come? Emily Cotterage? It would be well if they came. More women. The thought that Andrew might even now be in this very cabin put an awful fear into my stomach. I took up Mairi's hand as she sat beside me on the bed.

"Don't be nervous," she whispered.

Then the people hushed and I knew Chauncey had entered. The minister's voice welcomed all those who'd come to witness this marriage. Michael drew aside the curtain and beckoned me to his side. Mairi adjusted the shawl over my hair and gave me a little squeeze. I could hardly see, I was that nervous, and would have stumbled surely if Michael hadn't held me firmly by the elbow. The little cabin was packed, but an aisle had been left from the bed to the wall beside the door where Chauncey and the minister waited for me. Chauncey stood straight and tall beside the minister, who was dressed all in black. My Chauncey wore a new buckskin jacket with long fringes and bright quillwork. He smiled as if he were the sun warming me. All my fears vanished.

The ceremony was over quickly and there we were, married. My brother Michael rushed to give me the first kiss, as was tradition. He needn't have worried. The only women present were Jane and Mairi, held back in the crush as well-wishers crowded us at the door. Chauncey kept an arm tightly about my shoulder.

"To Grills," someone shouted.

"Mr. Grills offered to host a little celebration at the store, food and drink. It's a bit bigger than this place," Chauncey said close to my ear.

"We don't have to go, do we?" I whispered back.

At that moment Mairi and Jane reached our side and gave us hugs and kisses. Both Mairi and I started to cry and laugh at the same time, for here I was, finally a married woman, and it felt terribly joyful but sad. Jane pressed a small parcel into my hand, saying, "A little token. May you have a long and fruitful life together." Then Daniel hugged Chauncey and me so fiercely I could feel his every muscle strain.

"We can still go fishing, can't we?" he asked Chauncey. "Even if you're married?"

Chauncey laughed. One of his Indian friends standing near murmured something and Chauncey smiled and told Daniel that his friend had just offered to take Daniel fishing when the ice was thick enough on the lake several miles northeast of the village.

"When the ice is on the lake?" Daniel exclaimed in disbelief.

"They use spears!" laughed Chauncey, ruffling Daniel's hair. "Through a hole in the ice."

Paddy McGann approached to give us his congratulations and to make excuses for Lorna. She sent her best wishes but she was feeling poorly today, too close to her confinement to venture out on a day threatening more snow. I looked past him into the afternoon gone grey and chill. How quickly the weather had changed. I hadn't thought that huge bank of dark cloud would fall upon us quite so soon. I asked Paddy to convey my best wishes to Lorna for her recovering health and to tell her that now she could call upon me for help with the children when she needed it. "As a friend and neighbour," I added. He thanked me and turned away. Chauncey squeezed my elbow and I looked up at him. We both had to stifle the impulse to laugh out loud. We'd never have wished to hurt Paddy's feelings.

Most of the people had left the cabin by now. The minister apologized that he couldn't stay to celebrate with us, but with snow threatening he'd best be on his way to his next engagement. I dearly wanted to shut the door on everyone and retire with Chauncey. But with several hours of daylight left, my haste to be alone with him would've been the subject of much teasing. The noise from the store, which served as both tavern and inn, grew louder by the minute. Michael poked his head in our door, "Best to make a little appearance, eh? The party's begun but most people will be going soon. The storm is almost upon us."

"Michael, you're staying, aren't you, and Mairi and Josie too?"

He shook his head. He had to go, a milk cow needed tending, but Mairi, Josie, and the baby would be staying overnight at Lorna McGann's, where they were already. In the swirl of the crowd leaving almost all at once, I hadn't seen them go.

"Come on, you two," Michael urged. "Just stay for ten minutes and then everyone will let you go. You can hear them calling for you."

It was true. A roar of male voices called out for Chauncey and me. Fear pierced me at the sound, but Chauncey laughed, and his laughter banished my fear again. His laughter could not exist in the same place as fear, which fled from such a joyous sound. I threw my arms around him, "I love you more dearly than anything in the world, and especially your laugh." At which he laughed all the more.

AS WE ENTERED THE store, a chorus of hurrahs greeted us. Chauncey knew so many people! The storekeeper himself, Mr. Grills, a little man with a round wrinkled-apple face and a fringe of sparse white hair, presided over the celebration. The room reeked with strong spirits. The crowd toasted us, wishing us long life and happiness and many children. Then Mr. Grills, perhaps fearing that his stock of spirits would run dry without compensation, warned that the weather had turned for the worse. Best to cut short the celebration. Those travelling should leave before the main snow began. The inn could accommodate no more visitors.

"Wait, Mr. Grills," Chauncey suddenly called out.

My heart squeezed unpleasantly. Chauncey leaped up onto the store's counter. Everyone hushed.

"Oonagh and I thank you all for coming. We much appreciate your presence here today. Now please do take care going home in this weather. Thank you."

The crowd applauded his few words as he leaped back down from the counter and to my side. I gathered up the shawl close to my neck as we ran out of the door and down the road through the snow that had begun to fall. It was only when I entered Chauncey's cabin and closed the door on the world that I finally realized why I'd been so uneasy at the store. The Monaghans and the blacksmith had not been there. I was sure of it suddenly. Had Andrew and his gang even been at the wedding? Why this made me apprehensive, I couldn't have said. I decided to keep that apprehension to myself as Chauncey had flung himself down on the bed laughing.

"We did it, Oonagh girl!" he said. Then as swiftly as he had lain down, he jumped up to attend the fire in the hearth. He rubbed his hands together for warmth.

"Do you find it cold in here?" he asked me in concern.

"No, it's pleasant."

"Then why do you still stand there shivering in that shawl? Come by the fire."

He made me sit on the settle and close my eyes. "No peeking," he ordered. He had me a gift! "Open your eyes now."

He held before me a lovely little corn broom decorated with birch bark woven in, wild grapevines, and pine cones.

"Did you make this?" I asked, admiring the fine workmanship of the weaving where the broom attached to its handle.

"My Indian friend whose wife made this jacket made this for us. His wife also made you a buckskin dress but I couldn't get it to you in time for you to wear."

He took the broom back from me.

"Now we're going to have our own private ceremony," he whispered, holding out his hands for me.

"We both going to sweep together," he whispered. He made me stand in front of him, his arms around me, and placed his hands on mine on the broom handle and slowly we swept a circle around ourselves, the two of us moving in unison.

"This is a very old custom going back into foggy time," he said. "We're sweeping out the old life and sweeping in our new." His hands on mine were warm; his breath set my neck ashiver. I could hardly breathe. Then our circle was done. He gently laid that gaily decorated broom down in the centre of the floor. We stood side by side, arms tight around each other's waist, and he said, "Oonagh and Chauncey, as one. Jump!"

We sailed over that broom as if we were indeed one.

I untied one of my bundles and withdrew the thick grey vest I'd knitted for him. I pointed out the pattern in red yarn, yarn I'd salvaged from an old garment, wool gathered, spun, and dyed in Ireland by my mother. He stopped any further explanations with kisses.

When the snow began to fall in earnest I didn't know, for we were so cozy under the blankets. Our freedom to be together quite overcame us. Once Chauncey rose and stoked the fire and returned to the bed carrying a plate of toasted bread with slabs of roast venison. We need our energy, he laughed. After eating we snuggled in companionable silence, listening as the wind whined under the eaves.

"Have you ever gone to bed this early without being sick?" I asked.

"It's dark already. Could be midnight, couldn't it be?"

Snow rattled against the window in a fierce gust. The wind was picking up force. Trees squeaked and groaned in the forest nearby.

"I hope all those people travelling have found shelter by now," I whispered. He mumbled something sleepily and squeezed me closer. Could we be any closer, our bodies meshed together in this delicious peace? If there was indeed a Heaven, how could it be finer than this? I listened to his slow breathing and a small snore escaped his lips, but sleep eluded me, my mind too busy. I suddenly remembered my stone relic from Ireland still packed away. I crept out of bed, but as I returned, clutching the stone, Chauncey awoke. I showed him my special stone. He inspected it closely, admiring the design, then said he wouldn't mind at all if I wished to place it under our pillows, since it was obviously sacred to me.

He was wide awake again. I apologized for waking him and he laughed, declaring he'd never gone to sleep voluntarily so early of an evening, but then he'd never had a boisterous wife in his bed. *Boisterous, is it?* I dove under the quilts and tickled his ribs and he subdued me easily.

"Careful with me now," I said as he threw a leg over me. I patted my belly, raising my brows and he shook his head saying, "It don't happen that fast!"

"Oh yes it does. A woman knows." He teased me then, declaring he could hardly wait to see his skinny beanpole fattened up into a mama. He got serious and suggested that maybe we should think of moving to York or Kingston where there were other black people. He didn't feel all that welcome here now. Not welcome? After this day's celebrations? He voiced the same misgivings I had. We talked about trust and love and who we could believe were our friends. I cried for I didn't want to think I'd have to leave my family here. He sighed heavily, stroking my arm, and I was stung to remember that he'd left his own loved ones behind. My incorrigible curiosity revived. I reminded him that in telling me the story of his journey, he'd left me in suspense, himself hiding in someone's cellar.

"How did you get from that cellar to Canada?"

"Ah, I knew it. You married me for my storytelling." He obliged me, first exacting the fee of several kisses and caresses.

IT WAS SO DARK in that cellar he couldn't see his hand held up right in front of his face. Like being buried alive. Smell of earth, wet stone, mould, and the smell of the man, Abel, sleeping beside him. Powerful odour! Abel began to snore so loudly Chauncey thought he'd bring down the cabin. He kept nudging Abel to shut him up. He couldn't sleep himself, although he knew he had to trust this Taylor. Didn't Taylor have this hidey-hole all set up, and didn't he say he'd been looking out for Chauncey?

He finally fell asleep and then woke up, startled, when Abel clapped his hand over his mouth, shushing him. Outside, horses were stamping amid the jangling of bridles.

"Taylor, open up now!" a man yelled.

Taylor called, "Sure enough, boss."

Chauncey and Abel were still as mice.

"Mind if we look around your place again?" That loud voice was now right in the cabin and the floor pounded with boots. Slave catchers. The same loud voice said, "Nice little gal you got there, Taylor, like I always say. Nice little family. Y'all go back to sleep now. Ain't nothing here. Let's go."

Taylor said in a whining voice, "Boss, why you always hunting this time of night?"

"You a good nigger, Taylor. A damn good waterman. You be sure let me know you see any runaways, you hear. We'll split you the cash money."

"Oh sure, boss," he said. "I'd like that money. Sure enough would like it."

"Yeah, you'd sell out your little woman there, wouldn't you, for some cash money." That bunch laughed when Taylor answered, "Oh, sure enough, boss. Sure enough. How much you gimme?" They responded with further lewd jokes.

They finally left and the family settled back to sleep. Abel whispered, "I been here five nights and they come by twice already. Second time they come by in the day when Taylor gone fishing. They trying to catch him, think something's up maybe. But missus, she cool as spring water. The children too." Then he shut up and went to sleep. But Chauncey stared a long time into that dark.

Three nights later Taylor came in late, long after supper, and told them to be ready to move quick when he said. Then he shoved the bed back over the trap door and the family settled down for the night. Chauncey and Abel sat up waiting in the dark; it was a matter of complete trust. And helplessness. And yes, faith in a man he didn't even know. The night dragged on and finally Abel lay down to sleep.

Suddenly those riders were sweeping back down upon the cabin, hollering and hooting and pounding on the door. Once again Taylor let them in and once again they made their crude jokes about his pretty little wife and his likely-looking children and that they'd better be sure to report any fugitives did they see any. Once again Taylor spoke in that cringing way he had, talking to the white men. But he scared Chauncey when he said, "Now, Master, I ain't had three good night's sleep in a row with you all come pounding down my door near every night. You know I don't hold with stealing. I don't believe in stealing a man. I'm a free man and I work hard for what I do got. I'd be much obliged if you all would just pass me by for a few nights while I catch up on my rest!" He laughed and the slave catchers laughed too.

The boss said, "Taylor, you a good boy and a hard-working water-man and sometimes I don't know why in hell I let you persuade me to set you free. Indeed I don't."

"Oh, pardon me, Master, but I paid you a good sum for myself, remember?"

Down below Chauncey held his breath, waiting for blows.

But the white man only laughed and said he expected Taylor could have those few nights of sleep he wanted as he was fed up himself with running around the countryside all night hunting niggers who were probably already gone north. Within minutes the night was still again.

Chauncey remained wide awake, waiting and thinking about how well Taylor had played the enemy: the right amount of sass that would amuse rather than anger them, the right amount of dumbness so they'd never in a million years think he was capable of doing what he now did. Within an hour of the slave hunters' visit, Chauncey and Abel were huddled down in Taylor's skiff and he was rowing out into the Chesapeake. He warned them not to make a noise and his muffled oars dipped in silently. Dark night, no moon. They rowed past the islands to the east and into the open bay shimmering in starlight. Taylor brought the skiff around and headed straight for the point of an island. Still a good distance away, he stopped rowing. He said they were just off Love Point, a few miles south of Baltimore, and that a sailing vessel had left Baltimore on the tide and was circling back to fetch them. It was bound for Havre de Grace at the mouth of the Susquehanna. The captain, a Virginian, hated slavery. He sailed the coast all the way from Norfolk, bringing tobacco and other merchandise north and more often than not picking up fugitives. He'd worked with Taylor often and had picked his sailors for their view on the subject as well as their sailing skills. He was going to set them off a piece before Havre de Grace for safety, and then it was up to them to make their way to the Susquehanna and follow it north into Pennsylvania. Taylor warned them to keep travelling only at night. Slave patrols rode up even into Pennsylvania. Upriver in Pennsylvania was a place called Peach Bottom, where a coloured ferryman would take them across.

While he'd been talking, a sailing vessel loomed out of the dark. It turned around to face north and rolled in the slight swell. A small light blinked aft. Taylor rowed forward. A rope ladder slung down. Abel threw up his small bundle and hands caught it. Chauncey said, "How can I thank you enough?" Taylor smiled and patted his shoulder. Abel scrambled aboard, then Chauncey swayed up the ladder. For a moment he watched at the railing as the skiff disappeared into the darkness. Then a sailor urged him down into the hold after Abel.

"Sam. You Minge's boy, right?" The captain held the lamp high. "I could've took you from Norfolk if I'd known. You look wore out."

Sudden bile burned into Chauncey's throat. He recognized the captain from a previous voyage he'd made with the master to Baltimore before he went to New Orleans. This captain often took on a load of the plantation tobacco. The captain grinned. "You're safe with me. I've seen the notices for you. Now boys," he said. "Come along." He led them through the dark hold, which was packed with tobacco hogsheads.

"You're pretty long, Sam. Be a tight fit. Once I shut you up don't stir nor make a sound, not for nothing nor nobody, until you hear me rap like this, seven times," and he twice demonstrated a beat. His lamplight revealed a hole in a false wall behind hogsheads, pulled out so that there was just enough space to squeeze by and get in. The captain slid a panel, concealing the space, as sweet a piece of carpentry as Chauncey had ever seen. The captain grinned at them, then slid the panel open. "Gentlemen?" he motioned for them to enter.

Chauncey crawled in first, then Abel squeezed in next to him, both men lying on their sides, tight as two forks in a drawer. Abel was lucky to be a much smaller man. Chauncey couldn't avoid scraping his lacerated back on the wall. When the panel slid shut he felt a few moments of sheer panic, wedged in between Abel and the side of the ship. Would he suffocate? Hogsheads were rolled back up tight against the wall. What if there was a storm, an accident, the ship floundering? They would meet death stuck in that tight coffin. Then he wondered if on his previous voyage with the master, all those years ago, there'd been runaways concealed like this, and suddenly he was breathing again, exhilarated that people like this sea captain existed.

Abel was trying not to giggle, his body pressed tightly against Chauncey's. He began to shake with laughter and sputtered, "If only you was a sweet little woman." Chauncey told him to shut up, but both were soon shaking with silent laughter, Chauncey wincing as his back scraped against the wall. The ship got underway; they sobered up to the slap of water against the planks right at their heads.

THEY WERE SET ASHORE some miles below Havre de Grace and made good time in reaching the river. Because the banks of the Susquehanna were heavily forested, they chanced walking by day, keeping a sharp lookout. But for all their vigilance, early on the second day an old woman called to them from behind some trees. They dove into the bushes.

"Where you headed, boys?" she said. "Aw, come on now, I seen you. You afraid of an old woman like me?"

Chauncey crawled out first, feeling pretty foolish. He couldn't tell if she was black or white, she was dark and wrinkled as a dried fig, carrying a basket and a digging stick, which she pointed at him.

"You better not be stealing chickens."

"Oh no, ma'am," he protested, spreading open his empty hands.

"So where you headed anyway?" she asked again, eyeing Abel, who came forward grinning.

"Pennsylvania, ma'am," Abel said.

"Pennsylvania? You already in Pennsylvania!" The old woman smiled. Chauncey figured she'd seen enough folks trudging north from Maryland to know what they were about and what they'd accomplished. From the way she was grinning, it wasn't the first time she'd seen grown men fall on their knees, crying and scooping up earth and kissing the very ground. And it wasn't the first time she'd seen grown men leap about like they was little boys hearing fiddle music. But it was probably the first time she'd ever been picked up like she was a little girl herself and whirled around in a mad, mad joy.

"Now. Now you boys've had your fun. Put me down," she ordered Abel. "If you coming up from Havre de Grace, you been in Pennsylvania for the last five miles."

"We trying to reach Peach Bottom," Chauncey said.

But they'd passed the place a mile back. She advised them to keep heading upriver all the way to the bridge at Wrightsville, where they could cross with no trouble. But travel by night; lay up in the bushes by day. "Judas lives, oh indeed, he does. You boys hungry?" She turned and led them through the forest.

They navigated through Pennsylvania like crossing a treacherous stream in spring flood, leaping from one solid boulder to another, trusting to the boulder to be there even when the flood hid it, trusting to strangers to take them in. When they crossed the covered bridge over the Susquehanna, they had to trust their guide, fearing all the while that the enemy lurked at the other end. In Columbia, everywhere black men and women were at work, but none were slaves. Here Abel found work at a lumber yard, but Chauncey was determined to continue on to Canada. When he landed at Mrs. Esther Lewis's place in Chester County, the good woman took one look at his festering back and declared that he'd be spending the winter. It was the first time in his life a white person, a woman no less, touched him with no malice or self-interest, purely in the spirit of healing. They were Quakers, a widow woman and her daughters, with healing hands and loving hearts. He spent the winter of 1829 there before he was passed on up into Canada.

"SLEEPY YET?" HE ASKED me now and we laughed, for he knew my insatiable thirst for his stories.

"You're the bravest man I know. And the sweetest," I said, pretending to nibble on his ear. We began to make love again, and this time as I touched the scars on his back and thighs I stroked over them softly, as if I could possibly sooth them away.

"I can't hardly feel your fingers through those scars," he whispered.

So I slid them around to his belly and every smooth silky part of him I could reach. *From now on only joy, no more suffering.* What passed between us that night I could only wish for every new bride and groom. But at long last he curled his long body around mine, wrapping me up completely in the shelter of his arms, and we fell asleep.

We awoke to a horrible noise outside our window, a great screeching and rattling and banging. At first I thought the storm was destroying the cabin. Then I heard men's voices howling. I was still foggy with sleep. Chauncey, however, was already drawing on his clothes. He leaned down and tucked the blankets in around my neck.

"Shh. Don't move from here," he said. "It's only a shivaree."

"A what?" I whispered.

The noise grew by the minute until it seemed the whole world outside our cabin had gone mad. The flicker of flames cast a strange light on the frosted window.

"Are they going to burn us out?" I was so terrified I sat up, clutching the blanket.

By now Chauncey had his coat on, but I leaped out of bed and clung to him.

"You can't go out there!" I whispered.

"It's only a shivaree. Some of the boys having a little fun. They'll leave when I give them some money to spend at Grills."

They were yelling for Chauncey to be a man and come out and face the music. Pot lids clanged. Sticks rattled against each other. Someone had a drum and someone else tooted on a horn. Then the battering began on the door.

I held tightly onto Chauncey's hand, begging him to ignore them and come back to bed. They wouldn't dare break down the door and it was firmly barred against them.

"Oonagh, it's the custom around here. We have to be good sports. All they want is a little fun. I'll show my face at the door, throw them some coins, and they'll leave."

"No! No, please! Don't go out there!" I spoke out of my natural woman's fear of a crowd of men, drunken and rowdy, but Chauncey was determined to put forth a smiling face and brave the wolves howling at our door.

He opened the door and a blast of snowy air swirled into the room. Then with a quick grin at me he stepped out and shut the door behind him. I slipped on my shift and huddled back into bed, waiting, scarcely breathing, listening to the noise outside, listening for Chauncey. It took several minutes for me to understand, to identify the various components of it. What had been pot lids clanging and horns tooting and men's voices calling out in rowdy song subsided into harsh swearing and grunts. Then I was out of that bed; barefoot and wearing only my cotton shift, I flung open the door to a scene of utter madness. The night writhed with dark shapes leaping about, flaming torches, snow driven horizontally in howling wind, and in the centre of the melee a cluster of men had stripped Chauncey of his clothes and tied him upon a rail. While some held him to it, others were beating him. Screaming curses I ran toward them, but someone with foul drunken breath grabbed me, gripped my arms back in a terrible hold, and slathered his tongue all over my cheek, trying to kiss my mouth. I shrieked, struggling, but this devil yelled that I was worse than a whore, a traitorous slut who deserved to die. He bit my ear and I lost all control then, screaming and kicking and biting any part of my tormentor I could. He punched me repeatedly across my face and head, yelling "Shut up." Other men grabbed my feet, lifting me up, ripping my shift, laughing as I twisted, trying to kick them. A shout went up and suddenly they dropped me into the snow. Someone kicked me repeatedly in the belly and chest and head. I fainted. When I revived, the pack of cowardly brutes was running away into the night, torches flung every which way. I struggled to stand but could only get to my knees, dizzy and nauseous. I crawled over to where Chauncey lay, the snow already covering him as it fell thickly. He was still tied to the rail and the snow around his body darkly stained with blood. I tried to raise his head, to pat him awake. I cast about for his coat and carefully placed it around him so that he could regain some warmth while I tried to loosen the bonds that held him to that infernal piece of wood. The wind drove the snow at us.

Suddenly hands were upon me. I screamed one continuous scream, struggling to get free, but someone wrapped me up in a blanket. I went crazy, struggling against what I thought were bonds. A voice kept calling out my name. I was sure it was Chauncey. No matter how I struggled someone held me tightly. I was being carried somewhere. Terror suffocated me and all went black.

I awoke to a low murmuring sound. I must have made a noise or movement because a face suddenly loomed over me. I didn't recognize Mairi at first. She was draped in a black shawl. Then she spoke and the murmuring noise ceased. She placed her hand on my forehead and said my name over and again until suddenly she began to weep and someone else's face took her place. Lorna. Lorna asked me if I could sit up. She had some hot soup for me. When I struggled to sit up, my whole head swam with dizziness, my body ached and cramped as if I'd been raking hay for days. When I tried to speak my face felt stiff, my mouth swollen. With this realization I looked around to see that I was in Chauncey's bed, in our cabin. A good fire crackled on the hearth. The cabin was crowded with shadowy forms.

"Where's Chauncey?" I asked in alarm. My head pounded.

"Shh, love. Have some of this good soup." Lorna edged a spoon into my mouth. I gulped warm soup down and looked for Mairi. What was Lorna doing here? She'd been too sick to come to the wedding, after all.

I shoved aside the next spoon, spilling the soup onto the bed. Lorna gasped and stepped back.

"Chauncey!" I called. Once again the murmuring in the room ceased and heads turned toward me. Mairi came forward and there was Michael too. Michael! I thought he'd gone back to his farm already.

Michael sat on the edge of the bed and took both my hands in his large rough palms. "Are you feeling better?"

"I'm not sick! I was beaten." I was suddenly so angry I wanted to scream at everyone gathered in our cabin. Chauncey! I wanted to see him. I knew he'd been badly beaten. Where was he?

Michael held my hands tightly. "Oonagh, you have to be strong now."

At his words, I ripped my hands out of his and cupped them firmly over my ears. He put his arms around me but I had turned to stone. I suffered his embrace coldly. When he released me I rose from the bed and everyone made way for me as I walked to where they'd placed Chauncey on the table. Candles everywhere. It's odd that I noticed this extravagance. It's odd how one's mind can detach and note the most mundane details at a time like this. They'd covered Chauncey with the very blanket I'd just finished for Martha McGann and hadn't yet delivered. Before I could draw back the blanket from his face, Michael caught my arms and murmured into my ear, "Oonagh, love, don't."

I shrugged my brother off and turned the blanket from Chauncey's battered face. Even then I didn't weep. I stared at my poor damaged husband. Someone had already washed the blood away but his face was terribly broken in several places. Still, he looked asleep. I leaned forward to kiss his cheek above where his lip was gashed open.

"Sleep well, love," I said. Then I turned and was lost. I took a step forward and fell into blessed unconsciousness.

Seventeen

The crowds spilling out of the new St. Lawrence Hall on King Street on the evening of April 3, 1851, were, for the most part, in a celebratory mood. For the past two hours they had cheered and clapped and listened intently to the great Frederick Douglass as he described the horrific cruelty of American slavery suffered by over two million souls in America. He shared personal details from his own momentous life. He described how this vile institution held sway over the US government and he denounced the complicity of the Northerners and the churches in its maintenance. His voice thundered as he described how the very churches that preached the love of Christ preached also that the Word of God upheld the institution of slavery. Hundreds of preachers owned slaves and beat them regularly, declaring that God's Word not only justified this treatment, but encouraged it! They quoted chapter and verse while applying the lash across some poor slave's lacerated back.

Certain pious souls in the audience, clergy by their attire, were made uncomfortable with his denunciations of the American churches. But they were in the minority that evening. His appeal to Canadians to use their influence with Americans to strike down slavery was met with rousing cheers and calls of support. The mostly white audience was firmly anti-slavery. When briefly he declared that a violent end was merited of those who attempted to hunt down slaves, those in the audience already uncomfortable with his denunciation of the American churches squirmed even more.

As the crowd emptied into the streets, arguments could be heard on all sides. Some of the Anglican clergy who had attended were angry. How dare Douglass have launched such a vituperative attack on the Church, which in essence was an attack on all Christians. Were there not an abundance of good Christians in the forefront of this struggle against slavery?

I called to Samantha, Mairi's youngest daughter, who had accompanied me, to keep close in this crowd and I hurried down the steps from the ballroom on the third floor where the meeting had been held. In the press of the crowd swirling in front of the hall, Samantha caught up with me. She touched my arm, startling me as I hadn't seen her approach. She beamed and I threw my arms around her.

"Wasn't he wonderful?" I asked. "Truly wonderful. Brave. Bold with the truth! About time, I say." I raised my voice. "About time, I say, that the churches take some responsibility for the heinous crimes of their brethren in the States."

Samantha glanced around in embarrassment at my loud voice. I'd spoken deliberately so in the direction of a group of clergy several feet away who were coiled into a knot, angrily debating the great orator's words. The men turned at my voice, then turned their backs. Probably they were muttering that I was one of those shrill female abolitionists who also clamoured for women's rights. It was well-known that Frederick Douglass also championed the cause of women's suffrage.

I muttered to Samantha. "They're insufferable! These pious men of God. Do you see how angry they are that Douglass said bounty hunters deserve a violent death themselves? Oh, how could a Christian utter such a bloodthirsty idea? Well, let these men of God, Almighty God in Heaven, just once come and see for themselves what pious men of God do in the name of God in Maryland and Virginia and Alabama and Louisiana!" Again I practically shouted, my anger getting the better of me. I wished to puncture their self-righteousness. One of the clerics detached himself from the group and walked toward me. His face in the dim light seemed red and swollen with emotion. Instinctively Samantha edged behind me. When he was but a couple of feet away, he drew himself up as if to gain height, then spoke quietly through clenched teeth. "Madam, watch your words in public."

"Indeed not. We should all be raising our voices to Heaven in protest!" I took a step forward as if to drive the man back. He was familiar but I couldn't place him.

He leaned forward slightly, his voice urgent. "Yes. But some must work in silence. You endanger yourself and those you aid by making yourself a public figure. I beg you."

I stepped back, alarmed that he knew me.

The man suddenly smiled. "We met once at Mr. Garrett's, in Wilmington. God keep you." He touched the brim of his hat and turned away. Several in his party had called his name, gesturing to where a carriage waited on the street. The crowd was shifting, floating, dispersing down the streets into the darkness of the spring night. The clergymen who had glared at me climbed into the carriage and were soon gone.

I deserved his rebuke for being so heedless, even in this city. I didn't recall meeting him at kind Thomas Garrett's, in Wilmington, Delaware. Mr. Garrett makes no secret of his views against slavery and has been a true friend.

Samantha tugged at my sleeve. "It's getting chilly," she whispered.

"Come, love, home we go," I now said.

We linked arms and walked east on King Street toward Corktown. The gaslights flickered, sputtering in the chill west wind that swept along the street. We tightened our shawls and quickened our pace. No one wanted to be out on the streets at night when the winds extinguished the lights as too often they did. Samantha's hand tightened on my arm.

"Who was that man?" she asked.

I shrugged. "A friend who knows Mr. Garrett."

IN 1833, THE YEAR after Chauncey was murdered, the British passed an act of parliament that would abolish slavery throughout the British Empire in 1834. Why had the British waited so long to do what was right and just? Long before that, in 1793, when this place was still called Upper Canada, Lieutenant-Governor John Graves Simcoe passed anti-slavery legislation, banning all new importations of slaves. Further, all children born of slave mothers should be set free at the age of twenty-five. Although it was not outright abolition, it was a start. In 1819 the attorney general of Upper Canada, John Beverley Robinson, decreed that people of African descent who lived in Canada were free with their rights protected. Their rights protected! And still it took until 1834 for the British to catch up with their colony. And although it grieves me deeply to acknowledge the race hatred that still exists among certain elements of Canadian society, the hatred that killed my own Chauncey, it is also abundantly clear that with our firm anti-slavery laws Canada stands as a beacon of hope to those so terribly oppressed south of our borders. That's why Chauncey and so many others found their way north, and why a veritable flood of anguished souls seek to cross our borders today. We should not hesitate to open our hearts and homes, schools and all institutions to welcome these refugees from that horrific condition still celebrated and protected by heinous law south of the border.

Last year the American Congress, to their everlasting shame, passed a despicable piece of legislation called the Fugitive Slave Act. Now people are considered criminals who do what they can to help fugitives to their freedom. Nevertheless, the flood toward freedom is rising daily.

We cannot rest content in Canada knowing that we have enacted anti-slavery legislation and yet not admit there are those in our own country who would treat persons of African origin as lesser citizens. There are those who would deny black children the full rights to an equal education with white children. There are even those who think it just to return the fugitive slave back to his brutal masters and deny him refuge in this blessed country. To that end they aid the bounty hunter who dares cross the border in pursuit of his blood money. We must none of us be complacent about those in our society who wish to diminish black people. Such racism diminishes us all.

Samantha asks me questions. How many times has she heard the story now? I've come to realize how few of her questions about Chauncey I can truly answer. I didn't have enough time to find out everything I longed to know. A year after Chauncey's death, my brother Michael told me that Chauncey had spoken more than one language. This greatly shocked me, for I hadn't known this. I was not comforted for days after hearing this, that I could have loved him so deeply yet known of him so little. Years later it was Daniel, grown solemn and thoughtful, who reminded me that any of us who had known Chauncey had known the man he wanted us to know, that is, he had given us individually the gift of himself. *Think of that, Oonagh, think of sitting by the river fishing with him.*

At seventeen Samantha knows well how to watch her words around strangers. She fully understands the work we do, the lives we hold in our hands. The first time I took her on a trip to Virginia, her cousin, my nephew Daniel, came along too. Mairi had been deathly afraid that something would happen to expose us to the American author-ities and she'd been unwilling to let Samantha accompany me. So to allay her fears Daniel accompanied us. Having travelled with me before, he knew I would take every precaution to ensure our safe return and that of the precious cargo we would be smuggling north. I've been doing this work now for fifteen years, and if fate allows me, will continue until the need no longer exists, or I myself perish.

Two summers after Chauncey's death I went searching alone for his family in Virginia, but to no avail. I found the plantation on the James River he had described, but with careful inquiry discovered that his mother, Ella, and sister, Sadie, had been sold south mere weeks after Chauncey escaped. Daniel had wanted to accompany me but Michael refused to let him and tried to dissuade me too, sure I would meet a dire fate. When I returned safely he tried to keep me home, but I travelled south again the following year.

The summer Daniel turned fourteen, three years after Chauncey's death, he insisted on coming with me. Although by now I held little hope of actually finding any of Chauncey's kin, everywhere we went Daniel asked discreet questions. We could find no trace of them. The conditions we witnessed throughout our travels in the States sickened us.

One day we found ourselves guests on a huge farm in Maryland. We'd been travelling under the guise of a mother and son looking for another son who had disappeared into the States. We found the story rendered us quite sympathetic to the Americans we encountered. They invited us into their homes. This day our Maryland host decided to give us a demonstration on how to discipline a slave properly. He wanted to impress us Northerners with his disciplining methods. He sent his son to bring a young slave from a pen where he had been tied up in chains for three days. His crime had been sleeping past the time of rising in the pre-dawn. Daniel caught my eye as the son dragged forth a thin shivering wretch barely clothed against the chill autumn air. His back was already lacerated from the previous day's whippings. With my eyes I did my best to warn Daniel against making any objection. I will not attempt here to describe the horrific scene. Daniel gripped my hand so hard I thought my bones would crack.

Later we determined to pass this way again on our way back north and steal away that very slave and bring him with us to his freedom. I cannot in this account give details of how we were able to spirit him away. Suffice to say that by this time I had already acquainted myself with several like-minded people in the route north and to describe anything further might be to endanger them. The times have become very dangerous, and never more so than for the brave men and women and children who attempt to flee to freedom. How Americans, people who declare in their very constitution that all men are created equal, can justify the Fugitive Slave Act and continue to uphold an institution that condemns human beings to such horror I cannot comprehend. What gives us hope is that there are so many other brave Americans, both black and white, who dare to oppose this law and break it time and again in their efforts to aid the oppressed.

On that first trip with Daniel, before that experience on the farm in Maryland, Daniel would often whisper, "It's just as Chauncey said and much worse. Can't we do anything?"

It was in attempting to answer his question that I embarked on what has become my life's work. If we couldn't find Chauncey's family, then all those wretched people would be his family and therefore ours. I would see an old black woman scrubbing mounds of laundry on a board, none of it hers. I'd catch her eye, only for a second, and it would be like catching the eye of Chauncey's mother as he had described her, her hair greying, her face thin with worry and work and never quite enough to eat. And sometimes a young girl, her head tied up in a cloth, would walk across my line of vision and I'd think, *Sadie!* although I never met Chauncey's sister and probably never will. But it might have been her, and maybe tomorrow I will see a woman who is truly her, although no doubt her hair will be turning grey, as mine is. If any of his family is still alive, we are all fast moving toward the end of our days. But our Chauncey will remain ever young, ever that tall slender young man with a flashing wide-awake grin and contagious laugh. He is alive in my very being and will never grow old, and that is both my joy and my sorrow.

Acknowledgements

IN SUSANNA MOODIE'S *Roughing it in the Bush*, a neighbour tells Susanna about an incident in which a black fugitive, a well-liked local barber, has the "presumption" to marry an Irish girl who is condemned for "her folly." On their wedding night, neighbourhood ruffians drag the groom out of his marriage bed and beat him to death. Who was this couple who dared such a union, a former slave named Tom in Moodie's book and the unnamed Irish girl? When I tried to find them in the archives, I found much information about the era but nothing I could directly link to the anecdote in Moodie's book. So I decided to write their story myself.

In an 1831 edition of the *Cobourg Star and Newcastle General Advertiser*, I saw an advertisement in charming verse for a barber, Chauncey Taylor, who was setting up shop in Cobourg. He adds that he also has a formula for cleaning all manner of clothes. Moodie's "Tom" had also claimed a talent for cleaning clothes. Finding no further information on the real Chauncey Taylor, I felt free to borrow him as stand-in for the character of the black fugitive.

Although most of the characters are fictitious, several I mention were real persons and deserve readers' interest: Thomas Garrett, and Esther Lewis and her daughters worked in the Pennsylvania Underground from its earliest days. Frederick Douglass became a powerful black abolitionist. A real ship, *Elizabeth*, sailed from Galway, whose passenger list I accessed via the internet, http://www.theshipslist. com and used for my shipboard characters.

I must thank my cousin Olga Stokes of Chadds Ford, Pennsylvania, who hosted me on a memorable trip through Pennsylvania and Maryland in search of the Underground Railroad, Mary Dugan of the Kennett Underground Railroad Centre, Kennett Square, Pennsylvania, who took the time to talk with us, Bob Moore, who toured us through the Civil War and Underground Railroad Museum of Philadelphia, and Millicent Sparks, the Education and Outreach Coordinator there who was so inspiring.

In Niagara Falls, Ontario, I discovered just how underground the Underground Railroad still is when I went to visit the Nathaniel Dett Memorial Chapel on a hot summer day. The streets of the city were full of vacationers. I found the small Methodist church in a quiet residential neighbourhood. The historic chapel was an important link of the Underground Railroad, a shelter for those newly arrived across the Niagara River. A large tour bus was parked in front of the building. Two men outside assured me I could enter, although there was a tour going on inside. I walked in and was astounded to see the church packed with men, women, and children. I thought perhaps they were from a black community in Toronto or Montreal, or even all the way from Nova Scotia. But when I asked a young mother with a baby on her lap, she told me they were from Virginia and were making a tour of UGRR sites. I'm so grateful for the experience of meeting that amazing group of people and for the kind people at the museum and the Norval Johnson Heritage Library next door who were so helpful. I must also thank my brother Allan Scott for his company (and car) on the subsequent search for the UGRR sites in the Niagara region. For their encouraging support and advice through the years, thanks and love to all my family and many friends, especially my son, James, who patiently took me through numerous computer snafus, and my daughter, Tasha, without whom this book would never have been written.

The following people were kind enough to read partial or complete drafts and give me much-needed feedback: my first and last reader, Tasha Tilberg; Jude Abrams; Heather Allen; Brendan Allen; Dave Allen; Margaret Behr; Allan Brown; Terry Brown; Valerie Charun; Don Coles (most timely suggestions!); Heather Gordon; Roisin Culhane-Sheehy; Sigrid Hawkes; Jack Hodgins for his encouragement and great advice; Val Hudson; Pam Hudson; Mary Ann Lammersen; Lachlan Murray; Barbara Nicholls; Kylee Nicholls; Danny Nicholls; Phil Russell; Lenora Sattmann; Natalie Scott (my amazing mother); Olga Stokes; Alison Taplay; Pete Tebbutt; Monty Tyrwhit-Drake; Laura Wilson; Louise Young, whose encouragement kept me going, and a huge thanks to Marc Côté, who took a chance on me and whose editing advice was amazing. Thank you all.

Sources

The following is a list of the sources I found helpful in gaining a picture of the people and the era.

Angus, James T. *A Respectable Ditch: A History of the Trent-Severn Waterway 1833–1920*, Kingston and Montreal, McGill-Queen's University Press, 1988.

Bordewich, Fergus M. *Bound for Canaan*, New York, HarperCollins, 2005.

Cahill, Thomas. *How The Irish Saved Civilization*, New York, Doubleday, 1995.

Courlander, Harold. *A Treasury of Afro-American Folklore*, New York, Marlowe and Company, 1976.

Delaney, Mary Murray. *Of Irish Ways*, Minnesota, Dillon Press Inc., 1973.

Drew, Benjamin. *The Narratives of Fugitive Slaves*, Toronto, Prospero Books, 2000.

Dubois, W.E.B. *The Souls of Black Folk*, collected in *Three Negro Classics*, New York, Avon Books, 1999.

Foster, R.F. *Modern Ireland 1600–1972*, Toronto, Penguin Books Canada, 1989.

Gates, Henry Louis, ed. *The Classic Slave Narratives*, Toronto, Penguin Books Canada, 1987.

Gray, Charlotte. *Sisters in the Wilderness*, Toronto, Penguin Books Canada, 1999.

Guillet, Edwin C. *Cobourg 1798–1948*, Oshawa, Goodfellow Printing Company Ltd., 1948.

Guillet, Edwin C. *Early Life in Upper Canada series: Pioneer Life; Pioneer Social Life; Pioneer Travel*, Toronto, The Ontario Publishing Co. Ltd., 1939.

Guillet, Edwin C. *The Great Migration*, Toronto, University of Toronto Press, 1963.

Guillet, Edwin C. *Pioneer Arts and Crafts*, Toronto, University of Toronto Press, 1968.

Hill, Daniel G. *The Freedom-Seekers, Blacks in Early Canada*, Toronto, Stoddart, 1992.

Hughes, Robert. *The Fatal Shore*, New York, Alfred A. Knopf, 1987.

Jameson, Anna Brownell. *Winter Studies and Summer Rambles in Canada*, Toronto, M&S, New Canadian Library edition, 1990.

Johnson, James Weldon. *The Autobiography of an Ex-Colored Man*, collected in *Three Negro Classics*, New York, Avon Books, 1999.

Keneally, Thomas. *The Great Shame A Story of the Irish in the Old World and the New*, Australia, Random House, 1999.

Kilbourne, William. *Toronto Remembered*, Toronto, Stoddart, 1984.

Lowance, Mason, ed. *Against Slavery, An Abolitionist Reader*, Toronto, Penguin Books Canada, 2000.

Minhinnick, Jeanne. *At Home in Upper Canada*, Toronto, Stoddart, 1994.

Mac Con Iomaire, Liam. *Ireland of the Proverb*, Boulder, Colorado, Roberts Rinehart, 1995.

MacKay, Donald. *Flight from Famine the coming of the Irish to Canada*, Toronto, M&S, 1992.

McFeeley, William. S. *Frederick Douglass*, New York, W.W. Norton & Company, 1991.

McLaurin, Melton A. *Celia, A Slave*, New York, Avon Books, 1993.

Mitchell Marks, Paula. *Hands to the Spindle*, College Station, Texas A&M University Press, 1996.

Moodie, Susanna. *Life in the Clearings versus the Bush*, Toronto, M&S, New Canadian Library edition, 1989.

Moodie, Susanna. *Roughing it in the Bush*, Toronto, M&S, New Canadian Library edition, 1989.

Richmond, Ben, ed. *Reminiscences of Levi Coffin*, Richmond, Indiana, Friends United Press, 1991.

Rolston, Bill & Shannon, Michael. *Encounters How Racism Came to Ireland*, Belfast, Beyond the Pale Publications, 2002.

Shadd, Adrienne; Cooper, Afua; Frost, Karolyn Smardz. *The Underground Railroad: Next Stop, Toronto!* Toronto, Natural Heritage Books, 2002.

Smedley, R.C. *History of the Underground Railroad*, Pennsylvania, Stackpole Books, 2005.

Still, William. *The Underground Railroad*, Chicago, Johnson Publishing Co. Inc., 1970.

Stowe, Harriet Beecher. *Uncle Tom's Cabin*, New York, Aladdin Classics, 2002.

Taylor, Frances Cloud. *The Trackless Trail Leads On*, Kennett Square, Penn., 1995.

Washington, Booker T. *Up From Slavery*, collected in *Three Negro Classics*, New York, Avon Books, 1999.

Weld, Theodore Dwight. *American Slavery As It Is*, New York, Arno Press and The New York Times, 1969.

As well, numerous sites and articles online were helpful, with these noted:

Russell, Hilary. "Frederic Douglass in Toronto" CRM #4, 1998.
http://www.followthedrinkinggourd.org
http://www.mdslavery.net
http://www.jamesriverplantations.com
http://www.theshipslist.com

ENVIRONMENTAL BENEFITS STATEMENT

Cormorant Books saved the following resources by printing the pages of this book on chlorine free paper made with 100% post-consumer waste.

TREES	WATER	ENERGY	SOLID WASTE	GREENHOUSE GASES
15	**5,469**	**10**	**702**	**1,318**
FULLY GROWN	GALLONS	MILLION BTUs	POUNDS	POUNDS

Calculations based on research by Environmental Defense and the Paper Task Force. Manufactured at Friesens Corporation